FALLEN FLAME

J.M. MILLER

Fallen Flame
Copyright © 2017 J. M. Miller

Cover photo and design by Regina Wamba—www.maeidesign.com
Cover model—Jenessa Andrea
Map design by Tiphs—www.tiphs-art.com
Interior by Champagne Formats—www.champagneformats.com
Editing by Lawrence Editing—www.lawrenceediting.com

ISBN-13: 978-1546309802
ISBN-10: 1546309802

To those unsettled,
the dreamers, the wanderers,
keep searching, keep fighting.
You will find yourself.

GARLIN ISLAND

WYNTOR
VINEYARD

CHATEAU ROAD

R E V E L A T I O N
WOOD

CRYPT CLIFFS

ONE

MY ROUGH SKIN HAD REACHED ITS WEEKLY LIMIT, THE pressure crushing, digging into my body. It was time for my cleansing.

With closed eyes, I let thoughts of the day drift into nothing, enjoying the seclusion. Aside from sleep, there was little time I had completely to myself. All the other hours were spent alone in a different sense, silently protecting one person, often in rooms filled with many others. My life as a Guard.

The old bathhouse groaned lightly, wood walls and well pipes settling as the busy daylight hours gave way to the still night. The quiet solitude soothed my tired mind and aching body. For while my daily presence usually required obedient silence, my mind and body were always active, always alert.

I breathed in the solace and held fast, knowing the next breath would be pained with the biggest agony in my life, what I'd always known as my weekly cleansing. Curling my hands along the rounded edge of the only bathing tank left in the empty Guard house—my personal bathing tank—I took that next breath then threw myself into the cool, clear water. My skin instantly seized, every inch held hostage as the burning pain took hold, the water unyielding as it attempted to break into the scarred barrier that would forever reject it. Familiar as the process was, it remained excruciating. My body never adjusted, never even so much as numbed its reaction to the sensation, despite all the days, all the years.

The coolness disappeared in a flash, the water absorbing the heat of my agony. I opened my mouth and released a scream that was instantly swallowed by the mass of liquid pressing in from all around. My outer layer sloughed off by the time my garbled cry ended, the water finally penetrating the hard, ashen skin and freeing it from the smooth layer that lay beneath. I stepped out of the tank, newly shed and exposed. The air kissed my red-orange skin with spiked lips as I watched the old charred flakes settle to the bottom of the tank.

I am human. It was a daily reminder, whenever I caught sight of myself, looked at my skin—whether charred and cracked or smooth and red. *But I am not like the others who surround me.* Their eyes stared with curiosity and disgust, but, more often, averted with fear of the truth. For when I was an infant, I was said to have been scorched by magic. Something only whispered about in lore and cautionary tales, about a time before all on our island were born, when magic was said to rule.

My very presence was a constant reminder that it was more real than they wanted, that the monsters weren't as far gone as the stories told huddled around supper spits and celebratory gatherings suggested. I had been burned too close to home, nineteen short years before.

Without a courtesy knock, the jagged oak door swung wide, hinges squelching at the sudden movement. I turned toward the noise, already pulling on underclothes to wrap my bare body, since there'd be no time for the rough outer layer to reform in the open air as I usually allowed.

Haidee's sharp eyes scanned the dim bathhouse then stopped abruptly as soon as they spotted my bareness, the vibrancy of my skin halting the urgent words that forced such an obtrusive entry. Only two people had laid eyes on my body immediately after a cleansing, and she wasn't one. I'd been careful throughout the years. Always fully covered, especially in the rain. The element of life had become my true enemy, an external weakness. My coal skin color had never been the issue and blended in with the array of Garlin's people, but red-orange would be a different matter altogether and likely more frightening than the outer texture they already feared.

"Vala …" My name slipped through her lips as unconsciously as her scarred hands had fallen from the blade at her waist down to her sides. Her whole being was clearly stunned by my appearance, even more affected than the day I'd marred her speckled russet brown skin.

"What is it?" I snapped, not bothering to hide my annoyance at her intrusion. She was my most trusted ally on the Guard, one of the only people who agreed to help me train when I was young despite the texture of my skin. Mostly because her mother, Saireen, had been the one to find me those

J. M. MILLER

years ago and kept me when my own mother had never come forward to claim her blood. Haidee was ten years older than me and started work as a chateau handmaiden like her mother before joining the Guard. She'd served more years than me, but I was the one who became the Guard's most powerful weapon, which also meant I'd been given one of the most prized details. The prince.

No matter how annoyed I was about her seeing me in this state, she had reason. And there was only one that mattered.

She shifted, the sword grip at her belt handled loosely once again, her eyes blinking frantically. "I apologize for—"

"No need," I interrupted, securing my mass of stringed hair plaits into one and moving for my outer attire. "What's wrong?"

"He's gone." Her lips turned down. "His room is empty. I was to take over watch, but there was no Guard on spot when I arrived."

"What? Leint was there when I left. Anything amiss?" I asked, quelling the immediate pangs of fear and worry and redirecting my focus. I slid quickly into my worn leathers, gloves, boots, and cloak, then affixed my long sword. With the royal greeting the following day, several ships had already made port at Florisa's Cove, on the low, northern side of the island. There'd likely be stowaways mixed with guests and normal traders, eager to see what our quiet island had to offer, tour our wondrous gardens, drink the wines they loved to import while standing on the very soil the precious grapes were tended. High alert was scheduled to begin at daybreak, a few short—no longer alone—hours away. Apparently, the Captain of the Guard should have started it a day in advance.

"No." She waited for me to position my hood and the

4

flap of material that masked my face before holding the door open for me to pass into the dense night fog. "There was talk earlier, about Prince's Night."

"Prince's Night?" Surprisingly enough, words I'd never heard. I was close to the prince—growing up and training alongside him, sleeping in adjacent quarters, breaking others' bones for him. His secrets were my secrets.

"It's a supposed tradition, or celebration, the night before a prince was to be assessed. The elder men must have informed His Highness or the little lords he calls friends."

"How did I not know of this?" I quickened my pace down the narrow path between the main Guard and handmaiden quarters, navigating the rutted ground toward Chateau Bylor as I had for years, recalling the prince at my side through most of it. Always together. Even as children. Why hadn't he told me about a Prince's Night?

She didn't respond, knowing her fault for not having mentioned it when she'd first heard. I knew her reasoning was built from kindness. Still, the kindness of letting a little talk slide, of allowing me to take an hour of solitude before a week of high-alert events, it was all dangerous. There was no room for kindness.

I accepted her silent guilt as a lesson learned, as punishment enough … if the prince was unharmed. I had to hope he was unharmed. "Any other information about this Prince's Night?"

"Overindulgence in wine or mead, possibly some form of trials."

"Of what sort?" I wasn't sure I was completely sold on the Prince's Night answer. Haidee wouldn't have disturbed me if she were entirely convinced of it either. If something else had happened ... I shook the emotional thoughts away and focused on my training and my knowledge of Caulden. Had anything bad happened, he would have left me clues. His west tower rooms were the place to start. I knew them well enough—they were my home as well.

"From what I've gathered, Prince's Night is said to be trying but humorous, to see how fit the prince actually is before meeting his potential bride. If he succumbs to the games, can't handle the fun, things could get complicated during the next day's introductions."

"Sounds grand." The entire affair grated on me—him meeting Princess Anja, being shown to her like a prize to judge and measure—but what it really involved was more than worrisome.

Since Queen Meirin Tamir of Islain's first born was female, and had recently come of age, it was time for her to select a consort. Family and land was taken into careful consideration, evaluated for not only their heirs but for skills and kinship as well. Of course, it was all anyone on our secluded island could talk of for months, especially after word had spread that both queen and princess would be traveling instead of summoning the prince, which was the usual practice for the lords of their lands. But this situation was entirely different, and it wasn't exactly cause for celebration like some of Garlin's people thought. Garlin had been separated from Islain for hundreds of years and had only reestablished trade connection within the last twenty, which led to Islain's greater interest of claiming our people, our land. A courtship between the prince and princess would only make that process easier ... and avoid a war we would assuredly lose.

A salty wind climbed the hills from the port, sweeping

an endless cloud over the chateau grounds, as it did most nights and many days. Nothing appeared unusual. I checked the chateau gate for signs of disruption first, posted Guards merely nodding at my presence. Peering through the iron slats, only the lights of the cove's towers could be seen in the distance, the dreary glow spreading out over the tumultuous sea, marking our presence and warning any transit ships of the uneven coast along our cloaked island. I turned around to approach the chateau, noticing that the lanterns were dimmed the same as when I'd left for my cleansing. Even in the darkness, the royal chateau's size and elegance was awing. Stones upon stones stacked in extensive walls and pillared columns. Colorful panes of glass fitted into wide-arching windows. The largest building, standing high on the southernmost peak, looked over the island kingdom with its strong presence and comforting assurance.

As I stared out from beneath the edge of my hood at the royal home, Prince Caulden leaving the island seeped into my mind's eye and swept a chill through me. No matter how many times I'd tried to ignore it, the thought kept plaguing me. We'd all thought he'd marry within Garlin and stay to rule. Marrying the future high queen wasn't exactly the most horrible fate for him to have. It was honorable. He'd help rule with the kindness I knew him to always have. But the thought of Garlin and Islain uniting, and him not being here with his mother, with me …

I moved around the front of the chateau and gazed up at Queen Havilah's blackened windows and balconies. "You told no one else?"

"I didn't feel it necessary to alarm Her Majesty or the captain. You know Caulden best." Haidee's words held no malice, no bitterness despite the envy I knew her to harbor for my position.

I moved noiselessly through the main courtyard, searching for any unusual shadows around the edged gardens and stone entry arches. The sentinel Guards at the great doors parted as soon as they spotted me, allowing room for ten men, and not even a breath passed between them in my wake. They knew better. They'd learned to keep away, having either caught sight of my daily training, hearing others' whispers, or seeing the burns another had suffered. From the corner of my eye, I glanced at Haidee's bare hands, their scars one instance of proof. Others walked around worse off, while a few who had dared threaten the prince now only moved with the sway of the sea, their bodies tethered to stone and tossed from Crypt Cliff on Garlin's southwestern side.

Our trained footsteps emitted the faintest of echoes into the main hall then up the western spiral stone stairwell. The dead quiet unnerved me more than usual, the unlikely chance of the prince's peril growing more possible with each second, each hurried step. The post outside the prince's quarters remained empty. While I was glad Haidee hadn't notified anyone else of his disappearance, it was also a risk. If we found that something more significant had happened, more lives than his would be at stake.

I opened the door to the main sitting room, taking in every detail. Half ashen logs blazed within the fireplace, the snapping of the large flames stealing my attention first, calling to me as they always had, humming a drawing tune, as if they had taken over my head as well as my skin. Another effect I had to live with. This one, though, I'd only ever shared as a child with Saireen, who had wisely told me to keep it hidden.

She knew that truth would only garner more attention and more fear—another cursed difference. So it remained our secret. Even on her deathbed two years before, she'd never said a word. Not even to her only true born, Haidee.

"There's water on the washroom floor," Haidee said, tearing my focus from the fire.

"He was bathing when I left earlier," I replied, moving toward the opposite hall where my room door stood ajar, exactly as I'd left it. The flames from the main room couldn't reach inside, folding my simple space in the darkness I preferred each night. The blankets on my bed remained untouched, two books still stacked at the side.

Haidee's muffled voice cleared when I stepped back into the main room. "I noticed the splashes before I came to get you, but what I didn't see before were these light smudges on the floor."

Walking over then crouching beside her, I confirmed, "Boot prints. No sign of a struggle. Leint has to be involved." I ran an exposed fingertip through the watery print, ignoring the stinging on my thickening skin. Some of it cast off, a dusted shadow of myself left inside the thin puddle. "Chatty, that one. Ever since his reassignment to this detail, he's been taking any chance to talk with Caulden. He's lucky the prince seems to enjoy their conversations. Otherwise, I'd have him removed for dereliction."

"Perhaps the Prince's Night celebration needed a willing Guard and an opportune moment."

"Opportune because of my absence." Noticing something red and orange in the water's drab reflection of the stone room, I stood and moved around the curve of the tub to the high wash basin. One mourning flower had been tossed inside. A few of its petals curved over the edge, like flames gasping for air as the rest of its delicate corolla and stem bathed within the water.

Some of Haidee's numerous thin brown plaits slipped over her shoulder as she nodded and ran a scarred finger over the water where mine had been shortly before. She was probably thinking more about my skin and what she'd seen in the bath house, or possibly considering only the task at hand. With her, it was difficult to tell. She'd left Saireen's house to become a chateau handmaiden right after her mother took me in, so we hadn't really considered ourselves sisters. Once upon a time, I would have liked to. Unfortunately, I felt she didn't favor the same sentiment. Her mother had loved me enough to risk burns throughout my childhood. No matter how many times Haidee had begged her to stop comforting me, Saireen always refused. Her argument was that children needed to be held, comforted with kind hearts and a loving touch, not fearful eyes and cold gloves. In Haidee's mind, I supposed I'd only caused her mother pain.

I blinked away thoughts of the past and stared at the flower again. There were only two places they were located on the island, and I was willing to bet my life that no one would dare drink wine and hold trials in the queen's private conservatory from where this one had been stolen. "Whether or not Prince's Night is true, at least we have an idea of where to look."

TWO·

THERE WERE TWO ROUTES TO SACRED LAKE. THE FIRST was faster—a more direct passage up one of the island's highest peaks, part of the climb guarded by a steep crevasse field. The second was more passable—a rocky path that looped around the south then went north to follow the eastern cliffs, treacherous enough to have claimed many lives of those who had braved them. Either way was dangerous in its own right. Once considered the most spiritual place on Garlin, people trekked there to show respect and honor to their loved ones, often swimming in the hidden lake's water. But years ago, when quakes had shaken the island, the paths had become more unsteady, the crevasses even deeper, halting the frequent visits. Most people stayed away, content to respect the lake for its connection to death and, if they held the beliefs from a past now only whispered about, not wanting to tempt any goddess into relieving them of life.

I'd been to the lake's cavernous entrance once. After learning of its spiritual connection on his sixteenth birthday, Caulden had thought the lake might communicate guidance from his father, King Wystin, who had died shortly after his birth. The Captain of the Guard found us and stopped our entry, then Queen Havilah forbade the prince from returning, thus me as well. She also ensured her order by noting the one thing that would steal all temptation: my affliction. Even though most people no longer traveled there, she said my condition would surely taint the holy place. That killed all thoughts of returning, even after Saireen's death a year later. I hadn't bothered to request the travel time to stand outside the entrance, where the mourning flowers grew in abundance, spilling like blood channeling from its wide maw. Even if I'd been tempted to break the rules for which I was bound, there was no hope in me helping guide Saireen to whichever goddess she had privately prayed.

Haidee's boots crunched along behind me in the darkness. "Going down into town to drink their fill at the taverns and hold trials along the docks at port would have been an easier choice."

I scowled at the harrowing path ahead, wishing it were daytime when shadows were less deceiving. "There's always a chance they could have."

"Why not search those first?" Her voice was a little more than a huff, the tone dripping with age entitlement. In times like these, when there was no one else of authority around, I knew taking my orders was even more of a challenge for her. She was probably better suited for the prince's lead Guard position. She was a stronger fighter in many ways, having trained for years before I could even lift a proper long sword. But I was the most feared, so I was given the post at an early age. It added to her animosity toward me, straining our working relationship further and placing more pressure on me and my eternal need for acceptance.

The gaps in jagged stone teeth widened, forcing us a little farther apart to balance on the narrow climbing ledges. "Because Caulden is no fool," I rasped, then ran across several spaced ledges as the path broke away under my foot. "If he'd been taken without consent, the room would have been wrecked and the flower possibly shredded with a fight." I couldn't consider any other alternatives. He had to be safe. He had to be.

"We already covered that." Her murmur all but disappeared into the depths of the fractured ground like the loose stones kicked under our feet.

I rolled my eyes then looked toward the hazy starlight along horizon, noting our direction. "Yes. And since we know he went willingly the flower is our main clue."

"That was also pretty plain to see."

"Perhaps if you knew so much, you wouldn't have asked such a foolish question," I ground out. I'd tolerate a lot, but she was testing the limits. My nerves were already on edge, senses sharpened in the event something was actually astray. When she chose smartly not to respond, I leapt swiftly to a ledge on the next taller rock pillar, my sword hilt smacking the rock face before I climbed to the next ledge. "Whether Leint brought the flower or someone else, it was picked bravely from the queen's conservatory, probably as an introductory test to see if Caulden knew where to go and if he'd back out."

"Hmm," Haidee hummed, mulling my theory.

"If he wanted most of this night undisturbed—and to stir my anger by having me thoroughly traipse the island—he would have taken the flower with him. Yet he left it. He wanted me to know he was safe, indirectly. I'm guessing his princely manhood would have been at risk of a good taunting had he stopped to write a letter to his Guard," I said, hustling over a few closely grouped tiers.

Haidee jumped to the place I'd been before then laughed through a labored breath, hugging the ledge.

"He also dropped it in the wash basin, an added clue to the lake." I jumped the last gap and looked onward over the even ground to the very end of the island, the eastern cliffs. The starlight coated the remaining path to the entrance in a soft, tolerable glow, highlighting the taller boulders and shadowing the sparse underbrush.

Haidee took her last jump and hunched over for a pause beside me. "We should have taken the cliffside trail."

I walked on, checking for any movement after each crunch of stone and dirt beneath my boots. "It's bad enough that the first half of this trail could have been on horseback had the captain's quarters not been adjacent to the stables, but you'd be willing to risk an additional hour of the prince's safety for your own?"

"No," she said flatly, snapping back into her detail. After a few silent moments, she asked, "What's your plan?"

With the ground now leaning into a gentle downward slope, the amount of land on the horizon disappeared, the ripping sea beyond growing larger as my dilemma grew closer. I would do what I could to save the prince if he were in danger, risk my life as I was called upon to do. But would people ignore my desecration if that was what it took to protect him? Mourning flowers greeted us along the trail shadows. Where most other vegetation ceased to grow in the dense, rocky terrain, their numbers spread like red and orange ground fire, with the fog hovering like smoke above them.

"Observe the entrance," I said, my tone low, barely heard over the sea crashing far below the cliffs and the Vitae River—a mere stream of peak runoff here at its beginning—trickling alongside us. "If there are any hints of a problem or we're unable to see or hear him, you'll go in." Surrendering that responsibility pained me. Haidee was more than skillful. She could settle island brawls and any discontent easily. I trusted her to aid in the prince's safety, but I wasn't eager to let her handle it alone.

The stream veered away from us, disappearing somewhere underground as it did, making the remainder of our trip silent with closed lips and every toe placed with care. The entrance curved in a low arc, like a drawn bow lying on end, and the mouth dipped into the soil, backtracking inward, away from the island's edge. I leaned on a boulder and peeked around, seeing only a faint firelight flickering somewhere beyond the blackness. The distance was worrisome. If something went awry, would I have time to get to them, to him?

After a few quiet moments, Haidee's hand clapped on the leather at my shoulder. "With honor and courage, to protect Garlin," she recited, then added, "I'll report back quickly."

I nodded and watched her climb down the sloping walls of the cavern, her silhouette an eclipse to the light deep within. Her extra caution was not lost to me—only a couple tumbles of loose rocks indicated she was even inside. I sat on the boulder, swinging my legs around toward the entrance, and removed my gloves before tugging the stem of the closest flower, snapping it away from the grounded net of its sisters. Out of all the kinds of flowers on the island, it was the only one I'd never touched. During the journey, my skin had fully regenerated, stiff and coarse and ugly. The fresh petals folded over my bare hand, the contrast of textures stark, like silk on stone. I waited for the flower to wilt as all others had ever done, my skin burning the life within. But surprisingly there was no change. I studied it for a moment then removed my hood and mask to take in a full breath of salted air, pondering the heartiness of mourning flowers. My thoughts shifted back to Caulden and the time to come. Several hours of night stood before the dawn. If this outing was truly about a jovial Prince's Night, Haidee and I would have to continue our distant watch until its end. That also meant the prince wouldn't be alone in the challenge of wakefulness the following day. I imagined the chaos of the royals' arrival to be horrid enough without having to watch with laden eyes. The high queen and princess' introduction, the assessment of the prince. No matter what type of woman the princess was, she would fall for him. All did. I had hopes she wasn't as wretched as the stories spoken of her mother. Stories that traveled the water, passing over the lips of sailors on trade ships. Had she really murdered her king as so many had claimed?

A yell echoed out from the cavern. There was no playfulness mixed inside its tone, no hint of delighted pitches in its depths. Worry hit me, launching my body into movement on instinct. Time had stopped and then sped up again within a few harsh breaths. Whether loose or fixed, the rocks held steady enough to support my swift boots. Caution had disappeared, though, and had taken my silence with it. Every ear inside would know I was charging. There would be no surprise. Had I been stupid in not going from the start? Had I surrendered the prince's fate because of rules, over my fear of tainting a once sacred place?

Light spread as the cavern's entrance widened, the fire's flame calling to me in a hum louder than most others. I slowed as it all opened up. My focus skipped over the pit with flames twice the size of most men, climbing halfway up the arched wall of sparkling wet rocks spotted with red petals, and instantly locked onto Caulden's body kneeling on a circular island in the center of a lake that stretched farther than the light dared to go. His bowed head pointed toward the vastness, draping his unbound, almost shoulder-length black hair forward over his face. His wrists were wrapped with twine behind his hunched back, and his ankles were crossed and tied too. Lanterns flickered all around him, illuminating the small island like an altar, possibly as it had been used years before. One narrow path led out from the water's edge toward the island, not fully connected. And off the opposite wall, water spat from fissures of varied sizes, pouring down the rocks— the Vitae River feeding the lake.

A tapping of rocks in quick succession snapped my eyes to the side of the cave where Haidee's slim form blended into the jagged shadows.

"Vala." Leint's voice drew my attention away from Haidee's hidden position. He stepped out from around the massive fire, another new set of Guard leathers already taut from his ever-growing muscles. Having been on the prince's detail for a few months, he'd seen me without the hood and mask and had already been through the range of typical reactions to my appearance. So the surprise that flashed inside his

bright blue eyes tonight was simply in response to my presence. He remained assured in his powerful stance, not the
least bit concerned about having broken his duty as a Guard
or worried about the possible lashings that could slice the
milky skin of his youthful back because of it.

"Leint," I replied calmly, watching him stop between me
and the pathway to the island.

Two of Caulden's closest friends, Lords Josith and Rhen,
were slower to join our exchange, staggering from around the
fire, eyes large enough to show they shared his surprise. Their
clumsy feet, however, didn't share his assured stance. Both
were sopping wet and clutched a bottle in their hands. Even
more bottles glinted from strewn positions around the fire.

Prince's Night then.

"Oh look, Torch has come to join the party. I thought
Caulden said his pet wasn't invited?" Josith asked in a slur
then slugged Rhen in the arm. Rhen let out a wail that held
the same tone as the one I'd heard in the cavern's echo.
Unaffected by his friend's response, Josith tipped his head
back so he could dump more mead down his gullet. Rhen
opened his wailing mouth again, as if to speak this time, only
to bend and retch at his own boots.

I glared at them, hiding my internal cringe at the nickname. Years had passed since I'd heard it outright, but I knew
it was still uttered by those who clung to the dominance
highlighted by their status and their mindless past. Since I'd
grown up alongside Caulden, I'd grown alongside them and
a few others as well. Their families considered lords or ladies
for their stately positions, either heads of maintaining Garlin's
farms, vineyards, or port trade businesses. I hadn't exactly been permitted to interact with them in our youth. They

had all visited the chateau for classes occasionally. Caulden even went to their places a few times a month, to be, as his mother had said, acquainted with his peers. I had no formal schooling, only Guard. But with access to some basic books from the chateau and an adopted mother who wasn't as willing to let me drown in ignorance, I could argue my intellect matched the lords'.

Despite all else, I'd had enough interactions with them through the years to know they didn't share Caulden's kindness. None of them had.

Leint's head tilted in question, waiting. He was a foreigner, who had traveled to Garlin two years prior from western Islain, but he didn't even flinch at hearing the nickname, which told me he had heard it enough, possibly even among other Guards.

I gritted my teeth, furious at the entire situation. The fact that Haidee hadn't bothered to join my side might have infuriated me as well, but I was glad she was thinking correctly. It was wiser for her to remain hidden in any circumstance, friendly or not.

"Untie the prince," I said, walking closer to him and the island's pathway. "We'll discuss why you left your post after we get him back to his rooms."

"I can't untie him. And clearly I didn't leave him, so I didn't actually leave my post." His footsteps countered mine while Rhen's and Josith's moved them back toward the fire, an empty bottle clinking to the ground along the way.

"There is no gray area. You know very well what you did and didn't do." I stared out toward Caulden, his body still despite the carrying noises within the cavern. Was he even conscious?

"He's here of his own volition. He wanted to partake in Prince's Night just as the kings before him." His large body stood its ground, refusing to back off.

"The only thing you have going for you is that you were wise enough not to fully partake yourself," I said, noting his coherence. An inch of the rocky shore separated the toe of my boots from the lake's edge. While the beauty of the water's clarity could be seen for the first few feet thanks to the fire's light, the rest welcomed the darkness as easily as the night sky. I understood why people praised the place and wouldn't want anything to risk its beauty or spiritual power. I'd never seen anything like it, even in some of the paintings in the chateau and illustrated books of the mainland.

When Leint didn't bother to respond again, I looked back at him with a hardened stare. "You will untie him."

"He was to untie himself after regaining consciousness for the last test. Surely, he can finish." His stern expression remained facing the water, not facing me, a superior, as Guard regulations required.

I swallowed the growl climbing my throat and calmly said, "He's not conscious. There is no need for him to finish." The fire hummed louder in my ears, flames licking closer beside me.

"There is a need for him to finish. If you respect his wishes at all, you'll leave," he added, finally turning to look at me. His rusty-colored hair shifted with the movement, the short strands flickering as if it held its own firelight. Then his focused icy eyes peered into mine. "I don't want to fight to give him this, but I will. Besides, I'm pretty sure you aren't allowed to be here. You wouldn't want anyone finding out you were, definitely not that you could have swum in the Sacred Lake.

As of right now, no one else will have to know. Because this night is not about us. It's about him."

He was challenging me, about my respect for Caulden, my respect for the Guard. About my integrity and my honor. "Everyone will know because I won't keep the truth to myself." No matter the repercussions. A new detail. A barred cell. Or would it be more? My utter obedience through my years on the Guard hadn't yielded the punishments I'd seen others endure, so the consequences I'd face were a mystery.

"Who needs to know? His mother? That's precisely the point of this night. For him to prove to himself, show that he's his own man, that he's capable of leaving, capable of ruling one day." Leint turned back toward the lake and shook his head. "He's been sheltered here, by her, protected here, by you. He needed this, this crack in the egg that has been his life thus far."

His argument hit exactly as he'd intended, knowing how my life was for the prince—for his progression as well as his safety. But I couldn't shake the feeling that there was something else, like another way to test me, my control.

I let out a fast breath and pulled in another, preparing to choose what I thought was best for Caulden and for myself. For the first time, the answer wasn't so clear.

The sound of rocks sliding filled the cavern and my attention snapped to the tunneled entrance. Haidee had moved inward, only the very corner of her head visible from her position within one of the large cracks in the wall's facet. But the noise was not hers. Leint turned toward the noise too, with a hand on the grip of his Guard sword.

A shadow moved in from the entrance wall revealing a single man, then another, and on, until there were five. Their dark leathers suggested a clear reason they had come during the night. There was nothing recognizable about any of them and nothing outright distinguishing either. Their physical characteristics—hair, skin, builds—varied like anyone from Garlin. But knowing there were many new ships docked in Florisa's Cove, the men could've been from anywhere.

They all continued on, one lead stepping to the front as the others flanked. The lead drew his sword slowly and pointed its tip past us toward the island. "Archer, the prince."

THREE

HOW HAD ANYONE FOUND US? IF THEY WEREN'T FROM Garlin, their abilities rivaled the best trackers. Following prints on the rocky terrain to Sacred Lake took far more talents than a sharp eye. My studies of the mainland and the world beyond had been limited, purposely. I learned all the things any Guard needed but nothing that might take me away from Garlin. I'd been told at a very young age to abandon any thoughts of leaving. If I was feared here after having grown on the island, traveling anywhere else would prove much worse. So I learned the basics of Islain's high kingdom from some books and what little I'd picked up listening to the traders during the prince's trips to Florisa's Cove. This was especially frustrating as I stared at the men walking toward us. Their stances, weapons, and leather armor could hold some minor details, some symbolism, yet I saw nothing.

The sanctity of Sacred Lake was no longer concerning as soon as the unknown assassin drew his sword and ordered the prince killed. Time wouldn't allow for talks or quarrels. They had come for blood, so I would show them their own. Drawing my sword with one hand and unfastening my cloak with the other, I leapt into a run, honed in on my first target: the archer pulling an arrow from the quiver at his back. I reached him before he had a chance to nock it, swinging my blade. His eyes squinted then widened when he focused fully on my uncovered face. I took advantage of his confused or fearful hesitation and sliced clean through his bow before swinging around once more and burying my blade into his chest. Haidee had appeared swiftly at my side, a body already falling in her wake. I turned again, counting the final three as one charged at me with a determination that lasted a few strong strikes. His blows were heavy but, unfortunately for him, nowhere near swift enough to battle two Guards. When his life dissolved through a final scream, the count left two. The lead assassin had reached the water's edge as Leint lost ground with the last. Haidee moved to help him, and I charged on.

The lead's sword was sheathed, his large frame preparing to run the narrow pathway when I swung on him. My sword pierced the crest of his dominant shoulder, forcing his body to dip. The strike was meant to change his direction and focus. Since he had led the group, I wouldn't end him until he gave all his information. Using the momentum of my attack, his body turned with a swing of a fist. I shifted too late, and his knuckles grazed my jaw. The hit wasn't enough to throw me, but it clipped my head sideways and splintered cracks in my skin, like every hit I'd ever taken. The smell of burnt flesh tinged the air along with the sound of his pained grunt. As the shock trapped his attention for a moment, I caught sight of something in the shadows behind him, moving quickly, past Haidee and Leint fighting the last man, past the curve of land around the fire where Josith and Rhen lay drunken on the ground. It was faint and fast, and it had evaded my line of sight. A splash sounded, snapping my attention farther around the curve, the final stretch of ground along the lake's edge. Ripples spread away from the rocky waterline, growing wider and wider toward …

My breaths slowed. Someone else was in the cavern, and they were now in the water heading toward the prince.

The lead's sword glinted with firelight as it swung in front of me. He'd had enough time to evaluate the damage to his hand and determine I was a big enough threat to engage. But he'd lost that chance. After dodging his advance and leaving him for Haidee and Leint to dispatch, I ran toward the narrow pathway, sheathing my sword, eyes still on the prince's listless figure.

"Caulden!" I yelled. With how swift the shadow had been, there was little chance to reach him first. Each stride closer, Caulden's subtle movements grew clearer. They were minimal, barely keeping his drunken and bound body upright. Nothing more. If the shadow was to attack, he had to be more alert. "Wake up!"

He stirred, and his curtain of black hair swung lightly then parted as his head lifted and turned in my direction. There was a moment, as his unfocused eyes met mine, that the situation blended into everyday training, everyday living—seeing those same dark eyes looking energetic and mischievous above rounder cheeks, angry at another defeat, curious at our proximity, broken after his first hunt and kill, sad at Saireen's death, comforted in my covered arms.

"In the water!" I yelled, my feet continuing to push closer and closer to the tiny island, the span of water between it and the pathway growing larger and larger. The leap would have to be one of the longest I'd ever managed. Otherwise … My heart stuttered at the thought of my body sinking below the water for the second time in the span of a few hours—the tenderness from my cleansing still very much alive in my mind despite the already restored skin.

My leg muscles burned but thrived as I willed them to work harder, eating the last few steps faster than one full intake of air. And then, I leapt. I didn't bother to look down into the depths. The darkness wouldn't reveal the water's secrets even if I had. Instead, I kept my eyes on Caulden, who had been able to turn on his knees to face me, still bound. When I landed, more hope built. Mere steps separated us. But it all crashed when a figure emerged from the glassy water. Hands then arms and only the top of a head breached the surface and hooked Caulden's bound arms, snatching him backward into the water.

No! I dove and expected to hear the terror in my voice for both Caulden's fate and my own echoing back at me from the cavern walls. Yet the scream so clear in my mind never crossed my lips, and so I heard nothing but my final breath before the water welcomed my body with its cold, crippling embrace.

I bared down around the breath, waiting for the familiar pain that was woven into every piece of my life. Only, it never came. Although the absence was sublime, there was no time to rejoice. Caulden remained my biggest concern, my lack of swimming experience following closely behind. With my arms outstretched, I touched something solid and frantically clasped my hands around to hold tight. Leather. Straps. Buckles. Caulden's boots. The dive leveled out and the boots continued to drag me along through the water.

Questions rolled in an unending stream through my mind, but the fear of drowning cut through every one. If we died beneath the water, it wouldn't matter who was dragging us or why the lake water wasn't affecting my skin. I reached for the dagger at my waist with one hand, and on a hopeless whim of gaining my bearings in the darkened water, I dared to open my eyes. The lake was not how it had been above. A soft haze of light surrounded me, enough to see Caulden's boots. I used the blade to sever the ties at his ankles and noticed the water wasn't the light source at all. The light was coming from me, streaming out from breaks in my clothing. I walked my grip higher up Caulden's legs, feeling his muscles tense up in response. Reaching his bound hands was essential for escape, even though they were the hold for whomever was dragging us. Regardless of how impossible the task, I had to try.

Before I could pull myself farther up Caulden's body, a deep, insurmountable rumble sounded within the lake. An intense vibration was fast to follow, shifting the water around us with enough force to tear Caulden from my grasp. As his body disappeared from reach, from sight, I caught a glimpse of who had been pulling us, their body tumbling around, light peeking out from the breaks in their dark clothing.

My foot hit a solid, immobile form and I twisted to grab hold. As soon as I felt the dense rock at my fingertips, I let out my breath and climbed toward the surface to fill my aching lungs. Breaking through the water with a grateful gasp, I quickly took in my position while looking for Caulden. He was nowhere to be seen, but it was too dark to see much of anything. There was no large fire, no entrance. No main cavern. We were in another area.

The ground rumbled again, breaking rocks from the walls and ceiling and dropping them into the water below. I tucked my dagger away then hauled my body onto the rock ledge. The reddish light from my skin dimmed as air cocooned me, stabbing my skin like tiny blades. As the glow disappeared from my body and my rough outer skin began to form again, I noted two other sources of light. The closest was a beam of starlight pouring in from around a curve in the cavern's wall, a salted, misty wind twisting throughout. The other source had a red hue much like mine, moving within the lake, water rippling around it.

I rushed around the lake's edge, tumbling over the uneven rocks along the way. There was still no sign of Caulden. But the mysterious fighter had already gotten out of the water a few steps away.

"Ahh!" His scream boomed inside the cavern with so much force I could almost feel his pain. He was injured.

I leapt forward, drawing my sword, prepared to take advantage. Though, when I got closer to the man, close enough to see the water falling from his silhouetted short hair and chin, I stared at the dimming light encircling his face and hesitated. Slices of light pushed out from behind his clothing just as mine had. But what had happened to the water, to him, I couldn't care about. He had come here to kill the prince. I swung my sword and lunged forward.

The fighter screamed again—this time, a rough grunt to mask the pain—and hurled his body out of my blade's path, rolling carelessly over the jagged ground. I attacked once more, but he dodged another time, bounding back onto his feet and shuffling out of range.

Darkness had all but taken over. The sea's turbulent song seemed to grow louder with the night, waves punishing the bottom of the cliffs in a way I'd always envied. Constant. Unyielding. Tenacious. Even though my relationship with water had always been pained, I admired the waves and often tried to emulate their strength. Hearing their battle beyond the cavern was another reminder of who I was and why I had to fight.

I chased the sound of footsteps. The starlight barely highlighted the open split in the cave, but it was enough to show The Shadow's silhouette again, splashing through the edge of the water as he ran toward the opening. Either too injured to finish his mission or convinced it was already done, his intention was to flee. His grunts and heavy breaths continued with each stumble. I willed myself to move and got close enough to take another swing, determined to end the fight he had started. He heard my advance and veered off, finally unsheathing his own sword. My body stood in his way, steps from the narrow opening.

His sword swept through the air smoothly. It would have been a solid blow had it landed. I parried and countered, but he had recovered in a heartbeat and was able to catch my blade with the flat of his. The metal slid together, cutting a sharp tang into the air and bringing us closer. I was prepared to jump and thrust my head against his or kick whatever was in reach. Unfortunately, the soft starlight ended my plans, shining its glow upon his face, revealing skin as charred and as rough as mine.

"Not possible." His voice was thick and wild. And though he fought against it, his tone wavered with strain or possibly fright. It wasn't just me seeing him. He was seeing me as well.

I opened my mouth, gasping as I inhaled a shocked breath, unable to respond. Instincts and training urged me to move, yet my eyes refused, transfixed on the reality of him—the rough coal skin coating a youthful face not much older than my own.

Our quickened breaths tangled for a moment more, staring at each other with a paralyzing intensity, then his blade slid from mine and his body darted away, escaping through the cracked wall.

Had I not heard splashing and a cough from somewhere behind me, shock may have held me captive for hours. But the worry for Caulden pushed my body faster than my own thoughts, leading me away from the starlight and back into the blackness.

"Caulden!" My voice echoed, hollow but resonant inside the vast space. I stopped at the waterline and moved cautiously along its edge, not knowing exactly how large the second cavern area was.

Another splash was followed by a sputtered cough. I ran blindly, my balance faltering after a moment and throwing me face first into the water. Once again, there was no pain but there was light pushing out from my clothing. There was a small current leading into the darkness—an exit for the Vitae River, flowing down its path inland. Before the water's depth threatened to take me under, it shallowed with uneven steps to an embankment where a figure lay.

"Caulden!" I rushed to him, my hands sliding over his half-submerged body without thought, all formalities of duty shoved aside to ensure his safety. My guilt for chasing after The Shadow before finding him could be heard in my frantic breaths. If he was permanently hurt because of my choice, I would never recover.

He coughed again, wet and forced. "Vala."

Another rumble shook the cavern, the lake. Fractured rocks fell and splashed down around us.

"How are you? Are you injured?" Blood, tears in fabric or skin—nothing was visible in such little light and feeling for them was next to impossible.

"I'm fine." Another cough. "My hands." His body turned, rolling onto his side with his face leaning into the water.

I grabbed my dagger and slid the blade between his hands to free him.

"Ahh." Once the ties fell away, he sighed and rolled onto his back. "What hap—your skin …" His hand lifted to my wet face, hovering an inch away, the subtle light casting brighter upon his skin.

The tang in his breath and the slight slur in his words suggested his view could still be hazy, adding even more confusion to what he was seeing. Whether he would comprehend or not, I would explain if only I knew the answers myself. "I …"

"Beautiful. More so than I remember." The whispered words were barely recognizable as his widened eyes shifted around, taking me in. My light shone on him enough to see his amazement—the wonder in his stare, his slack mouth, the curious arch in his eyebrows.

I breathed in, recalling the time he'd seen me after my

cleansing a year before, how he'd looked at me then, how he'd asked to touch my smooth, vulnerable body.

His fingers moved closer, and I instinctively tilted my face away. I wouldn't make this night worse by returning him to the chateau with burns. His skin had never been harmed by my bare touch, and I wasn't about to let that change. My movement didn't dissuade him, though. His hand reached higher and his fingers slid some wet plaits of hair from my cheek. I waited for the hiss I'd often heard from Saireen during my young years. The red skin was no different than my outer layer. Flesh burning, life taking.

So when that hiss didn't come, when more of his hand made contact, gliding gently across my skin, I inhaled sharply. The feel of a simple bare touch was surprising. Gentle. Exciting. As comforting as I'd always wanted it to be, as soft as I always thought his smooth, tawny-colored skin would be.

"Vala," he whispered, reaching his other hand to hold the other side of my face. "Thank you."

I closed my eyes, wanting to cherish the feeling but also contain the tears welling inside. It wasn't just my skin. It was my heart. I'd never been as close to someone as I was to him. After a breath, I opened my eyes to find a closer view. He had leaned in near enough that his eyes jolted back and forth to look into each of mine. And then his lips brushed against mine and those eyes disappeared behind heavy lids.

My body shook under his touch, overwhelmed and overcome. Through the years as his Guard, I'd seen him touch girls in the same way. I'd even wondered how it would have felt if I were them, able to be touched by him, by anyone. My thoughts, my dreams, they had been nothing in comparison. They were a single drop of water, and this, the whole sea.

The air stabbed at my skin once again, and Caulden's hands and lips disappeared with that fearful hiss I had expected.

Embarrassed, I backed farther away, letting the darkness hide my shame. I'd known it wouldn't last, and yet I had let him continue, wanted his touch for another second, another minute. I hadn't wanted it to end. "I—"

"No … I'm … all right. And I'm sorry. I … I wanted to thank you for tonight. Though, I'm still unsure about the details," he admitted, his voice slowing, still loose from drink.

I followed his lead, choosing to move on from the topic. "You decided you'd be safe playing with your idiots alone."

A broken intake of air was all to be heard, his amusement unmistakable, until he collected his words. "Suppose I won't make that mistake again."

"Not when so many outsiders are visiting Garlin," I chastised. "What do you remember?"

"Finishing another bottle. Being tied. After that, your voice. Then the water. I was worried about you following."

I brushed off his concern for me, needing to end the emotions of the evening before it all turned sour. "Are you sure you feel all right? Nothing out of sorts?"

"My problems have little to do with tonight. My mother is less than happy about the queen and princess coming, about me possibly being chosen." After a pause, he added, "And having to explain what happened here tonight won't help."

"No, it won't," I agreed, already contemplating my punishments for nearly letting him die and for desecrating Sacred Lake, not even counting if his lips and hands had gotten burned.

"What did happen, Vala? The light …"

He'd only seen my body once after cleansing. He was the only one besides Saireen. But even if he'd forgotten all the details of that chance viewing, he knew glowing wasn't normal. For anyone. It hadn't happened to his body tonight. And yet, it had happened to me and to …

"And who grabbed me?" he finished his thoughts and mine as well. The Shadow. *The assassin.*

"I wish I knew," I answered honestly. "I will explain all that happened after you're able to rest, and we'll try to make sense of it all. Right now, we need to discuss our exit. The others are back in the main cavern. If they hold their breaths long enough to find us here, we'll be expected to go back the same way. I don't think it's wise for them to see my skin submerged in any water, especially not this water."

"I agree. What's the alternative?"

I turned toward the split in the cavern wall where the assassin had escaped. "We climb."

FOUR

THE WHIP CRACKED AGAIN, SLICING INTO MY BACK FOR the third time. Despite its hard texture, my skin gave way beneath the severe force of the plaited leather, the surface splitting and splintering worse than any hit I'd ever taken. Tiny pieces cast off to the stone floor at my feet, dark gray crystals splashed with blood. I clenched my fists above my head and tugged on the straps that bound my wrists to the vertical wooden beam in the middle of the chateau's empty prison chamber. More pain came as the dank cellar air sank its cool bite into the fresh wound, my skin forming a new barrier, healing, rebuilding.

I opened my eyes and gazed up at the highest point of the stone room, watching the dawning sky beyond the bars of the single uncovered window as the reality of my punishment settled. A tear slipped from my eye only to sizzle into vapor before reaching my cheek.

In the hours following Prince's Night, Caulden and I hadn't even discussed what had happened. We'd expunged all remaining energy by climbing out of the hidden cavern then backtracking to the main entrance. Haidee and Leint had been so relieved that the prince was alive that they didn't push questions about the assassin. They simply followed my orders to tend to Josith and Rhen while I escorted Caulden back to the chateau. Discussing anything while his head remained clouded with drink would have been useless anyway. I'd hoped to sort the details after a few hours' sleep, prior to reporting to Captain Baun and Queen Havilah. But I'd been wrong to assume word wouldn't get to them earlier.

A raven landed between the bars, the dark silhouette blocking the sky. It cawed and twisted its head, eyes taking turns to view me, staring hard as if it wanted to speak. The hinges of the chamber's door squelched, scaring the raven from its stone perch, and solid footsteps entered the room.

"How many?" The captain's voice cut through the air as sharp as the whip.

"Three," the chamber guard, Orimph, replied in his dull tone.

"Leave us."

"But, sir, you said the queen requested six."

"And what am I saying now?"

"Yes, Captain," Orimph murmured with obvious disappointment. Being a chateau prison Guard, he saw very little activity. And he'd never liked me much anyway given that when the prince and I were young we used to steal the extra pastries he'd often smuggle from the kitchen. His clothes made a rubbing sound as his massive body moved then disappeared after another squelch of the hinges and a hard thud of the door.

Captain Baun didn't say anything right away, only stepped around the open cell doors and approached my right side. Having tucked my face back down between my arms during their exchange, I watched his boots stop beside mine. They were his nicest pair, polished well enough to reflect the subtle morning light casting in from the window. Motes of dust and dirt they'd kicked up with their steps swirled above their smooth, pretty surface. I didn't need to look higher to know he was wearing his best ceremony garments for the royal greeting.

His fingers grabbed the bunched fabric at the back of my neck, releasing my shirt to fall over my exposed skin. Then his hands moved up to the straps at my wrist and began unfastening. "Your actions dishonored us all."

For the second time in the gentle dawning hour, I regretted not having slept with the dead assassins at Sacred Lake. Maybe Queen Havilah wouldn't have been so quick to have me tied and lashed if the evidence of the night's events had been seen by retrieval Guards first instead of relayed by another account. As it was, she wasn't one to wait for testimonies. I'd been seized from my bed and led to the prison without having uttered a word in my own defense.

"I don't believe my actions did, sir." The words felt heavy, both exhaustion and pain weighing my tongue. "If I hadn't entered Sacred Lake, the prince would have been killed." Surely my visit to the lake was the reason the queen didn't think twice about having me, a loyal servant to her and her son for most of my years, punished this way. She had every right to treat most Guard delinquents harsher than Garlin's people. But I'd always thought I was regarded on a different level, my actions only ever selfless, only ever for the royal family.

"And yet, if you had done your duty correctly, he wouldn't have been compromised at all."

The straps at my wrists fell away, releasing my stretched arms. I lowered them to my side and stepped back to look upon Captain Baun, standing tall to properly address him. His steely gray eyes studied me the same way they had for years. The fair skin above his blond beard—heavily pocked and scarred, even on his bald head—twitched as he gritted his teeth, anticipating my response.

"Leint holds that blame for allowing the prince to endanger himself. If *he* had done his duty—"

"And you suppose the prince would have listened to Leint had he told him to stay in his room?"

I had no direct argument for that. The prince was stubborn when he wanted to be and was capable of persuading most people without even brandishing his title. "I left him with a trusted Guard for an hour. What else could I have possibly done to—"

"All of you are to blame. All of you failed to notify me of the situation. But you … as the lead on the prince's detail, I expected you to know that protection doesn't just require a sword and a swift hand."

"I chose not to wake you over some ridiculous secret celebration."

"It is your responsibility to inform me of anything involving the prince, to include ridiculous celebrations, and especially when you have no knowledge of the prince's location and no way to predict a potential threat. We've been lucky here. Garlin hasn't endured opposition since our people left the mainland all those generations ago. We're far enough off coast that most forget we even exist except when our coveted exports arrive. But we knew everything could change when the prince came of age. And now that Queen Meirin and Princess Anja are here ... Others might choose to sabotage the visit, hoping to give their own lords a better chance of capturing the princess' heart and hand. And with last night's obvious attempt on Caulden's life, we can't afford to make such passive mistakes."

Hearing his tone soften, watching his eyes shift around the chamber, I knew what was coming. "Captain, I'm fully capable of performing my Guard duty. If I hadn't been there ..."

With a long blink, he inhaled evenly then opened his eyes to mine, their stern stare cutting through what little hope I had left. "Vala ... you've been stripped of your lead position. You will remain on Guard for now, with restrictions."

His words knocked the breath from my chest.

The rigid stance of his mountainous frame relaxed with a visible exhale—a slip in bearing not shown to many others. He'd been Captain of the Guard since before I was born, was the one who had overseen my introduction and appointed me to the prince. He'd been my guide through the years, second to Saireen. So naturally he had become another surrogate family member to me, and I believed a mutual feeling for that connection to be the reason for his occasional relaxed disposition. It all could have been based upon pity to start—aiding the outcast, a girl so different than most—but I'd hoped with my years of dedication, to the Guard and to the prince, that what was once pity had grown into some form of respect.

Though, respect only went so far given that his own title held limited power, which was evident by the ruling that came next.

"With my recommendation, the queen is permitting you to remain on the prince's detail. You're to aid in anything the lead Guard or the prince needs, but you will not call orders. I have a feeling she's only tolerant of this decision because there are guests on the island. She's not happy about Islain's intrusion on Garlin and would rather them leave quickly with nothing, save what they came with. So don't give her a reason to strip you fully and toss you to the street or to the sea."

I wanted to object to everything, but I had no words. With everything I'd put in to my duty, all the years I'd given to the Guard, such an easy dismissal without hearing my account was hard to ignore. And it stung. I blinked with a solemn nod. It was all I had.

"Before we assemble for the arrival, I want to hear your information to make sure we adjust our security measures appropriately. Is it true that their origin was unclear and that one escaped?"

"Yes," I confirmed. "He was the one who managed to pull the prince through the water to a separate area. He was more skilled than the others, moved through water and along the cavern swift and stealthy, like a shadow." And his skin … I glanced at my hands, at the cracked layers of rough char I'd never seen covering another person. Until last night.

"Haidee and Leint mentioned an opening in the cliff where you and Caulden climbed from. Is that where he escaped?"

"Yes."

"Do you believe he was able to make the climb?"

"Possible, yes. He acted slightly injured, but I still think he was too skilled to fall. He had enough time to climb and disappear while I searched the dark cavern for Prince Caulden and checked his health."

"Did you make the choice to climb instead of swim?"

"I did," I admitted. Unlike many others, Captain Baun knew my affliction made water my weakness, but neither Saireen nor I had told him what happened when my skin was submerged or how much it truly pained me. I didn't plan to change that or expand on the real reason Caulden and I had made the choice to climb. "If I'd felt swimming beneath the water was best for Caulden, we would have traveled back the way we'd been pulled. But with his drunkenness and my un-skilled swimming abilities, the cliff was a better choice."

He nodded his acceptance of my decision. "And the re-maining attacker was injured? From your hand?"

"I …" I recalled the fight and finally had to admit, "I nev-er landed a blow. He was intuitive and very quick." So how had he been injured? His skin was like mine, but the lake's water hadn't hurt the same as my usual cleansings. Perhaps he'd been reacting to the air. The regrowth. Though, to me, that was nowhere near worthy of the screams he'd released.

"If he was quick, and you're unsure of any injuries, he undoubtedly survived. Which means he's still a threat. We need to pass on as much information as possible to prepare all the Guards. What other details can you give?"

I glanced at my hand, my skin, doubting what my eyes had seen despite the clarity I'd felt a few short hours before. Words caught inside my throat again. This time it wasn't pain and disappointment holding them back. It was apprehension, and it was fear. I could admit to him that the man I'd seen was like me, that his charred skin was more unmistakable than I'd like to admit. But after being lashed and stripped of my position, questions began to churn inside. How might he or the queen react to that information? And alongside those doubts and fears rose something even more dangerous. Curiosity. The assassin's skin was like mine, and from somewhere deep, I longed to know more, to know who or what was to blame. He could have answers.

"He was a man," I finally admitted, "with a build as solid as stone but movements as agile as air." I stared at my hands again and shook my head. "The lake. The cavern. Darkness made it impossible to see. I was fighting a shadow." One who looked like me.

FIVE

A S I MADE MY WAY UP TO THE PRINCE'S ROOMS FROM
the prison chamber, the chateau's empty west stairs
and halls were as eerily quiet as the previous night.
I passed three Guards along the way, their eyes tracking me
more openly, not used to seeing me uncloaked and without
leather armor. Most of the chateau's inhabitants were likely in
the dining hall or the kitchen, prepping for the start of the big
greeting day. I wondered now what part I would have to play,
no longer positioned closest to Caulden.

The prince's rooms were deserted. I recalled the final moments of our evening, walking him past the calm flames in the
sitting room's fireplace and into his bedroom where he kicked
off his boots then promptly fell into the mass of blankets on his
grand bed, moving no more. I closed his door before seeking

the comfort of my own bed. A few hours later, the dim glow of fireplace embers had showed me his door in the same state while Orimph shoved me toward the hallway.

I stepped inside my own room, now bathed in morning light, and glanced around. It would be the last time I'd call it mine, unless I found a way to regain my position. Yesterday's underclothes sat in a heap by the wall, the skin I'd shed from the lake dried into a lining of ash within. As instructed by the captain, I changed into my best garments then packed my small amount of belongings. I'd likely move to the Guard house, giving the others ample time to gawk. Or if Haidee felt kind, she'd allow me to share Saireen's place just outside the chateau's grounds.

"Vala." Caulden's soft voice entered through my opened bedroom door some time later.

I stiffened, the final packed bag in hand, still facing the window overlooking the west grounds. The fog was light, showing a view of Revelation Wood and beyond to the southwestern sea, a view I'd grown to love. My island. My life. As much as I wanted to discuss what had happened the previous night, I didn't want to turn and face Caulden. I felt betrayed, and I couldn't help but to direct some of the blame toward him.

"Are you hurt?" When I didn't answer, his voice hardened a tad. "Look at me."

I turned then, a routine response to a command. His hands fidgeted at his sides, tugging the edges of his silver and green embellished doublet and straightening his black dress cloak—a nervous habit often brought on by having to wear fancier clothing for special occasions. With his face cast downward, his eyes stared at me through a thin layer of black hair hanging past them.

"Are you hurt?"

"Not physically, no," I replied honestly, forcing my eyes to remain focused on him no matter how painful.

"You're still assigned to me," he said with a sigh. "I couldn't change her mind about everything else. I tried. Please, believe me." His head and body straightened with a deep inhale, pulling his shoulders back and expanding his chest, showing his full stature. Sweeping a hand through his hair, he brushed the strands from his face. "I didn't want this. It won't be the same without you so close."

His words were pitched with the same hurt I felt inside. I couldn't blame him. His only crime was taking part in a tradition that had spanned numerous princes before him. It was his right to partake, just as it was his right to move on with life, with change. The princess would be here soon, and there was no doubt in my mind that she would claim him for her own. Despite knowing that nothing would ever truly come of our deep connection, that he was destined to marry someone more befitting, to become someone more than this island, my heart still wasn't prepared. Especially after he'd kissed me.

"I will still do my best. For you," I replied. Because no matter what, I would. It was my duty. My life.

He stepped closer, holding my eyes with his. "Knowing that makes me feel …" His hand reached out to mine, touching my gloved fingers gently. "I was afraid, after what happened, that you'd want to leave. That you wouldn't want to be with us. With me."

I wanted to reply with all my heart, to tell him everything that had been locked inside for most of my life, to tell him that I was also afraid of him leaving Garlin, leaving me, but I was more afraid that my confession would only become more of a burden. I could never truly tell him. Perhaps it was best that I was no longer his lead Guard. If he felt the way I did, perhaps it was better not to know.

"I'm honored to stay, Highness. I want only the best for you." The truthful words came automatically. But they were also stiff, a reminder of my place … and his.

"Yes, well …" He backed up a step and shifted his eyes away, as if snapping out of a trance. "I'm sorry that my actions hurt you. If I could change it all, erase the night, I would. For you." His words were slow as he looked nervously behind himself, eyes somber while checking that his Guards remained out in the main hall, out of listening range.

"Thank you," I replied. Knowing I might not get the chance later, I decided to discuss what had happened at the lake. "Do you remember more of last night?" When his eyes shot back to mine in question, I clarified, "About the assassin who got away?"

"It's all hazy. I can recall some things." Again, the words were slow, hesitant, and his eyes focused on the floor. "But I already told Captain Baun that I'm not sure of his appearance. It was all very fast and too dark. The water. The cavern." His stance shifted and he threaded his fingers, fiddling. "You, though … Your skin in the water …"

I inhaled sharply, knowing he remembered enough.

"It was like a dream. It felt like something else changed there too. There was a quake. Do you think it had something to do with you being there?"

"I'm not sure," I admitted. There had been a quake. Two actually. Both times, I had been in the water, which made it hard to deny the possible connection. "If your mom believes that, I can understand why she stripped my position. I ignored her warning, even if I was trying to protect you."

He dropped his hands to his sides and his lips turned down. "I think it has more to do with our visiting guests. All of Garlin had to have felt it. There hasn't been a quake for several years, about the time my father died. That doesn't help, as I'm sure it scared her even more. Then to worry about Queen Meirin and Princess Anja's visit and their safety …"

"It is a good deal more than she usually has to deal with, but I'm sure she is handling everything as it should be."

"Not everything. She could have shown you mercy." He paused, waiting for my eyes to meet his, but I couldn't bring myself to look anywhere but out the window again. "For saving me." His lighter, teasing tone was meant to soothe my hurt, as it had for years of whispered torments and disgusted looks from others. But this time the pain was different. The crack the queen had created might have spread too deep for any words to repair.

I offered a tiny nod.

A knock sounded from behind us, and we both turned.

Haidee stood in the doorway, polished black and green accented leather covering her chest, bags hanging in hands. "Sorry to interrupt, Highness."

My stomach twisted. She was taking over as the prince's lead.

"No, Haidee, it's fine," Caulden said, glancing at me before crossing the room. "I expect you need to get settled. Have the guests arrived?"

"They arrived at port. The queen requests us to be in the courtyard in a half hour to greet them."

"Good. Vala, that will give you time to relocate your things?"

"Yes, Highness," I said, fighting back the emotions again.

"I'll be in my room until then, Haidee."

She nodded as he swept past her through the door without looking back, taking all the air with him.

After a breathless moment, I slung an arm through the strap of my first bag.

"Vala, I'm sorry."

"You have nothing to be sorry for," I replied instantly, not wanting to hear apologies, not wanting to hear anything. She'd been with us last night, but she'd followed procedure, notifying me and then obeying my orders. Captain Baun had made the best decision appointing her as my replacement. No one else was good enough for the position. Though, everything would still take time for me to digest. I just wished I had that time alone.

"You know you can stay at Mother's instead of the Guard house. Food and firewood are already stocked." She extended a hand with a single key.

"Thanks," I said, feeling the weight of it as it dropped into my gloved palm. "I should move my stuff before the greeting."

"Do you need help?"

"I'll manage," I said, slinging another bag over an arm and picking up the last. I didn't have much, but what I had wouldn't look the same in another place. This room had been home for half my life.

"Wait," she murmured, keeping her voice low as she pushed the door until it was nearly closed. "Do you think he'll return? The one who fled?"

"Yes. Why he fled, I'm not sure. He could have had an injury I didn't see. But he obviously had a mission and a target. I have no doubt he'll return."

"I want you to know that I respect you, Vala. Just because

you're no longer lead doesn't mean I won't listen to anything you offer. Our priority is the prince."

"Do you think I'd risk his life because of pride or despondency?" I asked curtly, bothered by the insinuation.

"No, I don't believe that at all. Despite us not being as close as you and Caulden, I've always been honest with you. And I feel you've grown into your post well and with merit."

With the circumstances, it was hard to ignore the pity driving the admission. The words felt honest enough, though. "Thank you, Haidee. I feel the same for you. I'll meet you in the courtyard as soon as possible." I drew my mask and hood then moved through the sitting room, stopping at the main doors to take a final glance at Caulden's closed door. Then after a heavy inhale, I moved out into the hallway, unable to shake the heavy feeling of finality.

SIX

GUARDS LINED CHATEAU BYLOR'S COURTYARD WITH polished boots, leathers, and swords that were unsheathed, hilts in hands and tips resting on the ground at their feet. Some had been pulled from their port posts or called to continue their midnight details for the greeting. I wasn't sure that was the smartest choice on the captain's part, knowing the threats we had encountered the previous night. Though, I supposed it didn't matter much since we were on high alert. All Guards would be working longer hours for the duration of the royal stay. Hopefully, their senses would remain sharp with the added work on less sleep.

After having barely enough time to run my bags to Saireen's house, I'd arrived to the courtyard as Caulden exited the chateau. The long front strands of his hair had been plaited away from his face and tacked. His sword was sheathed at his side, more than half of it visible under his cloak as it billowed behind him. I waited for him to descend to his position at the base of the main entrance steps, catching his eye for a brief second, then walked to my place between Haidee and Leint, who were several paces off his side.

Bouquets of extra flowers were nearly as plentiful as the Guards, positioned anywhere in the courtyard that potentially lacked a pleasant scent or color. White thin petals sat near the stone archways of the intricately carved oak doors. Golden curved petals flanked the courtyard entrance columns. Blue layered petals overflowed a pot held by a handmaiden as she exited the chateau alongside Queen Havilah—the blue flowers a welcoming gift, to honor Islain's royal colors no doubt.

The queen stopped dead center at the base of the stone steps, and Caulden turned to address her. She wore one of her best gowns of Garlin green with long, flowing sleeves and silver lacing embellishments that matched the jewels on her wrists and fingers. As he spoke to her, she looked straight ahead, pointing to handmaidens and grounds servants to move things around in the courtyard. I'd always thought her demeanor was cold but fair. She'd allowed me into her Guard because of my affliction, but also despite it. She herself was one with skin a little different than others, mostly displaying a deep umber hue as rich as Garlin's soil but with visible patches on her arms and face that were as white as fog, like a purposely unfinished painting. It was almost a shame the quality had not been passed on to Caulden. It certainly made her more beautiful in my eyes. And I often wondered if that added to her hospitality of me, having a small commonality of uniqueness between our vast differences.

Her black hair had been knotted in sections and twisted up and back, the mass heightening her stature and creating a framed perch for her wiry crown set with several green jewels. She gazed around the yard, light brown eyes falling upon me for a moment and hardening to a glare before darting to Captain Baun, who had just finished checking all the Guard positions and was taking his place in front of Haidee.

"After a few of our men struggled getting back to the lake due to quake damage, the bodies there were checked." Captain Baun turned slightly to address Haidee, Leint and me. "Their armor and blades weren't forged here. No one recognizes the craftsmanship of either. The only possible lead is the archer's arrows. The fletching feathers are from a pheasant—a game bird native to Islain."

"Eastern Islain," Leint spoke up. "There are a couple of families in those territories that would have eligible lords wanting to wed the princess." When Haidee and I simply stared, he added, "I was raised in the west, near Ruere Canyon and The Borderlands, but we had studies about and interaction with the other regions."

"Would you be able to tell which family by looking at the bird feather?" Haidee asked him.

"Not likely," he replied.

"Shame not many of us have studied bird breeds. Garlin only has the gulls at the port, the farm chickens, and the occasional carrier pigeon," Haidee commented.

"And apparently ravens," I supplied, recalling the one I'd seen at dawn. Their faces turned to look at me. "One landed in the prison chamber's window during my lashings this morning." Captain Baun straightened, glancing at the queen and prince, and Leint and Haidee's lips turned down, both sorrowful but with noticeably different depths. "I saw a drawing of one in a lesson as a child," I noted.

"They're black, right?" Haidee asked.

"Yes," the captain answered. "It could have followed an inbound ship or traveled on one. Did it have any tags?"

"Not that I noticed."

"Keep an eye out for more. I believe they can be trained messengers like the carrier pigeons Islain uses to communicate with us for trade information and ship arrivals. So intercepting one would be an asset. Meanwhile, I'll spread the word that any free time should be used searching all available books for more information—"

"Captain," Queen Havilah's stern voice called over his. "Is there something we need to be concerned with?"

"Not pressing, Majesty," he replied with a bow of his bald head. "We were discussing precautions and procedures."

The queen raised an eyebrow and her focus went back to Caulden, who had a solemn stare fixed on me. Noticing, the queen cleared her throat to call his attention.

Before the captain could elaborate further, the Guards at the walls snapped their feet together and Queen Havilah's covered carriage moved through the iron gates and stone archway of the bailey, entering the courtyard. After word of their arrival, she had ordered three carriages to port earlier in the morning to welcome and escort Islain's royal family to the chateau. All bodies stood tall, watching the horses trot along the path toward the main entrance. The other two coaches followed closely, carrying guards, servants, and baggage.

My eyes scoured the yard while all others watched the arrival. I hadn't forgotten The Shadow and how important it would be to find him before he made the next attempt on Caulden's life. Images from Sacred Lake spun through my mind as I attempted to extract more details about him. His height matched Caulden's, but his build was less bulky and his movements more lithe. From his shadowed silhouette, I knew his hair was short and his jaw wide and strong. His dark eyes had been frenzied until they'd connected with mine. In that pause between us, there was shock and maybe fear in his stare. He had said, "Not possible." What had he meant? Was he as surprised as me to see someone with the same skin? But as I thought more about his movements and actions, especially in the water, it was even more confusing. He could have slit the prince's throat right in front of me. Why waste the time to pull him through the cavern?

A nudge from Haidee snapped my focus back. Guards in cloaks of blue positioned themselves around the front carriage while the women exited. Queen Meirin was as tall as the male guard at her side. She wore a long-sleeved, blue gown with brown and gold trim that tied at her chest and cinched closer at her waist. Her mass of golden hair had been fastened much like Queen Havilah's, appearing to create a cushion in front for the weighty golden crown to rest atop her head. Princess Anja exited right behind her mother. She was short in comparison, her round, wide-set eyes on the same level as my own as they scanned the greeting party and locked on Caulden. A pink hue tinged her sandy-colored cheeks, and a smirk played upon her thin lips as she slid her hands over the long belted sash at the waist of her iridescent gown. Her ash brown hair was loose, waves of it falling well past her back.

The royals offered one another head bows and shallow curtsies while everyone else bowed slightly lower to honor them all. Queen Meirin extended a hand to Queen Havilah with a smile.

Queen Havilah took her hand gently. "Welcome to Garlin and Chateau Bylor. Please, let us get acquainted in the dining hall."

"Thank you. That's very kind," she replied, letting her guide them to the chateau.

Caulden flashed a timid smile at Anja before stepping to his mother's side. Several Islain guards followed their queen and princess closely.

"That went well," Haidee said in a whisper as we started after Captain Baun, his body shielding our view of the others.

"More than well," I noted, feeling a stab in my chest, thinking of the look Anja had laid upon Caulden.

We entered the dining hall as the queens settled into their chairs. With only two added guests, there was no cause to replace the queen's eight-place table with the extended one used for larger occasions. Though, it was still nearly as amusing to see them seated so far apart at the heads. Caulden waited for Anja to sit beside her mother and then took his a seat on the opposite side next to his mother to view the princess more clearly.

Guards spaced themselves along the walls, and chateau handmaidens carried trays of food and carafes of wine from the kitchens.

"You are welcome to the kitchen at any time during your stay. That is also extended to your escorts. I'm sure your trip was lengthy," Queen Havilah said as a handmaiden poured wine into the goblets around the table.

"I admit there are many other ways I'd prefer to spend

my days than on a ship, but I could not pass up a visit to your island. We've heard so many things from our trade and port men over the last several years. Mostly about this wine, of course," Queen Meirin said with a soft laugh before taking a drink. "By the looks of your glassware, I'd say our ongoing trade has done us both well."

"Yes, it has. Islain's fine white sand has supplied us the means to make more glassware and windows for buildings and greenhouses. The sand on our coasts is far too tolerant of heat, so yours has helped tremendously. I do hope our wine has served as good of a purpose."

"My people have never been happier." Another laugh.

I let my gaze wander. Their accompanying guards looked normal enough—good heights, solid builds. I could see the definition of their arm muscles beneath their sleeves from across the room. None were hooded. None were women. None looked to have my skin.

"Speaking of, I think this trip might yield more than the original intent," Queen Meirin continued, making Caulden and Anja both shift in their seats. She ignored them and went on surveying the plates of food in front of her, reaching over the grapes to pick up a piece of orange melon. "Twenty years ago, when our husbands—may they forever rest with honor—opened communication between our kingdoms again, deciding to end the long silence between our lands … Why not forgive and move on? After all, it had been nearly a thousand years since your people had chosen to flee from the three united human kingdoms, sailing here instead of standing with us to fight the war against the cruel magic lands of Craw and Vaenen." She paused following the insult at Garlin's ancestors, slipping the melon into her mouth and lifting her eyebrows while chewing. "But when my husband visited those years ago, you did not have the plentiful variety you show here today. Your soil produced the same sunstarved vegetation as ours. And now, your grapes make the best wine, your gardens obviously flourishing. What led to that change? I can see that our sky is much the same, hours of sunlight blotted by the cursed fog. So what can it be? Is there some secret you're willing to share?"

I glanced at Caulden, the back of his head visible over the chair. He had stiffened at her words and his fingers clamped down on the side of the chair's arm in restraint. I didn't know much about the kingdoms' histories, only the common stories Saireen had told me. But I knew the queen was truthful in her insult, and Islain still harbored a very deep hatred of Garlin's ancestors for leaving when the human kingdoms had been attacked by Vaenen, the lands of the fae at their northwest, our far north. After they had fled, it was unclear to our people what had stopped the fae king, Izaris, who had controlled Vaenen and all those who lived in Craw—the other magic dwelling land that lay between Islain and Vaenen—as well. We'd heard rumors through the years, spread from ships after the kings had reconnected and began trading a mere twenty years before. Some claimed Izaris had grown too powerful in his quest to extend his reign to the human kingdoms, the unbridled magic becoming too much to bear and crushing him from the inside. Others believed those closest to him—the goddesses Alesrah and Herja—claimed his life. While the rest said King Ataran Tamir of Islain had discovered a way to end Izaris and all magic, then united the surviving humans by seizing control of the other two fallen kingdoms, Astone and Urelya.

Queen Havilah's lips turned up slightly as she lifted her goblet, the dark red wine swirling inside. Her eyes squinted some—a contemplative look I'd grown accustomed to seeing through the years, often when I'd catch her peering at me. "It's the island," she replied to Queen Meirin in a lazy tone. "That's really all I can say. It has evolved over the years, changed as much as our people have. I suppose it has become more stable and tolerant. It has learned to hold onto the warmth despite the cursed fog that has settled over all our lands following the war." Her response was light but the message unmistakable— she wouldn't tolerate insults in her own home.

Captain Baun adjusted his stance, a subtle confirmation.

I looked at Caulden again then toward Queen Meirin, waiting for her to respond, only to lock eyes with Princess Anja instead, her stare as sharp as the blade at my side. Not bothered having been caught, her face tilted the tiniest bit as if she were attempting to see under my mask and hood. I was accustomed to stares, but not those given by curious royalty with no fear or care of reprisal.

"We drink to change then," Queen Meirin replied with a laugh, raising her goblet. Everyone's focus was back to the high queen, including Anja, raising goblets together. "For it may bring us closer than we've ever been very soon."

SEVEN

ITH CALMER DISCUSSIONS OF TRADE AND Garlin's notable sights and resources, the remainder of the greeting had been cordial. Islain's queen and princess expressed their fatigue from travel and regretfully requested to be shown to their rooms at the southern end of the chateau. They accepted an invite to dinner and settled in without complaint. While other Guards received orders from Captain Baun to go into town to do research or to take the time to rest and eat, Haidee and I stayed on detail.

"What do you think they're talking about in there?" Haidee whispered before taking a huge bite of bread we had grabbed en route to the chateau library where the queen and Caulden were now talking behind closed doors.

I inspected the piece of bread in my hands while I finished chewing what I'd already bitten off. "Everything."

She nodded. "Do you think he'll marry her?"

"Do you really think it's up to him?" I shoved more bread into my mouth, needing to quiet my stomach as it twisted from emptiness and emotions.

"No, not really. I was just wondering how you think he's handling it. He seemed indifferent before they arrived."

"He wasn't. He's been concerned since word about their coming, more so with how Queen Havilah's been handling the entire process. She's not happy."

"And she has every right to not be," Haidee agreed. "That discussion in the dining hall proved this is not just about a marriage."

It was my turn to nod as I scanned the hall and listened hard for any approaching footsteps, from outside and inside the library. The last thing I needed was to be caught talking. Captain Baun said not to give the queen another reason to reprimand me, and with how bad the day had already been—for all of us—I wasn't prepared to test her tolerance.

"This is about regaining control," Haidee continued, staring blankly at the opposite wall. "It's basically a polite way of seizing Garlin and all our goods. She covets what our queen has, and she continues to loathe our people for something that happened ages ago."

"She is also the one who makes the decision. She knows that Garlin holds no position to deny her. Our Guard isn't large. We lack the ships they have, the defensive weaponry, a formal army. Their forces could take our peaceful island with little damage to the goods and soil they covet." I paused, leaning back against the wall. "Of course, marrying Caulden and

Anja would ensure their claim here, but she might not be too keen for Caulden to take the throne in Islain, even if it's only a consort title and the Tamir name maintains rule. There is hope, though. If Queen Havilah gives her a fair enough trade deal, maybe Queen Meirin will choose to forgo the marriage and let the Bylors keep Garlin."

"I hate to think how the queen is feeling. She has to be hurting. For the prince. For our people."

We let the silence spread, listening to the intelligible words behind the door, the distant chatter downstairs. In all the silence, I could feel the one thing the queen felt more than hurt. Fear. She had no options, no choices. Her hands were bound. Even if Garlin remained our own kingdom, Islain would forever own us. And she was afraid.

Leint took over watch during the afternoon, posting at the prince's rooms where Caulden had retreated until dinner. After speaking with the queen in more detail about the findings at the lake, Captain Baun gained permission to enter the chateau's library—ordinarily off-limits. Along with a group of other Guards, Haidee and I returned with him to seek any possible information about the assassins' origins.

Captain Baun unlocked and pushed through the door, his body taking up the entirety of the frame, almost having to duck and turn to fit. "Focus on anything about the united kingdoms. Islain, Urelya, and Astone. Look for anything about family specialties, traits, and skills." With a glance at me, he added, "Also, birds."

All the others spread out as the captain slid the curtains away from the wall of thin, arched windows at the far end of the room, spilling daylight onto the floor's center. I stood next to Haidee, watching her eyes gleam and her mouth slacken as she took in the massive library. Aside from a fireplace, the wall space was comprised entirely of shelves stacked with books, small paintings, and sculptures. I recalled having the same look when Caulden had allowed me in to study with him the first time. My visits inside the library had been few, but I was awed every time. And even though it had been years since I'd stepped inside, I'd read quite a few of the books, Caulden often passing what he'd recently finished to me before returning them.

"Let's move to this section here," I said, tugging Haidee's hand with a soft laugh.

"This is …"

Like me, she'd stood outside the doors numerous times. But watching the prince or the queen pass through, catching a glimpse or even staring in, never compared to stepping foot inside. "I know," I replied then frowned some as my stripped position came to mind again. "You may not come in here often, but living so close to the prince has other benefits. He'll surely pass some books to you." I ran a finger across a few bindings then tugged a book from the shelf and opened it wide, too lost in thought to truly see the content.

Her shoulders dropped, the excitement falling a notch with understanding. "That's if he stays here at all. Or if we stay here at all."

I looked up from the pages as she grabbed her own book to search. "If we stay?" Her words surprised me. "Even if the prince leaves, our people will stay. Queen Meirin will make sure our island provides for Islain."

"No, I meant us, as in you and me. I overheard two Guards near the dining hall earlier, just before we came here. They were discussing something about Guard Trials to decide who accompanies the prince if he is to leave."

I narrowed my eyes and cut them to the captain. Naturally, the queen would want to send some of our own with the prince to better ensure his safety. "I hadn't thought ..." I had never really considered leaving the island. This was home. Caulden and I had talked as children, daydreaming of what was beyond our island. We had lain in the courtyard one day and stared at the fog, watching as its movements formed grand ships and foreign castles. The queen had heard us and dismissed the idea quickly, the ships dissolving back into fog behind her while she lectured us about our home and duty. He was never really meant to leave. And being his lead ensured I wouldn't either.

But change had come.

"Captain," I said, calling his attention and watching him stalk toward us.

"Did you find something?"

"No. But I did hear something interesting," I replied, removing my hood and mask, ignoring the looks from the other Guards in the room with whom I wasn't as familiar. Haidee shuffled her feet—a nervous habit.

"Oh?" he asked suspiciously, crossing his arms over his expansive chest, reading my tone and actions well enough to know my next words might cross an insubordinate line. He tipped his head back slightly, blond beard hairs twinkling as they caught the sunlight.

"Is it true there are to be Trials for us if the prince is to leave? I would think that his own detail would already be chosen and notified."

His eyes flitted from side to side, noticing that all movement had ceased within the room. "If the prince is to leave, yes, there will be Trials for the Guards wanting the honor of accompanying him to Islain. If those on his detail want the chance, they will have to participate as well."

"Why not just address us as we are? We are his detail." His avoidance of our positions was vexing. "So you're saying that we will have to run these Trials also to prove our abilities when it's already known that we are worthy enough?"

"Yes, his detail will have to run the Trials," he replied stiffly only to relax his arms to his sides and release a tiny sigh. "Though, that does not include you, Vala."

Haidee coughed in surprise beside me but didn't dare speak.

"What? I am on his detail still. Are you saying that I will not participate?"

"Yes, you are. But as I told you earlier, the queen allowed you to stay on his detail with restrictions. This is one of them. You will not be permitted to go with him if he leaves, so there is no point for you to participate."

I slammed the book at my fingertips and gritted my teeth, anger flaring from the deepest part of my being. The judgment was not fair. "If he were allowed just one, it would be me. I am the most dedicated—"

"This is not the time—" His words cut across mine.

"The first one who would welcome death if it meant his life," I pushed through his words without pause.

"—or the place, Vala," he continued, his own words raising in volume as he cast a hardened glare from his steely eyes.

"You know I speak the truth!" I pressed on. "The queen knows. My whole life has been for him!"

If it were possible, the room had gone even more still. The only noise was the captain's slow intake of breath. "Perhaps that added to the queen's decision," he replied in an even tone. "Perhaps you've gotten too close."

I scowled at his accusation then slung the book across the table.

"I suggest you take leave before I'm forced to report your actions. I'll send word if and when you're to take post."

Haidee bit her lips together as I loosed an uncontrolled growl. My world was crumbling, all my years falling around me like heaps of inconsequential rubble. I had been nothing but loyal, honest. Dutiful. And now it was being stripped away as if none of it had mattered, as if my life had been worthless from the start.

I could feel the heat of Captain Baun's gaze following as I stalked away without acknowledging his command.

"Back to your duty!" his voice bellowed inside the library when I cleared the door.

Valued grounds servants, handmaidens, and Guards with families lived along Chateau Road—the main road connecting the chateau to Florisa's Cove with the crossroads to the eastern farms and vineyards in between. They rarely were individual houses, most only simple stone buildings divided into shared sections, no larger than two floors. Others who held details in town kept residences there, while those who were young and without families stayed in quarters on chateau grounds.

Saireen's was among the oldest and closest to the chateau, bunched with a few others, each with a single room and small garths of land between them and in the back to cultivate a garden, though not many had one. Whenever I'd travel the island with the prince, I would look upon the house, nostalgic for the woman who had dared to raise the scorched girl she had found abandoned along Chateau Road. If our lives had been switched, I wasn't sure I would've been so brave.

Earlier in the morning, prior to the greeting, I hadn't had the time to dwell. Standing at the front door for the second time in one day and with more than enough time, memories of her took their hold. In the years prior to her passing, we only spoke at the chateau. I was always with the prince, and she had continued to work for the queen, so we never had time for a proper visit. Maybe in some ways I had avoided one, hoping to let go of such a vulnerable past.

So it had been years since I'd stepped foot inside her house. Now I was to live there once again. This time without her.

In my years away, the space had shrunken as if the roof and walls had been beaten upon a blacksmith's anvil. I reached up and grazed the boarded ceiling with my gloved fingertips, feeling as giant as Captain Baun in such a tiny space. Through a child's eyes, everything had looked different. I picked up my bags and walked past two cushioned chairs in the sitting area, past the fireplace that also made up the kitchen with its wide hearth and stone stove, then opened the door to the bedroom and washroom. I placed my bags on the floor, noticing some of Haidee's clothing still hanging from a drying line beside the bed. Beneath them lay a basket of carved wooden toys and cups, those Saireen had used to soothe me, to feed me.

My heart stung for her, all she'd done for me and for how she had lived. She had never complained.

Hours had passed and the sun had set, a blanket of darkness settling around me. I stared at the cut logs readied inside the fireplace, but I wouldn't dare start a flame. Even though some light would be nice, the warmth wasn't something I needed. My skin was protection enough, keeping my temperature even. Despite everything else, fear was the only true reason. The fear that had ruled my life. No one knew what had happened to me those years ago. Was it a curse? Real magic? Taking any risk around the flames seemed like a death wish or maybe worse. Could it be me? There was no way to ignore how my body responded whenever I neared a fire. The flames grew louder than most everything else, as if my ears only wanted to hear them speak. My skin also reacted, tingling in a way, differently than what was caused by fear.

Hoof clatter drew my attention from the empty darkness. Maybe the anger I'd roused in the captain had quieted and he decided to finally send news. I was outside in a few short strides, sword at my side, hood and mask on, waiting in the shadows for whatever message was to be delivered. But it wasn't a single rider as I'd expected. There were two riders leading the way down the road. The queen's horses trotted along behind them, towing her carriage as they had earlier in the morning. The moon was still hidden, no different than the previous night, but through the starlit fog, I saw two more riders guarding the rear. With hardly time to consider who was traveling, the first horses passed the house. And then Haidee's familiar whistle hit my ears.

EIGHT

WITH SEVERAL SHIPS FROM ISLAIN DOCKED AT port, Florisa's Cove had become a different level of lively. It wasn't the normal kind of rowdy often seen during the nights visiting traders docked or when our own would return home from Islain. At the edge of town, the smell of wine hung in the air heavier than the reek of fish, and the voices and music carried louder than I'd ever heard. Streets were brightened with every lantern available. Windows of houses and shops were also alight, everyone too drunk on the prospects of more business to shut down for the evening.

Along the ride, as we'd gotten closer to the glow of town, I confirmed that the Guards leading at the front of the carriage were Haidee and Leint, which ensured Prince Caulden was a passenger. And because he wasn't riding his own horse, and since the guards at the back of the carriage weren't our own, I surmised that Princess Anja had requested an evening out.

The piebald mare I'd taken from a house near Saireen's neighed uneasily as I slowed our pace, keeping far away from the carriage to remain unseen. Haidee wanted me there, but whether she informed anyone else would stay unknown until we could speak. The carriage bounded past the keep tower—the silent beast of rock that guarded Chateau Road—and turned onto Trader's Row, leading away from the main docks and toward the shallow end of the cove, where the merchant shops and taverns stood. I followed until the buildings grouped more densely, where people spilled out onto the road along with the music from one of the largest taverns, dancing and staggering about. To ensure a ride home, I hitched the mare to a post beside a bucket of water at the rear of a fisherman's shop displaying handlines, longlines, and nets draped over sorted racks.

I wasn't surprised to see the carriage stop at The Siren Den—the darker-stoned tavern with wooden shingles sitting at the backside corner of the row. Caulden's favorite. Not many people shared his affection, leaving only a few patrons at a time, which made it the most logical place to take her. We'd been there enough times, knew the owner well enough to trust his information, and knew the regular drunken patrons enough to pick out anyone suspicious. I wasn't exactly happy about him trudging around town after almost having died at the lake, but I supposed if we had to be in town, The Siren Den held the best odds in avoiding foul play.

With my eyes on the carriage, I crossed the road, cutting

through the low lying fog along the edge of the buildings, using the shadows to avoid any sober eyes. Haidee dismounted her horse first and moved toward the entrance. After stepping inside to secure the area, she exited and spotted me at the corner of the building, well behind the carriage and guards. She held her hand up with a wave, calling me over.

The rear guards eyed me as I passed. Despite a wicked urge to glare, I chose to ignore them then stopped in front of Haidee just as Leint had. I nodded and skipped a friendly exchange for what was more pressing. "Did Captain Baun have a message to go along with the call to join you? Perhaps a few angered words involving my spending another morning with Orimph in the prison chamber?" At this point, after what had happened in a single day's time, I wouldn't doubt I'd wind up there again. Especially if they thought they could keep me out of the Trials to accompany the prince.

"Actually," Haidee said with a quick glance at Leint, who raised his eyebrows, "he doesn't know." When the carriage made a noticeable movement, she added, "We'll talk inside."

Leint grabbed hold of the carriage door while I stepped aside, my back to the building and my eyes on the perimeter. Princess Anja exited first. She had changed gowns from the morning, choosing to wear a dark shade of blue similar to what her mother had worn. Her hair remained loose, some strands falling off a bare shoulder as she turned to take in her surroundings. There was no denying how beautiful and decorative she was, a fact even more pronounced as she stood on the dull and dirty Trader's Row. I stole quick glances at her from the corner of my eye as hers fell upon me and stayed. Caulden hopped down from the carriage step and made to grab her arm until he noticed me as well. Leint closed the carriage door behind the prince, and I turned slightly, preparing to move inside. An easy smile appeared on Caulden's lips as he locked eyes with me. "Vala." A quick nod. "Shall we?" he asked the princess then guided her through the tavern's door.

I waited until all the others had gone in then eyed all the shadows and all the people down the road one last time before regrettably following the others inside—guarding the door suddenly felt like a better post. When I walked inside, the stench of sweat and mead wrapped around me like an old friend—an embrace tolerated but not fully welcomed. The barkeep greeted me with a silent nod, showing a little less hair atop his head since I'd last visited. I returned the gesture. We'd done the same any time Caulden came to unwind or to unravel completely.

The place was empty, save for a few drunken heads, most already well past their nightly limit, leaning on their tabletops or on the bar. Haidee had secured a table at the back where Caulden and Anja were taking their seats. The princess' guards stood between two other empty tables in the back, while Leint moved toward the bar and Haidee remained posted off to the side of Caulden's table. I went to join her, wanting to hear what she still needed to tell me.

"Would you like something to drink?" I heard Caulden ask Anja as I neared. "I promise the mead here is delicious, better than any other place in town. And I am sorry that it's less occupied, but I'd much rather hear you speak tonight," he babbled.

I stepped beside Haidee, shoulder to shoulder, about a table length from the babbler. The night would be longer than most others, filled with compliments and gushy courtship questions I cared not to hear.

"It was him," Haidee whispered, not bothering to look at me. "When you weren't stationed at dinner, he found out what had happened—that the queen forbade you from the Trials and how you reacted when the captain gave you the news."

My heart knocked in my chest while I watched Caulden stand from the table.

Haidee adjusted her grip on the hilt at her side—a reflex at his movement. "He wanted you here tonight."

"Vala." My name from his lips startled me, but I stepped to his side with the usual urgency. "Help me with the drinks?"

I didn't respond. I doubted I could utter the words even if I'd had them. Why ask me when the barkeep would have brought the drinks himself?

He waited until we were at the bar to speak again, ordering first. "Four meads." The barkeep went about the order. "I needed to tell you how sorry I am. I will speak to my mother tomorrow." He kept his face forward, and I stood still at his side, not daring look at him while I could feel sets of eyes upon us. "I find it ridiculous that she wouldn't want you to go with me should I travel. You're invaluable." The barkeep placed the tankards down in front of us. "We can talk more at another time, I hope. Take the other two tankards to her guards. I don't much care for them. Maybe this will spill them from their horses on the return trip." I grinned behind my mask then stifled my mirth before grabbing the meads and following Caulden as he added, "I'll owe you, Haidee, and Leint some of your own at another time. Tonight, I need your clear thoughts."

"For your men," Caulden said as he approached Anja, who eyed me as I handed her men the tankards. "I think they'd like to taste a drink of this caliber."

"Thank you, Highness," the men said respectfully after the princess nodded her approval.

I moved back to Haidee, this time keeping my back to her and facing the rear door, leaving no room for surprises.

"This tastes so nice," the princess commented after sipping her mead. "But I still prefer your wine."

"Shall I replace it?" Caulden asked.

"Oh, no, thank you. This is fine for now."

"It's probably best for you to drink it slowly. It is very potent."

"I will, thank you." After a silent beat her voice quieted. "I'm curious, who is your guard with the mask? Was she injured grotesquely?"

I felt Haidee stiffen behind me, felt the nervous look from Caulden that I couldn't even see, and I took a heavy breath, awaiting his answer as eagerly as the princess.

"Her name is Vala. She was burned and abandoned as a child and raised close with me. She is one of the finest on the Guard."

"Oh? Then she is the one some traders have spoken of. Only gossip from bored sailors, I suppose, but they claimed she's been cursed by those goddesses no longer worshiped, or maybe something more. Something impossible. Something like magic."

Caulden laughed. While full and soft and jovial enough, I knew the tone that lay beneath. He was bothered by the rumors of me. "Some also gossip that the fog will soon disappear and the wind will once again carry a dragon's breath."

"I suppose it does sound silly." She laughed lightly, gentle like a smooth melody. "My mother swears there have been changes in recent years, though, since around the time of our birth."

"Yes, well, I think things just get better as time goes on, the further we are from The Final War and everything that happened so long ago."

"Yes," she agreed. "I apologize if I offended you."

"No, you haven't offended me. Curiosity is understandable, especially when you've never visited here. The truth is, many fear Vala. Her skin is not soft like ours, no. But she is skilled and true."

Those words were directed toward me. An excuse for the princess' open inquiry. A subtle apology. There had been so many in one day, I was growing sick of hearing them. Despite an urge to ignore him, I shifted my stance in acknowledgment anyway, the way I'd done a millions times to communicate with him through the years.

Silence took hold of their table for a while, long enough to hear the bottoms of their tankards tap the table a couple of times.

"Tell me," the princess started a little tentatively, "what is it that you like? There was only more talk of trade between our mothers at dinner, what they each might gain whether or not we ... decide on a joined future. But I'd like to know your thoughts."

"My thoughts?" Caulden asked.

"Anything. What you like. What you believe."

"I think about Garlin's people. I believe in treating them fairly no matter what our ancestors chose."

"I understand. My mother wasn't very considerate when bringing up our histories. I want you to know that I don't harbor the same resentment for such an antiquated stigma on your people. I do, however, think that history is important. It is what I enjoy thinking about most, actually. The older tales most of all. Do you know many of them?"

"Around the time of The Final War? Goddesses and dragons, faeries and witches? Sirens?" Caulden shouted the last word and heads shot up at the salute to the tavern name with half-hearted calls of "Aye!" mixed with large belches. Caulden and the princess both laughed. "Is that what you mean?"

"All of the kingdoms during that time, yes. I think there's a lot to learn, from the information we have and what we have yet to see. We'd be fools not to educate ourselves properly, damning ourselves to repeat it all. I'm just curious as to what you've learned, here on this island, separated from the rest of the world. No disrespect, I simply don't know what your people may have brought with them or handed down to teach the histories when they relocated to this new place."

Caulden let out a pleased sigh after taking a drink of his mead. "I've learned some, but I bet you have far more information, from that time and well before. Maybe you can share with me. Teach me."

She released another melodic laugh. "I doubt I'm the best teacher, but I'd love to share with you."

"Please," Caulden prompted.

"We know there was never entirely peace throughout the kingdoms, even before the war. The division between the magic of Vaenen and Craw and our human kingdoms was large enough to make conditions uneasy at best. But the majority of Vaenen and Craw's inhabitants held no desire to take what us lowly humans had. They had an entire continent to our west that curved far into the north where many of the faerie families lived. Craw at our border, where most of the witches and underlings dwelt, had a lot of turbulent fights. The fae and creatures who tolerated us the most also lived there, some were said to even be allies, coming to our defenses if any turmoil had arisen. We were curious as to what loomed farther beyond, sending people to explore, often never to return.

"From what I've learned throughout my studies, change happened when the northern fae families began to war over territories. One triumphed over the rest, taking control after he had slain his own family and anyone who stood against him. Izaris was powerful, but that alone wouldn't have been enough to conquer so many. He was said to be cunning as well as magnificently handsome. Some stories claim those traits were the reason he was able to ensnare two of the three Disir—the guardian goddesses of our world who many of us had worshiped for thousands of years. With two goddesses at his side, he held an unfathomable amount of power, controlling many of the Vaenen creatures, choosing those who died in battle, stripping their magic for himself."

"I've learned some of the same," Caulden replied. "Only there are a lot of holes about the aftermath. Since our people left before the end of the war, we've only speculated about the demise of Izaris and of magic."

He was keeping his information close, not fully trusting the princess. I smirked at the realization. How much he was hiding, though, I did not know. His schooling had been widely different from my own, and it involved things he didn't care much to discuss during off time—when we were more inclined to interact freely. He wasn't only learning history but preparing to be a king as well, learning about trade dealings with Islain, traditions, customs, managing our people and the land. Also preparing for this day, to sit at the same table as a princess he might wed. All while I stood outside closed doors, ensuring his safety.

"We don't have as much information as we'd like. When the end came, it was fast, as if magic of the entire world had been snuffed out with a single breath. The only trace of it remained at the borders where we could no longer cross, land or sea. Our lands were left with relief, confusion, and scattered remains, of our own and theirs alike. Dragons. Faeries. Witches. Many of their bones remain still."

"Dragon bones?"

"Yes," she replied, and I could hear the smile in her voice at Caulden's interest. "I'd love to show you."

"So for all these years no one's been able to cross into Craw or Vaenen with no idea why or if magic is truly gone from those lands?"

"Through the years, our people have traveled along the edge, land and sea. The fog that lies at the border is too thick, like a wall hiding everything beyond. It's the only magic left that we know of. Any attempts to cross have led to sickness or death. If any other magic had lived, someone would have found a way to cross."

A loud thud beside their table captured all of our attention. The skinnier of the princess' guards had collapsed to the floor, an empty tankard clattering beside his head.

Caulden laughed as the other guard bent forward to help his comrade, only to stumble himself. The guard looked upon the princess with wavering, apologetic eyes.

"What did you do to my men?"

Caulden's laugh subsided enough to say, "It seems your men enjoyed the mead, Princess. Maybe a tad too quickly."

Indeed. Caulden had wanted a laugh tonight, and he had surely gotten one.

With my hand tightened on the hilt of my sword, I

surveyed the rest of the tavern. Most of the other patrons were snoring, heads pressed to their tables and the bar, completely oblivious to what had happened. The doors remained closed. I turned to Haidee and received a gleeful smirk.

What we hadn't expected was the princess to join in with Caulden's laughter, but she did. Her tone rang loudly through the room, letting loose as if it had been repressed into that soft melodic version for years.

After another few moments, she settled, a few dainty coughs sputtering into even breaths. "We should probably return to the chateau. It's been a very long day."

"Yes, I think you're right," Caulden agreed. I turned, watching him tilt his tankard fully, draining it before setting it back down. "Haidee."

"Your Highness?" she replied, already prepared to go.

"Please help Leint move those who are incapacitated into the carriage. The princess and I will ride their horses."

Haidee nodded then walked to Leint to move the drunken guards. I stepped hurriedly outside, checking for any threats and alerting the carriage driver. As Haidee and Leint hauled the other guards into the carriage, a bird's caw sounded over the dying noise of the crowd down The Row. I looked at the edge of the tavern, spotting the raven as it landed atop an empty hitching post. Its head turned, studying me as it had inside the prison cell.

Haidee and Leint finished with the guards as Caulden and Anja exited the tavern. They began to untie their horses when the raven cawed again.

"Is that a …" Leint's surprised words dropped off.

"Vala?" Haidee called to me in a worried whisper, her eyes on the raven.

I focused harder on the bird, past the slight shimmer of starlight on its inky feathers, through the darkness and fog. A shadow moved.

"Haidee, take them," I called back to her, unsheathing my sword. "Now."

NINE

H AIDEE WASTED NO TIME, SIGNALING PRINCE CAULDEN and Princess Anja to mount their horses. I was instantly thankful that they had switched places with the drunken guards. Caulden was better off on horseback—not contained in a box to be an easy target—and the princess' horse would follow his back to the chateau whether she was a skilled rider or not.

They galloped off, Leint and Haidee guarding and guiding from the rear, guaranteeing the solid pace. The carriage left last, trailing far behind, an obstacle to help block should anyone give chase.

"Show yourself," I demanded, stepping closer as I stared behind the curious raven where I'd seen the movement, watching the immobile outline of what was definitely a hooded, cloaked man.

With such little light, it was impossible to see more. But when the figure suddenly turned, the hood moved, revealing a small glimpse of his face that, while still shadowed, appeared to be smooth and of a lighter shade. Not charred. He leapt into a run, cloak billowing behind him as he followed the path the prince had taken. Coils of fog swirled in his wake, swallowing his figure. The raven squawked in protest at the movement, lifting up from its perch and flying up and away into the night. I gripped the hilt of my sword tighter and set off after The Shadow, refusing to give him another opportunity to get close to the prince.

He sprinted through the now sparse crowd of wandering people on the darkened road, easily dodging the bodies with heads too clouded to notice or care about our chase. There was no denying his speed. I had to stow my sword, saving my arm strength for a potential fight. His form darted past the fisherman's shop where I'd hitched the mare. Not knowing if he'd remain on foot, I decided it was best to continue on horseback. After losing only a few moments, I was back on his trail and gaining ground quickly. Hearing the hooves pound at his back, his body took a swift turn through an alley and then another, taking all options to throw me off his course. As he navigated through the smaller roads closer to the water and docks of the cove, his main direction kept aim at Chateau Road. Without a horse, there was no way he could catch them, but I wouldn't gamble with Caulden's fate by abandoning the chase. It would only give him reason to return, to try again another day.

He turned and disappeared between another set of buildings, so I slowed the mare and cut the turn the same as I had all the others. Only he hadn't continued running as he had before. Right after I made the turn, his body leapt at me, dropping from the ledge of a high window. There was no time to react. A hard body collided with mine, knocking me from the mare with enough force to steal my breath. Both of us tumbled into the packed dirt below but were up with swords drawn at nearly the same speed and far more grace.

"Who are you? Why are you after Prince Caulden?" I asked while advancing, pushing the words out in the fiercest tone I could muster despite the sharp ache in my chest.

A rasping breath sounded from beneath his hood, pinched with shock or pain. "Who are you?" he asked in return, retreating the steps I'd advanced.

I moved again, more questions blinding my immediate thought to kill. "Tell me who you are! Who sent you here?" I lunged with a wide swing of my blade, engaging but not intending much damage.

He turned and lifted his blade, blocking my attack. A hard grunt followed and then a hiss. His blade kept lowering the slightest bit between hits, as if it were a struggle to lift even though his expert parrying suggested otherwise.

I'd had enough playing. He was a threat, and if he wouldn't answer questions, then it was time to end him. I swung again and was met with another block and then another. I kept pushing him forward toward the edge of the building, toward the last road where everything opened wide to look upon the water and the cove.

He groaned with another block, smacking my blade forcefully enough with his own that his cloak's hood fell away from his face. After another swing, he cleared the building's corner, standing directly under a swaying cone of light from a hanging lantern post along the deserted waterline road.

I gasped and froze at the sight so clear, so close. My eyes had to have betrayed me by the tavern. There was no way to deny it here, no way to ignore it. Dark, rough, and cracked, his face was like the rock at the cliffs, like the flesh coating my own body. The entirety of him looked far more intimidating under the light—his height, his size, more powerful than I'd realized at the lake, but obviously not cumbersome enough to slow or hinder his abilities. As all shadows did, he dressed in all black, only his face visible now. Hair that mimicked the night sky topped his head, cut fairly close, not obstructing the view of his parted lips, narrow cheeks, and broad, flaring nose. His marbled gray eyes mirrored the night—fog laden darkness—and my own. They were wide with shock as he heaved excessive recovery breaths.

"You …" It was all I could manage at first, stunned at the sight of him once again. How could it be? Had he also been struck down by some mysterious curse of magic like I had? Had someone claimed his human life in the same way? The memories of my youth ripped through me, demanding answers to the questions that had haunted me an entire lifetime. What had happened to me? To him?

He grunted and hissed air through his teeth, not making a move to attack me again, just watching, waiting. Defensive. Only defensive.

I extended my sword, leveling it with his chest, and moved even closer. "Why are you here?"

His lips pressed together as if he were considering a response. He kept his sword arm low, angling it slightly downward. With a small twist of his hand, the blade glinted and its smooth curve caught my eye, so unlike the straight one I had pointed toward him.

"Answer me!" I demanded, taking another step forward, placing myself within striking distance.

"You," he began, his tone rough, pained. "You have to tell me who you are. What you are." He lifted his other gloved hand and touched his cheek tentatively, as though it were tender.

"I am Vala of the Guard, and if you do not tell me who you are, I will take your head." I forced the words out. The thought of taking his life, never getting the answers to the questions burning within, hurt in an unimaginable way.

"I came for him, yes," he finally said. I pulled back my arm, settling into a striking position, and he quickly added, "For information first. I dragged him away to ensure his survival from the assassins. If I had intended to kill him, I would have done it immediately. I had more than enough time."

I released an even breath, feeling the guilt of the truth we both knew. He'd had plenty of time at the lake. I hadn't been fast enough to save the prince, and he knew it. "Who sent you?"

"That, I cannot answer," he replied in a more relaxed tone. His shoulders pushed back and his chest lifted as his body straightened. "But I can tell you why."

"Why then?" I urged, wanting any information he was willing to give.

He inhaled deeply and stretched his limbs then worked his empty hand open and closed. "The visiting queen and princess look to be deciding the future of their kingdom and yours. But what if I told you the queen could have other reasons for being here, something she isn't divulging."

"Why would that concern me?"

"You protect your prince, this island. I'd say it would very much concern you."

"And why should I believe you?" Islain could very well dismantle Garlin whether or not the princess chose Caulden as her consort. The idea that the queen had other plans seemed absurd. What could be worse than that? "What's your reason for telling me this information?"

He shrugged in an easy, comfortable way. "Because this island, these people, may not be the only ones affected should the queen find the information she seeks."

"Is this some form of rival trickery? Do you work for one of Islain's lords? One who would like nothing more than to see Prince Caulden dead so they can sit upon the throne themselves?"

"No. If I were like them, commanded by them, surely I wouldn't be here with you right now. Their intentions were made very clear, and you know as well as I that those intentions didn't involve talking."

True. Though, I wouldn't admit that to him. How could I trust what he was saying to be accurate without knowing him or his purpose? "What are your intentions then? What is it that you want to know? Is it the same information that the queen is seeking?"

"Possibly. But when I came across you … let's just say things have changed."

A sense of foreboding riddled into my bones, a cautious warning I couldn't ignore. We had an obvious resemblance that neither of us had yet to admit aloud, and the easy talk between us could have been because of it. But what if all of it was a lie? He had been sent by someone. Was he just waiting for me to feed him something useful? Would I have the information he was searching for?

I glared at him as his words drifted away, putting myself

in check. "You now know who I am, so tell me your name. If what you say is true, you can at least tell me that."

"At least? I think I've given you more than I even should," he said, glaring right back. "In fact, I think you owe me something."

I stiffened, tightening my fingers around the grip of my sword, preparing to defend myself with the change in conversation.

"Who are you, really? And how did you come to live *here*?" His face turned in either direction, surveying what could be seen through the fog rolling in off the water, his upper lip pulling away from his teeth in disgust.

"I am from here," I replied, instantly regretting my hasty response.

"I know for a fact you are not, so quit lying."

"And how is it that you know? Where are you from? Why do you have skin like mine?" There it was, out in the open, the question I'd been wanting to ask since I'd first seen his face in the cavern.

"So you aren't lying." His eyes flashed and his head tilted, observing me. "Interesting. You truly believe that with skin like yours you are from here? Do you know nothing beyond this island?"

I seethed, letting the anger roll from me through heavy breaths. "I know enough."

"Apparently, less than you think," he replied and had the nerve to lift the corner of his lips in a pleased smirk that set my soul blazing with more fury than I'd felt in a long time.

The frustration and pain the day twisted together, building into something dangerous inside. I ignored the calm, controlled voice to which I had listened all through my years on the Guard and swung my blade at him. I held no care if he died. He'd given me enough information, whether I chose to use it or not. I wouldn't now, however, be fooled by appearances of likeness, or of sweet acting princesses, or of queens filled with arrogance and greed. I'd trust no one, especially if I were to accompany the prince to Islain, save those I'd known for many years.

His blade lifted, smacked mine away, and swung back around to counter. I dove into a forward roll, dodging his movements then turning with another thrust of my blade. He laughed out a breath as he stepped out of the path of my swing, the sound of it pounding my ears worse than the blood pumping through my veins.

"You are skilled, Vala," he said, lunging at me. I ducked to the side, hearing his blade slice the air. Close. Too close. "I'd like to think you could do better with a different kind of blade."

He was skilled too, far more than anyone I'd ever encountered. Even the captain. That feeling of disquiet returned, splintering through me like a quake on the verge of destruction. He doubted my life on Garlin, certain I was not from the island. His words were taking hold, filling me with so much doubt I could barely think. I wanted to end him for taunting me, for digging under the skin that had punished me since birth, for holding my lack of knowledge captive.

"Don't assume to know me, to know my strengths or weaknesses." My voice boomed through the chilling air, the noise of the night having all but disappeared as I advanced on him again, swing after swing after thrust of the blade. I waited for him to duck and counter then I kicked off the edge of the stone wall and turned, gaining enough height to crash my boot into his shoulder, shoving him backward into the open road. The water behind him in the distance was barely visible through the mass of nightly fog, the light of the cove's towers shining strong enough to see the smooth, reflective surface.

"I'm only interpreting what is plain to see," he replied, shaking off my blow and bounding toward me.

"Vala!" Haidee's voice called out from somewhere close, stealing my attention away for a swift moment.

But even I knew one moment was more than enough time to change lives, to end them. A fatal mistake. When my focus returned to him, the end of his blade was almost to my chest. His eyes widened, flitting with a look of disbelief or regret. I had no time to turn, no time to block, only time to watch the blade as I thought of Saireen's peaceful eyes. It felt like my end. The next moment came fast, a flick of his wrist in time to shift the point of the sword away from my chest and across my arm, the sharp steel biting in as he withdrew.

I wailed at the sudden pain before guarding myself properly, sword at the ready again even though I'd seen the change, knew he'd decided not to take my life.

He relaxed his sword, the blade falling limply to his side as his shoulder rounded with a heavy exhale. His eyes met mine again before he retreated backward a few paces.

I wanted to yell at him, to tell him not to leave. His actions had only left me confused. I needed more information, more time.

"My name," he said, as if reading my expression, my mind, "is Xavyn. Don't forget what I told you. Stay alert, Vala."

"I—"

"Vala!" Haidee's voice called from behind me, the thudding of her horse's hooves echoing between the building walls.

"I'm here." I turned back, watching her ease her horse past the piebald mare then travel down the alley toward me. I slid a hand over the wound at my arm and turned back to where Xavyn had been, only to see the swirling fog in his wake.

"Are you okay? Did he get away?" She jumped from her horse beside me. "You're injured."

"It's not bad," I said, shrugging off her attempt at an inspection. "My skin is already healing around it."

She was quiet for a moment, staring at me while I stared after the man who could have taken my life. "Caulden sent me back. He was … concerned. I volunteered to come find you to make sure he wouldn't return himself."

"Good," I said with a nod. It would have been much worse if everyone had seen who I was up against. But I knew the real problem with that statement, the problem with how Caulden had been behaving all day—he was more worried about me than he was about himself. I could hear in Haidee's voice that she was bothered by his reactions too. Had I become his liability instead of his protector?

"Were you able to get a better look at him this time?" The statement held no judgment, only determination and the drive to end a threat. Our duty.

"Yes," I replied, considering all that I'd learned in one day. "Maybe too good of one."

TEN

AFTER RETURNING TO THE CHATEAU WITH HAIDEE TO inform Caulden that I was still breathing, I was released by the captain to go rest with the order that I return in the morning to give the details involving the altercation as well as face punishment for joining in on the evening when I was not given the order to do so. The rest of the night I spent sewing the tear in my cloak and shirt where Xavyn's blade had sliced into my flesh. I was lucky, though. I might not have been breathing had he held the blade's intended course to pierce my heart.

Xavyn wasn't an ordinary fighter. There was something else about him that was different, something more than the obvious likeness to my skin. At first—like at the lake—he had appeared to be in pain. But there was no real indication of injury aside from his stiff movements and distressed noises. As skilled as he was, injuring himself when he'd first tackled me to the ground was unlikely. And the longer we had engaged, the evidence of any injury seemed to disappear. He was composed toward the end, relaxed. I'd go so far as to say comfortable, infuriatingly so, telling me that I'd do better with a different blade. Was he trying to crawl into my head even more than he already had?

I was late to rise the following morning, my body sore from the exertion of the fight and my mind exhausted from hours of contemplation. The chateau was bustling with activity when I arrived. Several farmers had pulled their carts for their weekly deliveries of produce, meats, and wine. With all the people milling about, they barely noticed me, which was a blessing since I didn't care to receive the usual gawks and stares. Breakfast had to have been served already, leaving the dining hall empty and the smell of fresh biscuits and eggs lingering in the warming morning air.

Any chance of having a few more moments of peace before the interrogations began were doused as soon as I knocked upon Prince Caulden's door and was greeted with a firm welcoming grunt from Captain Baun.

"So good of you to join us," he said gruffly, backing away from the door to let me in. "I suppose tacking on a small infraction of tardiness is nothing when you completely disregard orders to stay home."

I scanned the room, meeting Haidee's tranquil gaze from her position outside what was once my bedroom door—now her bedroom door. Leint's head of rust-colored hair didn't even turn from his position, peering out the window while Caulden lounged in one of the sitting chairs in front of the fireplace.

"I apologize for being late," I admitted, standing straighter. No matter what was to be discussed, it was better to start off on a good note.

"I think we have a bigger problem to focus on than Vala being late or my choice to have her on detail last night, Captain," Caulden spoke, tossing a book to the table as he stood. "I for one am glad she was there. Who knows what would have happened had she not been."

"Your Highness," Captain Baun acknowledged the prince's statement. "While I agree that Vala's skills are of good use, the queen wasn't very happy to hear that she disobeyed—"

"Enough about my mother, Captain. I trust her judgment, but not when it applies to my own Guard. I decided to have Vala there last night. My team works well together, and I didn't want anyone missing when the princess was out with me."

"Understood," Captain replied with a nod.

"Now, Vala." Caulden turned toward me with an easy smile on his lips. "Thank you. We've never experienced this type of threat and I want you"—he turned to look at Leint and Haidee—"and you both as well, to know that your efforts likely saved the princess and me from something serious. I hadn't expected so many members of Islain's court to be so threatened by this potential union. I just hope it all settles down quickly."

"With respect," Captain Baun spoke up, adjusting the lower metal plates in his leather chest armor. "I don't think it will settle. It's only going to get worse from here, Highness. With your courtship and the queen and princess' continued visit, we have to assume there will be other attacks, other threats. That is, until some decision has been made."

The captain's statement was accurate. Islain's courtiers would not back off for some time, possibly until they were seated at Caulden and Anja's wedding. And even then it wasn't guaranteed. Caulden knew as well as the rest of us. He was just being optimistic, maybe to calm himself about the strife he would have to endure from now on. Even the most serious of Garlin's internal threats against the throne—those that had even led to deaths and burials from Crypt Cliffs—seemed trivial in comparison.

The prince nodded and looked back at me. "Vala, we've already been over the events leading up to the visit from The Shadow last night, to include the odd presence of the raven bird. Please, tell us what transpired after you ordered us away."

The Shadow. The nickname they'd now adopted after I mentioned his ability to hide so well again last night when they'd attempted to question me immediately. It still suited him but felt weird to think now since I knew his name, but sadly not much more. The things I did know flickered through my mind. Skilled. Smart. Deft. Evasive. Strong. Maddening. Was he not human? Did that make me the same? He'd very well implied as much.

"Vala," Prince Caulden said, waving a hand in front of my face. "Are you all right? Do you need to sit?"

"No, Highness," I replied, catching Haidee's and Leint's eyes, both staring inquisitively.

"Is your arm still injured?"

Instinctively, I rubbed the place where Xavyn's sword had sliced my rough skin, feeling the soreness but knowing the skin had already regenerated, sealing the wound. "I'm all right. I was just trying to recall the events."

"You mentioned his appearance was still shadowed last

night," Captain Baun started in. "After a night's sleep, is there more that you recall?"

Some. But a dreadful feeling wiggled back inside as I thought of Xavyn's words. Could I really trust everyone here? They all wanted the best for the prince, for Garlin. I couldn't say they wanted the same for me. I trusted all of them, had feelings for each of them, even Leint to a degree. But telling them what little I'd learned about Xavyn felt wrong. It could be considered as cowardice, protecting myself from the judgment that would undoubtedly be placed when they learned that he had the same skin. It would only lead to more questions, questions with answers I couldn't give. Was it bad that I wanted those answers for myself first? Since Xavyn had insinuated the truth about my being born somewhere else entirely, didn't I deserve to know if I was somehow connected to him first?

I blinked several times. "He wore a hooded cloak this time. It was so dark and the fog even more dense, concealing most everything beyond arm's reach. After traveling a few buildings on foot, I chose to chase from horseback, not knowing his intentions and hoping for a better vantage point. He continued on foot, trying to lose me by ducking between several buildings. I got complacent." I shook my head. "I followed blindly, expecting him to continue on. But when I turned into the last alley, he jumped from a ledge and knocked me from the horse. We both stood quickly, swords drawn."

"And still you couldn't see his face?" Captain Baun urged.

"No," I lied, my eyes drifting to look at the floor. "We fought for a while. I kept on the offensive, pushing him toward the front road, hoping for a better view. But one never came."

"How did he manage the hit to your arm?" The murmured question was Leint's.

"He's had training, and he's very skilled. I thought more about it last night and realized he had remained on the defensive most of the time while I expended much of my energy. When I heard Haidee call my name, I hesitated for one second, worried that it was a call for help rather than one seeking me out. That's when he landed his strike." I wouldn't dare include what I really knew.

"And he just retreated after … because he knew I was approaching," Haidee said, the statement filled with so much doubt that it was almost a question.

"Yes. It puzzled me as well."

"There's not much to ponder," Captain Baun said. "His target was already gone. He knew it was far better to leave and fight another day than to face two of our Guards, whom he'd witnessed kill several assassins at the lake."

"Yes, but there was something off about the encounter," I added, deciding to release a little bit of the information to gauge their reactions, make them question his motives as I had. "He didn't seem to want to inflict that strike. It was almost as if he regretted it."

They were all silent at that, eyebrows rising as if they were concerned with my sanity. Perhaps they had reason. Leaving out the details about him … Was I a traitor for not disclosing it all?

"How could you even know that if you couldn't see him clearly?" Leint questioned, but the captain interrupted impatiently.

"Maybe he has respect for your skill. Maybe his only goal is what he was ordered to do and nothing more. Who can even know? There's no reason to analyze this. We just need to find him." Captain Baun crossed his arms, closing himself off to any more absurdity.

"That's not all," I said, looking directly at the prince now, needing him to hear me, to understand over the others. "I thought about it last night as well. If he were really here to kill you, why didn't he do it immediately at the lake? He had the time. I didn't reach you fast enough."

Caulden's face paled and his lips went slack. Everyone else went silent again.

"Think about it," I urged. "Why would he take you under the water? With one swipe of a blade, he could have sliced your neck open, draining your life into the lake."

"That's enough!" Captain Baun snapped loudly. "Are you wanting another visit to the prison chamber? I'm not sure what's—"

"No, Captain," Caulden interrupted. "There's no need for threats. It's something I need to hear. I want to be aware of everything. That includes the information hardest to swallow."

"It doesn't mean he isn't planning to take the prince's life," Leint said, keeping on track. "He made a choice. He could have planned to drown him after pulling him away from us, or tortured him. Perhaps that was why he neglected his dagger right off. He obviously knew about the lake's other cavern and the exit onto the cliffs." His blue eyes glared at mine, their intensity growing, challenging my thoughts and reasons.

"It's true," I said, understanding his logic. "But I doubt there was reason to bother. What would one gain by torturing or interrogating the prince? He hadn't even met the princess yet. He holds no inside information regarding her kingdom. And if he were an assassin sent by another court, he would have been as forthright as the others. He would have done it immediately."

"Any thoughts to why he didn't then?" Caulden asked. "Why go through the effort of dragging me away with no reason?"

I shook my head, not able to admit that Xavyn had said he had come for information and his actions at the lake had been to get Caulden away from the assassins. But I still had no idea who had sent him—if he was acting under orders at all—or what information he was after. And the bigger question was why he thought I needed to be watchful of Queen Meirin. "Maybe he's seeking something else."

"I don't want to hear any more of this." Captain Baun huffed in frustration. "We need facts. So far we have no description and no idea how to capture or end him before he threatens the prince or the royal guests again. I need to confer with the queen about our next course of action regarding this Shadow. In the meantime, more Guards will arrive from town to ensure the chateau is heavily manned. For now, I'll have others take the prince's detail, so you all are dismissed. I'll send for you later after I've spoken to the queen and her council."

"Yes, Captain," Haidee and Leint replied.

"I have a meeting with my mother as well, Captain. You being there will likely be beneficial. There are things she needs to hear regarding her recent judgments of Vala."

I swallowed hard, everyone's words ringing in my ears. The prince was defending me, but after my lies, after withholding information about Xavyn, I wasn't sure he should.

ELEVEN

"YOU LIED TO THE PRINCE," HAIDEE'S VOICE WHISPERED from behind me.

I sighed, knowing that my peaceful day had ended as I rounded the pathway to the longest bowered arbor in the chateau garden, where I'd been instructed to post and await the prince's arrival. I had successfully avoided everyone from the time I'd left the prince's rooms well into the afternoon, first roaming the grounds then eating and napping at Saireen's before reporting back to the chateau.

Hearing Haidee's words confirmed the evening was bound to be longer than even the captain could anticipate with everyone restricted to the chateau.

"You were injured last night, so I didn't want to push

you for all the details. But I had no idea you'd lie about it this morning," she said, tugging on my arm to slow me.

I let her move to my side and stopped, touching one of the vines with a fingertip and watching it curl and wilt in reaction to my skin. I dropped my hand and looked at Haidee, really looked at her. She held so many resemblances to Saireen. A pointed arrow nose set evenly on her diamond face. Plentiful lips so used to telling truths. Wide, warm eyes, like grassy hills flecked with golden flowers, drawing me in, inviting me to feel their comfort. It made me wonder if I could confide in her the way I had in our mother.

"What are you hiding, Vala? You told me last night that you'd had a better view of him." She sighed when I didn't respond right away. "If you are in trouble—"

"No," I admitted in a low voice, resolving to trust her. It was probably the reason I'd let the small confession slip on Trader's Row to begin with. After glancing around, I turned to face the back of the gardens. "I have to ask you something."

She tipped her chin and narrowed those warm eyes in response.

"Do you remember when Saireen found me? I know we haven't really talked about it …"

She shook her head lightly, her stringy plaits rippling over her shoulders at the movement. "I know we never talked … Yes, I remember when she found you. I hadn't moved to the chateau to apprentice as a handmaiden yet."

"Were you there when she brought me home?"

"What is making you ask these questions now, Vala?"

"Just, please … I need to know. Were you there?"

She sighed then looked quickly around the gardens to

ensure no one had arrived yet. "Yes, I was home, but I was asleep. I woke when I heard you crying."

"Did she ever tell you where she had been? Where she had found me?"

"She said you'd been abandoned on the road, that someone had dumped you. She never told me more, no matter what I asked after." Her eyes drifted to her hands, the scars she had because of me. I was certain, after realizing that I was different, she had likely asked many questions. And I wondered if that was the reason she had been sent to the chateau soon after.

I bit my lips together, knowing I'd have to search Saireen's house for anything else that might better explain my existence. Had Saireen herself known more, or was it as simple as being found on the road? After having talked to Xavyn, everything had become questionable.

"Vala, talk to me. Why are you asking these things? Did something happen last night?"

"Yes," I replied, lowering my tone again. "I did see The Shadow, Haidee. I had seen him at the lake too, but I just couldn't believe my eyes. He looks like me, with my skin."

Her eyes widened and she shook her head. "No."

"Yes. I spoke to him last night. During our encounter." And so I told her what had happened as briefly as I could, explaining how he'd doubted me and quickly changed course, thinking me naive or dumb for not knowing what lay past Garlin's sea.

"But what he's suggesting is …"

"More," I offered, not wanting to say the word out loud. *Magic.* Was I something more?

A shudder accompanied her deep breath. "What are you

to do with that information? How do you even know he's telling the truth?"

"I don't, but I can't very well ignore the fact that he has my skin. He knows something, and I can't ignore that. I can't pretend that I haven't seen him or spoken with him."

"So what now? Should we keep lying to the prince? Keep—"

"You won't be lying to anyone. Just please don't mention knowing until I can figure out what to do."

Her eyes closed with a nod. "And in the meantime?"

I looked toward the back of the chateau. The sentinels posted around the gardens all snapped to attention, signaling an imminent arrival. "I'll search Saireen's house when I'm relieved for sleep. And while we are on duty, we listen. If what Xavyn said is true, we might just overhear something from Queen Meirin or Princess Anja. The princess could be seeking more than the usual information from a potential consort." I was glad the prince had remained mostly silent the previous night.

"They've arrived," Haidee noted and began walking under the arbor again as several people exited the chateau. "The captain didn't seek me out after his meeting, so I'm not sure what the prince may have said to the queen. I don't think he'll be able to persuade her into letting you partake in the Trials. If they take place, that is."

A distant ache panged somewhere inside, the longing to stay with Caulden twisting with something different, something new. A raw need to know more about myself, to see more than this island, to learn more about everything. I steeled myself as I followed Haidee, resolved to keep an ear on what was being said, but also taking care so as to not let

Xavyn's words eat away at who I was and what my duty demanded of me. I was a Guard. My life was still for the prince.

"I'm sure I'll hear about it soon enough," I replied in a whisper at her back, then closed my mouth to the activity of conversing for possibly the last time in the day.

Prince Caulden wore his casual attire from the morning, a lengthy green tunic with pants and boots. The princess also dressed more casually than the previous day, no doubt saving her niceties for the eyes of more people. Various shades of purple material flowed around her in delicate layers, the little breeze in the garden caressing the dress as she walked.

Haidee fell in step behind the prince, dismissing the Guards the captain had charged with his detail while we were gone. I followed her lead, listening and waiting for any command.

"These gardens hold some of our foods, spices, and medicines. A good amount of our goods also come from the farmers. Their soil has become far richer over the years. A majority of the peak runoff flows in their direction." The prince continued his tour after an acknowledging nod toward Haidee and myself. The princess smiled brightly, turning toward us. I felt her eyes on me again, but I kept mine pinned to Haidee's back, ignoring her stare.

"Would you like to see the queen's conservatory since we're out here? The length runs beside the east towers along the garden there," Caulden said, pointing toward the stone building with the paneled glass windows and a row of spires.

I flinched at the idea. The queen was never thrilled to have guests, let alone the chateau staff visiting her conservatory, even for cleaning and tending to her plants and flowers. When Caulden was younger, he used to try and hide from me there, knowing the queen disapproved. Of the few times I'd been severely scolded during my youth in the chateau, the conservatory was the place it happened.

"I'd love to," the princess replied.

Fantastic. I gnashed my teeth. It didn't matter that it had been years since those accidental childish incidents during games of chase. I already had one foot over the fine line of Her Majesty's good graces. The last thing I needed was something else to happen. It would kill the sliver of a chance I had at participating in the Trials to leave Garlin with the prince, should he go. I worked my hands, opening and closing my fists to expend whatever nervous energy had taken hold. I was being paranoid. That was all. I needed to focus on my duty.

The prince and princess strolled toward the building, her hand cupped under his arm in a familiar, comfortable way. Caulden pointed this way and that, explaining each section of the garden to the princess. She kept a weak smile in place that failed to fully hide her disinterest. Luckily, the prince hadn't noticed, having gone into a studious trance, reciting the many things that had been lectured to him through the years. Or it was possible that he had noticed and chose to continue anyway. He wasn't exactly thrilled about being stuck inside the chateau this evening due to the mysterious Shadow threat and could very well have written off her somber demeanor for the same. I was certain the queen and the captain hadn't fully disclosed all their concerns to the visiting guests, but Anja had seen enough the previous night to know that leaving the chateau was probably unwise. And then again, maybe her disinterest didn't have to do with that at all. Garlin was a great deal smaller and undoubtedly quite boring compared to her extensive kingdom. Her lack of enthusiasm for Caulden's narration could simply have been her reaction to the entire island. After all, we didn't have dragon bones.

When they arrived to the oak and metal doors, the queen's usual Guards—Bransley and Lato, who she used more like sentinels—pulled them open and bowed their heads in greeting. Voices met us before stepping foot inside.

"Darling," Queen Meirin cooed, opening her arms from halfway down the conservatory's sizable main aisle. Her golden hair gleamed under the tiny rays of clear light passing through the window glass. She'd left a majority of it down, a mix of loose strings and plaits falling to her back. She also wore a more relaxed dress—hers with a crimson hue—its bodice section forgoing the restriction of a corset.

At her side, Queen Havilah stepped out from behind one of the stone pillars with raised eyebrows and a pinched smile. The fabric of her dress was a dark cedar, complementing the umber toned patches of her skin. "Isn't this a pleasant surprise?"

The surprise part was true, but I could tell by her posture and the clipped tone of her voice that she most definitely didn't find it pleasant. If the prince had any thoughts of relaxing alone with Anja inside, those plans were gone.

"Mother. Queen Meirin," the prince said, bowing his head slightly. "It's wonderful that you're here. We were walking the gardens, and I knew I had to bring the princess here for a proper tour." The words were meant to ease his mother.

"Of course," she replied, relaxing her tense lips. "I thought the exact same. Queen Meirin was just asking if you had met up again to spend more time."

"Yes, I am glad that you both aren't too shaken after what

occurred last night," Queen Meirin stated, bending a little to prod the group of small, white flowered tips of the anise plant at her side.

"It wasn't exactly horrible, mother," Princess Anja replied, eyeing the prince warily. "Prince Caulden acted very fast. And his riding skills are utterly superb," she boasted, slipping her hand farther down his arm so she could grasp his hand.

I couldn't help but to watch. The way she touched him was … purposeful, calculated. Or maybe it was simply her way of drawing him in, expressing her willingness for progression. When I shifted my eyes to resume their leveled and fixed position on the opposite wall, I got caught by a narrowed set of light brown eyes. Queen Havilah regarded me for a silent second until I hastily looked away.

"All the thanks has to go to my Guards. But last night's issue may not have been as bad as we originally thought," Prince Caulden noted, and I guessed this was a subtle way to address whatever he and his mother had spoken about during their meeting.

"Any issue such as that should be handled as a serious threat," Queen Havilah said, confirming my suspicions. The prince had shared my thoughts and questions about The Shadow with the queen. "It's bad enough that we have to worry about assassins of those who wish to end your life, in turn ending a potential union of Garlin and Islain, but we can't simply disregard rogue warriors because their intentions may be questionable. Nothing should be taken lightly, no idea laid aside because of its improbability or determined level of risk, especially what we think has no ill intentions at all. I'm certain that Queen Meirin deals with things the same way."

Queen Meirin's gaze had indeed slid to Queen Havilah's while she was talking, tilting her head. With a soft nod, she said, "We most certainly do. Nothing should be ruled out so easily."

I could tell following their words, behind the courteous smiles they'd exchanged, something else lingered.

"Your conservatory is lovely," Princess Anja said, clearing the uneasy silence that had settled as densely as Garlin's evening fog. "There are so many wonderful plants and flowers."

"Thank you, dear," Queen Havilah replied.

"Will you show me your favorite?" the princess asked her while stroking Caulden's hand. "I'm always looking for inspiration for our gardens back home."

I kept my eyes low, not wanting to meet the queen's again. The reluctance in her pause was telling and almost uncomfortable until she recovered and said, "I have some things to tend to, but I'd love to show you first. This way."

Haidee and I followed their procession down the pathway until it ended at the well alcove, the walls framed by pillars decorated with intricately carved flowers. At its side sat the queen's sitting bench and a simple clay pot atop a pedestal. And though it was basic in its decoration, like most the others that held dull plants or flowers with hues of white or yellow, that pot held the most vibrant flower in the conservatory. The queen's favorite.

"Oh, my!" Princess Anja said, drawing up the loose layers of her dress so she could step quickly to the pedestal. "I can see why it's your favorite. I've never seen anything so pretty."

"It's a mourning flower," Prince Caulden said, sparing his mother of having to give the information. "Do you not have them in Islain?"

"Not that I'm aware of. I've never even heard of it." She

reached a finger toward one of the flowers hanging like flames from the edge of the pot, suspended by the tangle of vined stems, one of which had noticeably been cut. Haidee chanced a peek back at me, her thought of the flower from Prince's Night same as mine.

The prince nodded his approval for the princess to touch the petals. "They must be rarer than even we believed then. They just began to grow around the time of my birth. I like to believe that's why my mother favors them," he noted, shifting his eyes to Queen Havilah who flashed a meek smile before cutting her eyes to me, catching me looking again. This time it was her who looked away first, leaving me to blink away my confusion until I finally shifted my eyes and caught Queen Meirin staring at me, her eyes wide with curiosity. Not wanting to offend, I leveled my gaze again, this time at the well, hoping to avoid meeting any more eyes.

"I didn't see any from the road when we arrived the other day. Where do they grow?" the princess whispered as she pinched a single red and orange petal between two fingers.

"Only in one place actually. At Sacred Lake on the eastern cliffs," Caulden replied.

"Is it possible to—"

"The lake is off-limits, I'm afraid," the queen interjected. A warning. "The paths there have claimed enough lives already, and the quakes we had the other night made the trek even more dangerous. So I've had to enforce my rule against travel there."

"Oh," the princess replied, her lips turning down a bit. Maybe she wasn't accustomed to being told "No."

"Better safe than sorry, dear," Queen Meirin tutted in response.

The prince grabbed Anja's hand, turning her to face the mourning flower again. "The Sacred Lake was once where lots of people went to mourn family deaths. That's why it got its name."

"Fascinating," she replied. "It is a shame, though, such a pretty thing being tied to death that way, being named for it."

"I'm afraid I must go," Queen Havilah interrupted. "I will see you all at dinner." Everyone nodded their understanding as she turned and left, one of the sentinels falling in step behind her.

"Forgive my mother," Caulden said. "She is very close to these flowers. I think they also remind her of my father's passing. It happened around that time as well."

"I'm so sorry of that." The princess turned to him, closer still, trailing her hand down his arm.

Queen Meirin had been watching their exchange from the side, then turned and left quietly without disturbing them.

"It's fine. Thank you. I didn't have a chance to know him." Caulden looked into her eyes for a few silent moments then cleared his throat and looked back at the mourning flower. "I used to not like these so much. I'm sure it had to do with how protective my mother was of them, of this conservatory. Perhaps I was a bit jealous." A faint laugh as he reached his own hand to the flower and stroked the petals. "But it's become my favorite, too."

"Why the change?" she asked.

"Let's just say my eyes were opened recently, making me see how beautiful some things really are despite what may surround them."

My breath caught, and I dared a direct look in time to see Caulden's head tilted to the side, casting a quick glance over his shoulder before his focus returned to her.

TWELVE

"They're going to the vineyards today," Haidee called through my bedroom door after having let herself into the house well before dawn. "They are enamored with the wine and want to study everything. I think they are very jealous of our soils. Maybe if they learn something they won't be as inclined to seize our island."

I groaned. It had been three days since the captain had restricted everyone to the chateau grounds. But the Guards he'd assigned to search for The Shadow—Xavyn—hadn't found him, and the visiting royals had slowly morphed into wild beasts trapped inside a cage of stone and glass. There was no chance for even the captain to tame their need for freedom ... or more information.

"Maybe if that happens, you won't have to worry as much about the Trials, about you leaving," Haidee said, hitting the door again. "About him leaving … you."

My eyes snapped open. After I had disclosed the truth to her about Xavyn and all he had said, Haidee and I had become … closer. It had only been a few days since our brief talk in the garden and yet it felt as if we'd bonded more during that time than all the years we'd known each other. When I was off duty, she listened intently to catch any hints of treachery from Princess Anja or Queen Meirin. On the little time she had off—from now being the prince's lead Guard—she'd report anything to me. She also helped search Saireen's house for clues that my life could be something else as Xavyn had suggested, anything to show that Saireen could have known. We'd found nothing except that new closeness, something we'd never thought possible. And now, with a comment like her last one, she was getting even more personal.

I threw my clothing on, secured my leathers, then pulled the bedroom door open. "Was anything said last night worthy of note?"

"I haven't heard anything of note." Before I could continue on that topic, she said, "I'd have to have been blind for years not to see, but especially over the last few days, since Prince's Night. It's even more obvious now, the way he looks at you. His comments." I gritted my teeth at her decision to press me on the matter, my jaw taking the brunt of my frustration. "Something happened between you two that night. It's not good, Vala. How can you even think that this … that you …"

"That he'd ever love someone like me?" I snapped, crossing the room and ripping the loaf of bread she'd brought in half. "I haven't been thinking about it. I know it's not possible." I took a bite, the soft dough as bitter on my tongue as the thoughts in my head.

"But?"

"Nothing. That's all."

Those eyes, Saireen's eyes, looked up at me from the table where she sat with her leather arm guards resting upon it.

"He kissed me that night," I admitted. "After I saved his life ... or maybe didn't save his life." Xavyn had said he'd pulled Caulden to get him away from the others.

Her mouth opened. "But, I thought ... how is that possible with ... your skin?"

I took a deep breath and released a long sigh. "I'm not exactly sure about that myself. And I haven't thought about it much since that night or the next morning after I'd been lashed." Haidee flinched, but I continued on. "Water usually hurts me. I know you probably knew—"

"I knew enough. Knew of your cleansings. Mother had told me you needed it done once a week, that it helped to relieve pressure from your skin. I'd heard your screams when I had visited the house a couple of times, years after moving out, when you were no longer a baby who had an excuse to cry at a bath. I thought she was hurting you. She reassured me but never let me enter. So I didn't know about the color—"

"Right," I said, recalling Prince's Night when she'd seen me in the bathhouse. "Well, the lake's water is different for some reason. My skin broke and sloughed off but the water didn't pain me. It only hurt again when I'd gotten out—the normal response to my skin reforming. And while I was in the water, my skin emitted a glow." I shook my head, disbelieving my own words as if I were remembering incorrectly.

"It seems like a dream now, like it didn't happen. My skin always burns anything alive—plants, people—but that night ..."

"You didn't burn him?" she asked, filling in the information. "He kissed you and your skin didn't burn him."

"No, it didn't. Until the water had been off my face long enough and my skin began to reform. Then it burned him. Not badly enough to mark him, though."

"So he saw you?"

"He had seen me once before, walking in on me accidentally during a cleansing. He never touched me because he knew he couldn't."

"But he did that night when you saved him."

"His head was still clouded with drink," I said, shrugging off what had happened again. "The next day, I tried to make sense of everything with him. We acknowledged what had happened between us, enough to dismiss it at least, knowing nothing would ever progress between us. But we never talked more about the water." I stared at the rest of the bread in my hand and let it fall onto the table, my appetite gone.

She tore some of her own from the loaf and took a bite, staring down at the table in concentration. After chewing, she whispered, "He was there that night. Xavyn."

"Yes," I confirmed, confused by the reason she would restate the obvious.

She looked up at me. "He was there too. Was his skin the same in the water? Did he look as though he noticed a difference?"

"His skin gave off a glow too. But when he got out, he was screaming. That was why I thought he was injured."

"Do you still believe he may have been?"

"I can't be sure. He seemed to be injured the night on

Trader's Row also. The longer we fought and talked, though, the less it appeared to bother him. It was like he was growing comfortable with the injury. I couldn't really make sense of it. What he asked, what he said—it's confusing. He said he was sent for information, possibly the same as what the queen is after, but finding me may have changed things."

"I don't think it's a good idea to treat his word as gold. You don't know him, even if you share the same skin. We have no idea where he comes from or who sent him."

"You're right. I just can't get it all out of my head. I've been over and over it."

"Well, we're leaving the confines of the chateau today. Maybe we'll get lucky and he'll decide to take his next shot at the prince, or seek more information as he told you, then we can put all of this to rest."

I nodded. "I'm just hoping we see him first." Because if someone else did … Secretly, I was relieved every time Captain Baun updated us, having no success in finding him. "I wouldn't mind hearing more of what he has to say."

"This is a dangerous game, Vala. Not being honest about the way he looks is bad enough, but hiding all the other information from the captain and the queen is grounds for a lot worse than lashings."

"I expect my actions would be deemed as traitorous, which would earn my lifeless body a dive from Crypt Cliffs."

Haidee's eyes didn't meet mine, but I watched her lips turn down. "I don't see how you can sound so cavalier."

I laughed once, the sound harsh and ragged in my throat. "Perhaps you'd see differently when your dedication to the throne, to the prince's life, is rewarded so graciously by a strip of position and a crack of a whip." When she didn't respond,

I added softly, "I was doing my duty, Haidee. You know I was trying to protect him. The queen's punishments have only made me question my value to them. Have I been viewed so poorly this entire time without knowing? Were they just waiting for me to fail? Or did it take one simple mistake, one poor choice to make them view me as others have for years? Ever since I was a child, the queen's eyes have assessed me strangely. But I thought there was some understanding inside them since she had allowed me on the Guard. Her judgments felt extreme, and not allowing me to partake in the Trials is the worst of it all. I never felt my physical appearance was weighted against ... until I was told I was not permitted to go with the prince. What other reason would she have to keep me here? One mistake over years at his side? It pains me." I let my shoulders fall, along with a single tear that was gone in an instant. "And now, hearing that there might be more ... The questions inside won't die. I cannot simply forget or even pretend to be happy at the possibility of the prince staying here. Because even though I still would give my life for him, still honor my promise ... I no longer know who I am."

THIRTEEN

THE DAY LAGGED AS IF THE COVERED SUN HAD BEEN tethered to my emotions. While the captain was not able to keep everyone inside the chateau for another day, he was able to convince them all that it was best to split the vineyard trip into two. Regardless of how many Guards could accompany them, having everyone travel at the same time was a risk he was not willing to take. The queens visited first, returning well after midday. The prince used that extra time—as he had on the previous confined days—training beside us in the courtyard. The princess watched for a while, content to keep her eyes pinned on the sweat dripping down his bare chest as he engaged in all forms of battle—wielding his hands, a sword, a staff, a bow—with his main sparring partner Leint. I was content to ignore the prince and princess both, working my frustrations blow after blow on Haidee and a few other willing Guards.

Captain Baun had also thought it wise to forgo the carriages, opting for the backs of the fastest horses. No one objected. The princess had even donned her most basic outfit yet—a white tunic lined with intricate blue threading, leggings, and boots, with a small dagger strapped to her waist. Her hair had been smoothened and gathered into a single tail left to fall down her back. Upon seeing her after they had both changed from the morning, Caulden's eyes roamed over her noticeably. I mounted my horse beside Haidee's, directing my eyes elsewhere. But not before I caught a look from Haidee, her eyebrows drawn with understanding.

"Princess, you look far too … clean for where we're going," Caulden stated. I could hear the smile on his lips that I no longer wanted to see, knowing he was helping her onto her horse.

"Why? Are we to make the wine ourselves? I passed my mother in the hall and she mentioned no such thing."

Caulden laughed. "Not unless you want to. Are you ready?"

"Yes, I'm excited."

"Good," he replied, then addressed Haidee. "Leint and the princess' guards can cover the front. I want you and Vala behind us."

Haidee and I fell back, allowing the others to pull ahead. Caulden and Anja rode closely together during the trip, and even though I was forced to watch them, I was grateful that Haidee kept enough distance that we were unable to hear their full conversation. However, judging by the bubbling laughs from the princess and the gleaming smiles from

Caulden each time he turned his head toward her, I could guess it was going well enough.

Enduring that for the hour long leisurely ride only made the day longer.

"The grounds are empty," Haidee noted as our horses walked along the perimeter fence of the vineyard's entrance. Lush bundles of twisted grapevines were lined in rows that stretched far down the hillside, disappearing into the fog. "Captain Baun mentioned he'd demanded the property cleared of unessential workers for today's visits. Though, Lord and Lady Wyntor are ready to receive us should the prince like a word."

"Good." I surveyed the rest of the property as we turned onto the entrance road, wooden gates spread wide-open in an extended welcoming. The manor house and storage building had Revelation Wood guarding their back. The towering oaks had thick interlaced branches spreading as wide and as high as the face of the western cliffs that dropped into the sea at the opposite end of the vineyard, where the air was too smothered with fog to see. With all the people cleared from the grounds, the main threat outside was the cover of the tangled trees. "When we arrive at the house, I will take the edge of the wood. Unless you have another plan."

"I agree. I'll have Leint and the others spread farther around to give the prince some space, but I'll stay close by his side."

I nodded, actually happy that she had been assigned my place. No matter what had happened through the years between us or even in the recent days, we were of the same mind with the same goal.

We drew the horses closer together and slowed their pace

approaching the manor house. I was accustomed to the vineyard being busy each time we'd visited, full of voices and movement. While the day's dull quiet aided our ability to protect the prince, I couldn't shake the unnerving tingle it caused, a caress at my spine.

"You know how I mentioned the stream during the ride? Vitae River, which moves underground in a few parts of the island?" Caulden asked Anja.

"Yes," she replied sweetly. "We didn't seem to pass over it along the way."

"Precisely. It weaves its way through most of the island, starting as a mere stream at the peak of the eastern cliffs, feeding Sacred Lake, then flowing above and in pockets below, supplying all the crops. But see"—Caulden pointed at the tree line to the side of the manor house—"right there? It appears here too, splitting the rows of grapevines then it coils back around, downward to the north and to the other vineyards and farms."

The water rolled lazily down the sloping grounds in between the rows of vines as Caulden had said.

"It's lovely," the princess commented, staring where the prince had pointed.

"It is. It didn't make much sense to have the water so close with the worry of root rot, but the grapes have flourished. The lord here believes it is why."

"And it's the main source of water?"

"For the most part. We use wells, of course, and there are other smaller rivers sourced from rain and the continuous fog. But Vitae is the main river of Garlin."

"I see," she replied, looking around the grounds. "Your mother mentioned quakes the other day. Do they happen often?"

"No. They aren't frequent. Did it worry you?"

"I was just thinking about this river, about your Sacred Lake and how much I'd love to look upon its beauty and the mourning flowers that grow there. How treacherous is the path?"

"Very, for even the most skilled now. I got to see the damage from the last quake … Actually, I was there when it happened and struggled to get home because of it."

I wanted to laugh at that, knowing I'd been the one who actually struggled to get him home from the lake that night. Had his head been clear, it wouldn't have been an issue. At least, not as big of one.

"You were there? Do you go there often?"

Caulden cleared his throat. "No, I don't go there at all really because of my mother's decree. But that night was … the night before you arrived and—"

"Oh, I see." The princess' words were saccharine. "You were dared to go for Prince's Night."

He turned his face with an amused grin. "Something like that."

"It must have been dangerous then."

Unable to control my audacity, I coughed. Haidee's face snapped to the side, shooting me a hardened glare while Caulden's back stiffened.

"It was. But the trek wasn't the most dangerous part of the evening," Caulden recovered. "That was where the assassins attacked. My Guards, as you've seen, handled the situation admirably."

"Yes, I have seen their skills. Admirable indeed," the princess admitted as the horses stopped a few paces from the manor's front door. Without waiting for Caulden, she dropped from her horse expertly then slid her eyes to me, openly staring. "Is there any news on the one your people are calling The Shadow?" she asked, keeping her eyes on me while the rest of us dismounted.

"None. I'm rather hoping we scared him away," Caulden replied. "That is probably wishful thinking, though."

"Well," the princess said, turning back to him. "I for one wish the same. Otherwise, the departing ball your mother plans to throw us when we do leave might be affected. As with the Guard Trials you mentioned."

I bit down on my lips, feeling the slap of those words strike the permanent hollow in my chest. They had talked about the Trials. And that meant they had talked more about being together. About him leaving. I glanced sideways at Haidee and found her already looking at me, her eyebrows pulled together a fraction. She knew. She had probably heard. That was why she had brought it all up this morning. I pinned back my shoulders and stood straighter, cramming the emotions deep and waiting for my orders. I was being ridiculous. I'd already come to terms with what could happen. There was no reason for all of it to affect me, and certainly not my ability to perform my duties.

"Yes." Caulden's response was slow as he handed his reins to a lone worker staged to welcome us, taking the princess' and repeating the process. "The faster he's caught, the better." After a moment, he turned around. "Haidee, I think we'll walk out here some first then go inside."

"Yes, Highness," she replied, then turned to me and handed over her horse's reins. "Watch the wood."

I nodded as she moved toward Leint to give him and the others their orders. They hitched their own horses on the north side of the house, and I followed the vineyard worker to the south side to do the same.

"Interesting day," the worker commented as I walked behind him. His tunic, pants, and boots were plain but in nice enough condition to show his work was likely inside the manor, not on the grounds.

"Yes," I agreed neutrally.

"I suppose quite a few have been lately," he continued in his smooth tone, stopping at the posts at the corner of the manor to tie the reins.

"I suppose they have." I moved around him and the prince's horse, eyeing the back of him more closely as I went. The top of his brown tunic was taut, spreading thinly across his shoulders. His hair was clipped close at his neck, which bowed a little as he looked down to tie the reins. I moved to the side and got to work on the other horses, catching glimpses of his movements over my horse's head as she bent to drink from the trough hanging below her.

"Do you also suppose they will continue?" A bold question for a vineyard worker. As if he'd known he'd overstepped, he added, "Everyone is curious, it seems. Mostly on whether the prince will choose to go. But also if the one they seek will be found or if he will continue to elude them."

I studied his movements in broken glances. He backed up farther in a bent position, leaving only the dark hair atop his head visible until his hand reached up and ran along the horse's back in a soothing movement. The skin of his hand was smooth and a sandy gray color like the inside of a freshly split log of oak. "Why are you so interested in the affairs of the royals?"

"Everyone is interested right now. It could be good and

bad. Wouldn't it be a shame to lose the prince to another kingdom?"

It would be. Though, it wasn't exactly as the prince had much choice. After witnessing the queens converse at the arrival, I was certain the only one making the decision was Queen Meirin. Now that Queen Meirin already knew she'd have the island either way, it was probably up to Princess Anja to choose whether or not she'd have Prince Caulden. No matter what he wished. What I wished. But I would not offer up that or any other information to a worker for paying gossip. "Indeed," I agreed simply. "Please, leave the horses here. It's uncertain how long the prince will stay," I added as a clear end to our exchange and took a few strides toward the wood. Despite Haidee's withholdings about the prince and princess' exchanges during our morning conversation, she had offered up good insight as to what might happen should the queen and princess find whatever they are looking for, be it information about our farming ... or something else. They might choose to leave Garlin alone. Finding and catching Xavyn would help ease that pressure too. But then, he had stated they might be looking for something that would affect us in some other way, affect not just us but others. I wasn't sure what to think. I didn't have nearly enough information.

The stillness within the wood was reassuring in its normalcy. I walked the edge, peering back out onto the vineyard first as Haidee, Prince Caulden, and Princess Anja lazily made their way down the middle of the vineyard, the princess plucking grapes along the way. Then I turned my attention to the thicket of trees, their branches spreading and twisting a massive barrier, fog lolling over them, filling the gaps throughout.

"So …" The worker's voice was so close I instinctively grabbed the hilt of my sword and spun around. "You're one of the prince's Guards. Are you participating in the Trials they mentioned?"

Looking directly upon his face for the first time, I studied him closely. Dark brown hair rolled backward in a thick wave, sides clipped short like the back I'd seen moments before. His cheeks more narrow than wide, curved down into a strong jaw. His eyebrows lifted slightly in question above a staring set of brown eyes flecked with an array of different shades of the same color. The shape of everything looked familiar, the resemblance hanging somewhere on the edge of my mind, yet not close enough to place him.

I shook my head, released my readied grip on the sword, and scanned the area again for anything unusual. He was no threat, but he was too curious for my liking. Most people, after taking a single glance at me, made an effort to stay as far away as possible, not seek me out. Even for answers. "Is there something else you should be doing? Perhaps getting refreshments for the prince and his guest?"

He laughed lightly and the tone of it registered as familiar too. Had he worked in the chateau at one time? "Shouldn't that be 'the prince and the princess'?"

I snapped my eyes back to him. "Watch yourself," I warned at his challenge.

"A mere correction, Guard. No need to get worked up. I won't tell them if you won't."

"I suggest you go on about your business."

"What if I don't?"

"Then you'll be impeding my duties, and you'll be treated as a threat. The lord of the manor might be burdened a bit when I hand over his dead servant, but I'm willing to bet he won't have trouble finding a replacement."

"And how exactly will I die, Guard? Do you have some other tricks up your covered sleeves or will you just burn me?"

I advanced on him, grabbing the front of his tunic with one hand and drawing my sword with the other so quickly he had no time to retreat. Pressing the blade to his neck, I sneered and watched his lips pull back into a fiendish grin before his skin began to ripple, its sandy gray color ... changing.

FOURTEEN

"WHAT'S WRONG, VALA? NO LONGER FEEL like cooking me and dumping me on the manor's doorstep?"

"What—" I held tight even though every part of my body screamed to release him and run. There was movement in his skin, a river of something below his flesh, something wanting to come out.

"I'm sure that captain of yours would be so happy if you ended their search," he continued, his words soft and very close to my ear.

Xavyn. It was him.

But …

"Ah," he said, an amused smile lightening his tone. "That look in your eyes is so telling. You've finally placed me."

"Your skin, it—"

"No, I'm not like you. But I can be. And that's what makes this all so curious. Did you find out more about yourself? I know you've been searching, and I'd love for you to share."

My grip tightened, my body still frozen in place, watching the skin under the edge of my blade harden into the likeness of my own then soften and pale into smooth flesh again.

He lifted his eyes to the sky and bared his teeth, sucking air between them.

"What are you?"

"What are you?" he replied, tipping his face down to look at me again. "You're not supposed to be here. Humans are the only ones who should be here, and you are not human."

"How do you know I'm not?"

"How don't you? Did they tell you something else? Raise you to think something different? But I think you've known all along. You just haven't admitted it to yourself. Or do you fear what they might do to you if they found out? They already know you can burn living flesh. They seem to have tolerated that along with the physical appearance of your skin. Do they know what lies beneath this skin, though? And do they know how the flames speak to you?"

My eyes darted behind him, frantically searching for Caulden, for Haidee. If they saw … if they heard …

"You're afraid. I can feel your heart beating. They don't know, do they? They don't know about that humming beneath the crackles of a flame, the tingle under the skin."

I hissed at him, seething that he'd spill my secrets out into the open air, allowing the fog to carry them away. "How do you know this? Are you in my head?"

"Ha!" He laughed, and I pushed my sword harder against

his neck, a droplet of blood popping out from beneath, coating the edge of the blade. Red blood. Same blood. After seeing his skin change, I half expected his to be different. What was he?

"You will be quiet," I said with a growl. "And you will tell me, or I will turn you in … or kill you right here." My feet began to pull us backward, moving us closer to the cover of the stone building that stored barrels of wine.

"I'm not in your head, no." He had to bend as he moved with me, not daring to stumble with the blade at his neck. "But as you have seen, I can change."

The corner of the building provided enough cover, especially with the wood at our backs and the distance of fog blanketing the grounds. It gave me time, and I was hoping it would be enough to get more information, to make a decision. "Tell me more," I demanded, forcing his back against the stone wall after securing our position, making sure we couldn't be seen from the front of the vineyard.

"You tell me more. Have you heard what the queen might be here for? What they're interested in?"

I huffed out a breath, releasing some of my frustration, knowing I had to give him something to make him talk. "They are jealous of our crops. They want our soil for their own. They will take this place whether the princess chooses Prince Caulden or not. We don't have the forces to fight them, and they know it." There it was, a heap of truth for someone I didn't know, someone I shouldn't even trust. But that need for more information ran deep enough to relinquish truths that were nearly common knowledge as it was.

"So they want to know why your crops are so good. Why are they?"

"What do you care?"

"I already told you why I care. It's not just Garlin that has to worry if they get what they want." His teeth clenched as more ripples crossed his face, charring then softening again. "There has to be more," he said in almost a snarl from pain or his own frustration.

"I haven't heard anything," I admitted, loosening my grip and backing off the pressure on the blade.

His eyes widened, realizing my slip. "You sure you want to risk that, Vala?"

"If you wanted to fight me, you would have already. You would have killed me when we were on Trader's Row."

My answer received an eyebrow quirk. "I almost killed you. I should have."

"So why didn't you? Whoever sent you will surely be displeased at your failure to kill me, to kill the prince."

"I'm not exactly bound by the same rules you might be, like getting whipped for protecting a prince."

My grip tightened again and I scowled at the memory of the lashings. He knew. "If you know so much, why seek me out for information? You should just get what you came for and leave. But if you attempt to end anyone, that courtesy ends and I take your life."

One side of his lips pulled into a humored grin. "I've already explained that my plans changed as soon as I saw you— someone who shouldn't be here and has no idea who she is. And I'm free to change plans if needed. I only fail if I can't find the information she wants. Finding something extra might be beneficial to me."

Ah. "And who might *she* be?" I pressed. If I was something extra, and possibly beneficial, he needed to give me more in return.

"Lower your blade all the way first."

I stole a glance around the corner of the building. No one was in sight, which only made my heart beat faster. But I still lowered my blade and backed a single, reluctant step away from Xavyn, hoping it wouldn't be the most foolish step I'd ever taken.

"Her name is Elige. And she, like me, is from Vaenen."

"That's not possible. All the stories say that no one can travel there."

"And yet, here I am," he replied in almost a bored tone. "Someone who you can't explain because you can't even explain yourself."

It was a truth I couldn't debate. "How then? And can others? Are there more?" Garlin's people vocalized no ideas or theories where this was concerned as far as I knew. We believed magic to be dead. But Islain was closer. Was it possible that they knew?

"No, no others can come here. But that's a conversation for another time. Look, I will promise not to harm or kill your prince, or anyone else unprovoked, but you have to promise that you will help me. There are things I can't see or hear. I need you to listen to what the visiting queen wants, what she is looking for. Anything. Even things that are nonspecific."

"How do you even know that she's looking for something? She might just be here to seize our island, to take us whether it comes with her daughter's marriage or not."

"There is more to the visit. I know she has been searching through historical documents and collecting things from hundreds of years ago, especially focused on the war, when magic was killed and the world divided." He gritted his teeth again, the muscles in his jaw flexing hard as a wave of char rippled over his skin. "I can't hold this form around you. My energy ... wants yours more than human. I've been practicing these last few days, trying to control it all more but—"

More than human?

A crack of a nearby branch silenced us both. Our heads pivoted for signs of movement, neither of us daring to breathe. I couldn't risk being found with him, especially like this, talking as if we were friends. And if his skin changed in front of them? I would likely be screaming my truths into Revelation Wood on the death march to Crypt Cliff, as many other criminals had.

"I should go," he said, studying the shock so clearly written upon my face. "You are going to let me go, right? I don't have to kill my way out of here?"

My eyes, still wide, looked into his, reading his same concern. He had a goal and needed my help. Without it, perhaps it wouldn't only be him who failed. I nodded with a surrendering blink.

"Then I'll see you again soon, Vala." He flashed a smirk and ran to the wood on the far side of the building, disappearing into the thicket.

After letting the shock settle, I collected myself and walked toward the manor house, passing the horses. As I turned the corner, I was met by Leint. His arms crossed at his chest, hands tucked neatly in to hold the position that looked alarmingly comfortable.

"Where have you been?" he asked, strands of his orange hair shifting over his forehead as his face tilted to assess me. Our exchanges had always been edged with competition. He had wanted my position—now Haidee's position—and made no effort to hide the fact. So him having any reason to report me wasn't good. Especially after he'd barely gotten reprimanded for his part in aiding the prince on Prince's Night, while I was tied up and …

I stopped in front of him and scowled, as I normally would at his questioning me. "That's none of your concern."

Those crystal-colored eyes narrowed briefly then looked toward the vineyard's horizon. "Haidee made it my concern when she asked me to find you."

I breathed in calmly, hoping my heart would slow its pace in turn. Had he seen me? "So you ignored the lead's order and stood here instead?"

"I didn't want to catch you at a bad moment." My heart paused as his words did. "I'm not one who enjoys disrupting someone tending to their … personal needs. So I waited." I sighed inwardly. "Transton and Prins went inside with them. I knew you had the back covered, with or without your pants down." He flashed a humorous smirk, and I found myself smiling in return, catching a surprised glance from those crystals. He couldn't see my mouth, but he obviously saw the amusement in my eyes. It was rare for us to share that kind of exchange. I wondered if the strain between us had softened a bit after Prince's Night. "They won't be much longer."

"Good," I replied as the relief rushed through my body and I took a position that mirrored his on the other side of the door.

Even through my scrambled thoughts about Xavyn— what had just occurred, what he was asking of me, what he could possibly be—I looked out over the vineyard and took in the silence, feeling the peace fill me. Maybe something inside begged it of me, knowing it could be the last time I might enjoy that kind of calm, my life splitting, no longer aimed to a single goal, the direction no longer as clear as it had once been. As much as every ingrained part of my being wanted to hate Xavyn, what he could be, the fear of it all, I couldn't ignore the voice inside that knew he was right about me. I was different. I always had been. As much as I resented the people of this island for fearing me, my skin, I realized I resented myself more for feeling the truth, knowing that I was something else but being too fearful of what others might think to seek answers. I was naive, like Xavyn had said. I knew only what had been told to me, and I believed it all, never asking questions. Fear, blind trust, and anger imprisoning me. And now … all of those same things from different angles, steering me down another path. One that didn't have an end already in sight.

Wings flapped in the air and a streak of muted black cut across the vineyard's horizon, ending my moment of silence.

The raven landed on the top of the closest vine post, head cocking first at Leint then at me before releasing a screeching caw.

FIFTEEN

"**H**AIDEE," I WHISPERED, MOVING HASTILY TO HER side as soon as the prince and princess were mounting the steps of the chateau, the final rays of the day's sun slicing through the fog and projecting sporadic specks onto their backs. "Tell Captain Baun that the princess should have one of ours to guard her as extra security. Suggest me. Leint and you are plenty for Caulden, and he can always pull others."

"Why?" she replied in a whisper over her shoulder.

I glanced around, checking for prying eyes but finding most had scattered about their duties—the stable boys leading our horses around the chateau, the sentinels stepping back to their stations after we'd arrived. "I need to be near her. To listen."

Her head twisted backward, eyes widened.

"Yes," I answered her silent question. "There's no chance to get the queen. But the princess could still give me a chance to overhear something. So I need you to recommend me for her detail. And if Caulden happens to be around when the captain starts our debrief, it'll be even better mentioned in front of him. I'm fairly certain he'll agree should the captain need added affirmation."

"All right. I hope you know what you're doing, Vala," she said, taking longer strides to catch up with the prince.

I pinned my eyes to her, watching the bundle of thin plaits shift back and forth between her shoulders with each of her steps. I hoped I knew what I was doing too.

The queens were in the main sitting area of the chateau, apparently each awaiting their child's arrival.

"Did you have fun, darlings?" Queen Meirin called cheerfully, standing from her seat not far from the large hearth of the burning fireplace, her hand wrapped around a goblet while strands of long hair slid off her shoulder to her back, like shifting rays of sunlight.

The fire hummed to me, stealing my attention for a moment. I stared at the flickering flames licking the air. *Do they know how the flames speak to you?*

"Everything's fine," Princess Anja replied to her mother, moving toward her and kissing her cheeks.

I noted Captain Baun's eyes as they snapped to Haidee, his chest puffing out with an expectant inhale. Haidee met his stare, shaking her head the slightest bit. The captain's chest deflated, realizing The Shadow hadn't been caught or killed.

"The tour was lovely. Lord and Lady Wyntor were very

kind to show us inside the manor. They also took us down to the cellar to taste some of their best."

"Caulden?" Queen Havilah took a step closer to him, worry straightening her back and flaring her tiny nose. She folded her hands in front of her to maintain a calm appearance, but was unable to fully hide her nerves as her fingers twisted together.

"Mother, it was a fine trip. No one showed up. There was no threat," he replied, casting a glance toward me then Haidee. A few drops of sweat glistened on his forehead and I wondered if he had exerted a fair amount of energy during the ride or if the room was too hot.

"Haidee," she said, ignoring Caulden's answer. He looked at her incredulously, but her focus has already shifted to his lead Guard.

"Your Majesty?"

"I'm not getting the honest answers I'd prefer to hear. So please tell me what happened," she said with a smile.

Haidee swallowed, knowing there was no use backing the prince in a situation like this. The queen's ability to pick up on things was an art form. During our time on his detail, there had been a fair amount of cover-ups on our part, keeping his little secrets from his mother. Most were inconsequential. Some weren't. Haidee had seen me handle enough to know this was one of the latter. "The raven appeared."

"Raven?"

"It's believed to be the same one we saw on Trader's Row when The Shadow showed."

"I see," Queen Havilah said. "But he didn't appear this time, correct?"

"That's why I said nothing happened, Mother," Caulden

said, shaking his head as he walked toward the wine table. "It's a stupid bird, probably someone at port's travel pet."

Queen Meirin's eyes and Princess Anja's met briefly, some unspoken connection.

"If I may, Your Majesty," Captain Baun interjected. "The prince is right that it could be nothing. But I'd still like to take precautions."

"Yes, yes," Queen Havilah said, her gaze sweeping from him to me then over to Queen Meirin. "Shuffle the Guards, Captain, and pull whomever you need from the port. I want that Shadow caught, but I refuse to lock us all up for even a single more day of their visit."

Queen Meirin nodded her head. "We'll remain cautious. If there's no reason to travel, we won't. This island is so small as it is. We've already seen much of it."

I glanced between the queens, watching everyone else do the same.

"Yes, well, it's a good thing, I suppose, that we have wonderful food and wine to keep us entertained."

"Indeed," Queen Meirin replied, scooping her hair onto her shoulder before grabbing her daughter's arm. "Come, darling. You'll have to tell me all about your visit while we get ready for dinner."

The room was silent as they left.

"If there's nothing else, Captain, I'll take my leave," Queen Havilah said.

Everyone bowed and waited for her to disappear out into the hall, four sentinels leaving their posts with a nod from Captain Baun to follow her.

"The bird," the captain said as heads turned, facing each other again. "We have found no information about ravens used in Islain, only the stories of their connection to Craw and Vaenen." I stilled at that. I had never known. What was the connection? Had it crossed as Xavyn had? Or was it Xavyn's bird? It had never been seen on the island before. The captain continued, "So we're back to focusing on the actual threat."

"Captain, I'd like to suggest something," Haidee said.

"Yes?"

"I'd like to suggest that one of ours be assigned to the princess. I realize that they brought a fair amount of Islain guards, but I think it would be in our best interest to protect her with one of our own. Vala is my recommendation."

Eyes cut to me. Even though it probably wouldn't matter if they'd discovered that I'd made the suggestion, I still widened my eyes the smallest amount to show some shock without anger.

"I don't see that as necessary," Caulden said, biting his bottom lip the slightest bit with a swift glance my way. "The princess is safe."

"With respect, Highness, you're covered well enough. I think it's our duty to focus on the guests, whether they are within the safety of the chateau or not," she added.

"I agree that it would be a wise decision to take more precautions, especially if the queen wants everyone free to wander," Captain Baun said, and I half wondered if the queen wouldn't mind The Shadow meeting her guests. Their deaths would likely start a war, some other courtier staking claim to the throne there and laying waste to our kingdom anyway. In some facet, death could be more appealing than surrendering Garlin over to become Islain's slave. "Highness?" the captain questioned.

Caulden nodded without a word then took a drink from his wine goblet and walked to the fireplace, keeping his back to us.

"Vala?" Captain Baun addressed me then, raising a scarred eyebrow.

"It would be my honor," I replied with an honest nod.

Princess Anja and Queen Meirin entered the dining hall not long after, refreshed and ready for dinner. Princess Anja had traded in her plain attire of the day, choosing to wear a dress of green silk for the evening, possibly to honor Garlin's colors or perhaps she had brought enough colors to go through them all. Dinner conversation had died considerably each evening since their arrival. The queens chatted more about trade, finding that to be the most neutral topic aside from that of their children, which always seemed to be the topic left for last, when the carafes had all been emptied and the plates had all been cleared.

"Can I walk you to your room?" Prince Caulden asked the princess when the queens both retired.

"I'd love that," she replied.

Haidee and I allowed the princess' guards—Transton and Prins—to follow first and we fell behind them, keeping a safe enough distance to whisper while still monitoring the conversation up ahead.

"Captain Baun informed the queen of your new detail before dinner," Haidee said, her voice barely heard over our footsteps.

"I'm guessing it went well enough since I didn't get new orders."

"She wasn't happy. He seemed a little shaken by their talk, actually."

"Really?"

"He probably shouldn't have been so forthright with me, but he told me that she had asked him all sorts of questions about it. Like whose idea had it been? His, Princess Anja's, or Caulden's. He explained that I had thought of it as an extra measure for safety, and she still seemed thrown off by it all, not behaving like herself. He said she looked nervous. And that she had asked about you too. How you'd been handling everything."

"Really? That is curious." Too curious. Why would the queen ask about me?

The prince turned the corner and held his arm out for the princess. "Thank you for joining me today," he said, breaking the silent start to their walk.

"It was really lovely, the vineyard," she replied, looping her hand up through his arm and taking hold.

"Yes," he agreed. "I like to visit them sometimes."

"I bet you do," she teased with that melodic laugh.

"What? Do you think I overindulge?"

"Well, you tell me about Prince's Night and then about special princely visits to the vineyard. What am I to think?"

He laughed a laugh I'd heard quite often but not recently enough. And it was for her. "Fair enough, princess. But I'm usually rather boring. You already know I enjoy reading. My friends, Rhen and Josith—who I'm sure you'll meet at least once before leaving, whether I invite them to meet you or not—are always trying to get me out more. They were the main culprits for Prince's Night, actually." The next laugh was soft, showing a fondness for his friends.

"Well, I like my fair share of fun, but I do enjoy reading as well. I can't wait to show you our palace library. The books go on and on forever. There are far too many to read even in an entire lifetime."

Her voice started drifting as my mind lost interest. We turned through another corridor and entered into the southern area of the chateau, which was practically foreign to me now. It had been sectioned for guests, yet Garlin didn't see many visitors. The queen's court and council all had their own manors, whether they sat upon farms with extensive land or were residences inside town at Florisa's Cove. With the island being small enough to travel from point to point within a day, there weren't many reasons for people to stay overnight. So the chambers had been left alone, mostly unused by anyone aside from rambunctious children of chateau workers sneaking about to play games, as Caulden and I had when we'd been their age. With empty closets and armoires, the southern end had the perfect hiding places.

"That sounds amazing," Caulden replied, sounding honestly enthralled by her. "I wished we'd had a fraction of that here. I've reread some several times over, mostly my favorites. Some about the knights of the ancient kingdoms, others about the faerie."

"I enjoy some like those as well. But I told you about my favorites down on Trader's Row. Most of them involve our histories."

"Ah, yes," he said with a sigh. "I would love to learn even more. One of these upcoming days perhaps. But for now ..." Caulden stopped outside of the grand door of the princess' chambers.

"That was the quickest walk I've ever taken," she said, turning toward him, closer than she needed. He laughed, the tone airy and sweet.

Haidee and I posted against the wall a distance back. Transton and Prins moved farther along to cover the opposite end of the hall.

"Thank you, again," she said, leaning in close enough for the silk of her dress to caress Caulden's legs and boots, close enough for her head to tip back and his face to tip down.

He ran a hand through his hair, pulling it away from his eyes. "Oh, I almost forgot to mention. With everything happening, we would like for you to have some extra protection by way of one of my Guards. Vala has been assigned to you for now."

The princess' eyes snapped my way, but I made sure I kept mine to the wall across from me. "Do you really think that's necessary?"

"I think so, yes. I want to be sure you're safe. And Vala … Vala will be sure of that."

Liar. The thought dug into my mind as I pictured the look on his face when the idea had first been introduced. But I quickly reminded myself he wouldn't disclose his hesitation. What would be the point except to get her to refuse me? And yet … that was an out if he really wanted one. He could kill the idea by accepting her refusal.

"I'm not sure it's necessary. But if you say it is …" She leaned in again, touching his other arm. "Then I'll accept the offer."

"Good," he said, clearing his throat nervously. My shoulders dropped. What had I been thinking anyway? That he would want to keep me for himself badly enough to change his mind, to go against what had already been accepted by his mother and the captain? No, he wouldn't. "Vala," he called me, snapping me from my bothersome woes.

I knocked Haidee's arm as a goodbye when I brushed past her. "Yes, Highness." I wouldn't meet his eyes. I couldn't. So I stopped a fair distance from them and stared at his chin instead.

"You start tonight. Unless the princess instructs otherwise, post out here until someone relieves you."

I nodded a small bow.

"Good night, Anja," he said, grabbing her hand and lifting it to his mouth to press his lips upon her delicate, smooth skin.

"Night, Caulden," she replied as he released her hand and turned. Haidee followed him, disappearing down the hall.

Anja's eyes slid to me then slowly looked me up and down, her smile long gone. A second later, she was inside her sitting room, Transton and Prins pushing past me to follow her before the door slammed shut.

SIXTEEN

THE FOLLOWING MORNING, I WAS MET WITH A RECEPTION identical to the previous night's icy dismissal. The princess seemed indifferent to my presence. She didn't address me or even speak while I was around unless we were in the company of the prince. The lack of acknowledgment could be routine for her, avoidance being a normal treatment of staff. I knew the reason wasn't due to fear. I'd seen fear in enough eyes to know hers held something else, something conflictive, like a blend of distaste and inquisitiveness. After her curious questions about me the night spent on Trader's Row, I halfway thought she'd bend to the desire to learn more by asking me about myself or about Caulden to aid in her decision on a future with him. But she hadn't shown signs of interest so far, making the possibility of gaining information from her despairing.

She had left her chambers late in the morning, moving to the dining hall for breakfast, where she ate alone and quiet, even her mother off doing something else with her time. Later, she'd attended the prince's training session as she had done every day during the week, watching him as he sparred throughout the side courtyard, his bare upper body glistening from exertion in the warmth of the autumn day. I stood with my back against the chateau wall as she sat on the low stone ledge that lined the entry steps. Haidee joined the prince in training as we usually did. While having time to relax would have ordinarily been appealing, my muscles twitched as I watched them train, wanting to be used for more than simply standing around.

Queen Meirin found Princess Anja midday as she retreated to her chambers for an afternoon refreshment. "Did you enjoy watching the prince this morning?" the queen asked Anja after a quick greeting. She trailed a finger along the wall while they walked, touching the bottoms of paintings and tapestries as if she were marking everything she wanted to keep or tear to shreds.

"Mother, please don't start," Anja answered with a huff.

"Forgive me," Queen Meirin said with sigh that sounded far from apologetic. "I'm bored. And he is nice to look at, nicer than many of Islain's available lords, nicer than any you've already taken to bed." Her thin fingers continued their assault on the chateau, wall after wall, dancing over vases and statuettes, sliding under the tapestries.

"Yes, well, the water here seems to grow nice things."

Queen Meirin barked a laugh as tall as her body. "This is true. Or at least things that are younger than a certain age. That captain they have isn't exactly—"

"Mother," Anja interrupted, her tone short with warning.

And as if to check if I had heard, Transton and Prins casted almost imperceptible glances over their shoulders to me. Even the queen's two guards, walking in front of everyone, appeared to react with head movements. I ignored them all.

"Oh, stuff your politeness, Anja. I'm sure this—Vala, is it?—would agree that her captain isn't exactly the most handsome man on this goddessforsaken island, whether she's attracted to men or not."

"You'll have to forgive my mother, Vala," the princess addressed me while continuing on their path, not bothering to stop or turn. "She was upset to learn that your queen doesn't keep a proper stud stable here and she's not used to being away from her own rotation of men for so long."

I didn't dare laugh no matter how hard one pushed to escape my chest. It was shocking. Laughter was one reaction I hadn't planned to have while around them.

"So true. Honestly, I think that woman would be worlds happier if she just had her own, a different man to visit her bed each night."

"Perhaps Queen Havilah still honors her late husband," Anja replied with a sharpness meant to cut.

Queen Meirin didn't flinch. "Perhaps. Or perhaps she maintains that fallacy in respect, while actually keeping one bedmate in secret, one who makes her feel safe while bowing to her control."

Captain Baun. I'd always had suspicions, but since it was none of my concern, I didn't dare seek confirmation. It was interesting that Queen Meirin had been able to pick up on it in the short time she'd been here.

"Enough of your ramblings. She is still a queen who can

do as she chooses." Anja tutted as they reached the door to her chambers.

"For now. But if you choose, these kingdoms will unite … peacefully," the queen said more seriously. The words panged around inside my mind, a cold splash of truth, reminding me of what was still to come. Queen Havilah would likely no longer be a queen of Garlin. Garlin would no longer be a separate kingdom.

And suddenly I felt sick for having almost laughed.

Queen Meirin planted a swift kiss on her daughter's cheek then began to walk down the hall to her own rooms before adding, "Then we'll make sure to supply only the finest men to the stable we create for her."

Another day had passed on the princess' detail. Waiting. Watching. It had been my normal routine since I was taken into the Guard. But I'd never realized how different it could be with someone who barely spoke to you, barely looked at you. At least Caulden spoke to me during off times. I wasn't even close to his equal, yet he acknowledged me like a human … *A human.* Maybe the princess kept her distance because of my affliction, the mystery surrounding me. It was understandable. I often wondered if the only reason Caulden treated me differently was because we had grown together. If our story were written in another way and I'd been assigned to him later, would he have treated me the same? I'd like to think that he was unique, that he would be kind in any manner. But there was no way to know, and I wasn't sure I would want to even then. I only knew that he was kind enough, and I missed being on his detail. And possibly more.

"Yes?" Princess Anja asked after Transton—or Prins, I still didn't know who was who and didn't much care—whipped her door open in response to my knock. She stepped forward past him and dipped her head out to peer into the hallway, her loose brown hair swinging around, making me retreat a step. Not seeing anyone else with me, she backed up and added, "What is it?"

I bowed my head. "Your Highness. I've been informed that dinner is being served in the dining hall." I had been granted a respite not long before and was told to bring word.

"Tell them I'm not interested tonight."

"Yes, Highness." I moved to go, but was stopped by her voice again.

"Wait," she said, pointing to Transton and Prins. "These two will go inform them and take time to eat a meal in the kitchens. You, stay."

I stood still as her guards swept fluidly around me, like water around a rock. I had been so used to staring at their backs, when I glanced at their sunset hair, bronzed skin, and the similar faces again, I finally realized their likeness was more than their blue accented leathers and their height and builds. They were siblings.

"They are attractive, aren't they?" Anja said, noticing my observation of them, then turned back into her sitting area and beckoned me in with a wave. "Close the door."

I did as instructed and stepped to the side, posting myself against the wall. The room was bright, every lantern lit and blazing, but the fire drew my attention from them, roaring with life, flames flaring as they consumed the logs piled high inside the expansive stone hearth. In the center of the room, in front of the flames, a low table sat with plush chairs positioned all around. Books of all sizes were stacked on the table. Some lay open, pages spread about even ripped from their bindings. At one side of the fire, draperies billowed lightly, catching a night breeze from the windows pushed halfway open. At the other side was another door, closed to the room behind.

The room was near stifling, even to me, but I tried not to think about the heat so much as my eyes gobbled up as many details as possible. I was not close enough to see book titles or read any of the notes she had made on blank journal pages.

"I didn't feel like dining tonight," she said to me, though it felt as she could have been addressing the silence of the room just as easily as she gazed into the fire. "In two days' time, I mourn the death of my father for another year. My mother is unaffected by the loss of him, but I can't deny the hold it still has upon me even after a few years."

I shifted my stance, watching her silently stare at the flames as I wondered why she was disclosing personal things to me. Was she simply speaking out loud, knowing that I was bound by my duties? Or simply not caring if I were to ever repeat her words? In another moment, her hands jumped to life, moving the books around and shuffling papers.

"You can come closer," she said, and I hesitated a moment before taking a few steps toward the center of the room. "I want to apologize for being so closed off these past few days. I'm not usually so quiet. But I've had a lot on my mind as you can imagine." Still, I didn't respond. I wasn't even sure she wanted me to. So I stayed my place.

She brushed her hair back from her face, her fingers

working to secure the top portion of her long strands into a plait at the back. When she finished she glanced up at me, a smile slowly easing onto her thin lips. "You are very well revered around here, Vala. I'm happy to have you on my detail."

I nodded with a blink to show my appreciation.

"You may speak to me. I hold no ill intentions and will not disclose what you might say to anyone else." An offer. Or a trap. That need for information had finally broken through her barrier. And here we were. Both of us wanting something, only one of us fully aware of that fact.

"Yes, Highness," I replied my acceptance. "Thank you for having me." Short answers. How I, as a Guard, had been taught to interact with nobility.

Her smile grew as she threaded her fingers and placed her hands into her lap, where the fabric of her light blue dress swallowed them like massive waves of the sea devouring a lone ship. "Good. I suppose we have Caulden to thank. He is very darling. And he thinks very highly of you. You grew up together, correct?"

"Yes, Highness."

"Please, Vala, since you are so close to Caulden, you can call me Anja when we're alone." The slight tilt on her face, the tone of her voice—it all seemed sincere.

I nodded again, understanding.

"He respects you and, I think, admires you in many ways." Not a question. A statement, possibly to gauge my reaction. I kept my eyes on her, waiting. She quirked that smile a bit more. "I think he might even love you."

My eyes widened. There was no way to stop them. I hadn't been prepared for her to say such a thing.

"It's true to an extent," she pressed on, noting my reaction and simply brushing it off as the confirmation that she hadn't even needed. "But maybe not as much as you'd like."

I couldn't breathe. It was all I could do to keep from passing out in front of her. The air. There was no air. Only fire—flames humming and cracking rhythmically.

"It's completely understandable that you have some feelings for him, and him for you. You have been together for a long time. You've saved his life at least once, and maybe in a way he's even saved yours. Wouldn't you agree?"

I inhaled, trying to keep the room from spinning. "Yes," I admitted, breathing more, calming myself.

"I know this and yet, I'm not quite sure what all this means to me, to him. That's what I've been considering lately. We have a connection, and I think he will make a wonderful king. He seems gentle but strong enough to make the hardest type of decisions. And I don't just mean ending lives of traitors and thieves. I mean leaving his home to come rule with me, cutting ties and seeking out threats to our kingdom … doing what needs to be done for our future. And I think he could love me, he certainly appreciates the way I look, the way I feel"—her hand opened and spread across her dress, smoothing the material—"and I believe he would like to move forward with me. But this also means that I would need to be certain you'll be a benefit to us, not a threat."

Her eyes stayed on me, watching carefully, calculating, her lips steady. It didn't matter much what I thought. Whether I agreed or not, I had to answer, "Yes, of course, Your—Anja," I corrected myself.

"Excellent!" she said cheerfully with a broad smile as bright as the flames close behind her. "Now that we cleared all that, I'd love to know a little more about you, Vala."

I adjusted my stance and my leathers, still reeling about the conversation and unsure what to really think. As I attempted to piece it all together, the only thought that flashed in my mind was the ripple of my skin across Xavyn's human face. *I need you to listen to what the queen wants, what she is looking for.* My only option was to stay on the course, listen and observe from the window the princess had just opened to me. Though after gaining access, I had to admit, I was even more uncertain about the evil intentions I was told to look for.

When I didn't respond, she asked, "I haven't asked Caulden because I was unsure how he'd react. But I can't help my curiosity. Do you know what happened to you?"

"No. No one does," I answered simply.

"Do you not have parents?"

"None that I know. The one who raised me was the one who found me. I considered her a mother since my own abandoned me."

"Sounds like a good woman. Is she still alive?" she pressed.

"No. She passed two years ago."

"I'm sorry." She chewed on her lip and glanced at the fire for a few moments. "What is it that you want, Vala? When the prince and I leave for Islain to wed, he will no doubt want you with him. But do you want to go or to stay here on Garlin, stay with Queen Havilah's Guard?" When I didn't respond quickly enough, she added, "Did you plan to compete in these Guard Trials that have been mentioned? I hear they have begun setting up some kind of course somewhere between the chateau and that Sacred Lake on the eastern cliffs."

I opened my mouth to respond and closed it again. *When.* She had said *when* they leave. She had already made her choice and was confident enough to not worry about Caulden's choice, or his feelings. And the Trials. I hadn't had a chance to talk to Haidee for the last two days, and the captain had no reason to disclose the information to me. "I would like to, yes, but …"

"But?"

The word had slipped. I could have just left it without acknowledging anything else. I didn't need to offer all the details. I shouldn't offer her *any* details. Especially when it is of no consequence to her. But that one little, stupid word had escaped. *But.* "I've been told I'm not permitted."

"Oh?" Her neat eyebrows lifted high above her eyes, which appeared to hold the reflection of the flickering flames held hostage inside, showing only yellow and orange and red within. "And who told you that? Your captain?"

"Yes, but it was ordered by Queen Havilah after Prince's Night."

"From what I've heard, you were the savior that night."

I wasn't sure how to respond, so I remained quiet while cringing inwardly at my mistake. I shouldn't have said anything.

"I see," she replied as if she could read my thoughts with a simple look. "I don't want you to fear reprisal for talking to me, Vala. What is said between us, will remain that way. I will, however, try to work my charms on the matter, and perhaps you'll be permitted to partake in the Trials. If you want to, of course."

I nodded. "Yes, Anja." And I did. I still wanted to very much. If it meant keeping my lifelong promise to protect Caulden, I would. Even more so now that it also meant a chance to leave the island, a chance to find out who I really was.

SEVENTEEN

A S THE PRINCESS SLEPT DURING THE NIGHT, AND A
few hours before and after, another Guard relieved
my post outside her door. I was conflicted about
the extra time alone. In some ways, it made me happy. Extra
time was something I rarely had when I was with the prince.
Haidee was dealing with that now. Though, I doubted she'd
ever complain since it was the position she'd wanted for so
long. And in other ways, having the time was distressing.
Without the active search of information while around the
princess, my mind wandered through thoughts, searching
endlessly for answers I didn't have, some I'd possibly never
find.

I finished dumping the last pail of well water into the
wash basin inside Saireen's washroom—my washroom. It

had been a week since Prince's Night, and it was time again for my cleansing. This time, though, there was something slightly different, aside from where it would take place. My skin would often begin to ache that final day, pressure gradually building to a point where I'd welcome the pain of the water. There had been no ache yet, nothing to remind me of what I needed to do. The lake water had been the only thought as to a reason. But I wouldn't forgo and risk breaking down in agony during my detail at the feet of the princess.

With my clothes and sword discarded on the bed, I moved into the washroom and stared at the liquid I loathed so much, watching it slow and settle. The peace before the condemnation. Was there a reason behind my weekly torture as well? A reason water was both my enemy and my savior, crippling and releasing. The lake water hadn't hurt me, though. I bit down hard on my lip, weighing if it would be any different this time. Before I had too much time to think, too much time to hope, I stepped inside, holding my scream as the life element attacked my legs. Lowering. Lowering. To my waist. To my chest. My skin cracked under the assault, the water slicing through, shredding its path. I slipped my face beneath, opening my eyes to the liquid above and the ceiling of wooden planks somewhere far beyond. So far away. Then I opened my mouth and screamed, letting the misery shed along with my skin, until the final bit of breath emptied from my lungs.

I emerged with the usual quickness, looking myself over for any signs of change. There was no glowing. Everything was normal again. Maybe the lake was sacred after all. The hidden cavern, the river feeding it, the location by the cliffs—it was all a part of the appeal. But did the people who once trekked there to mourn their loved ones know there was something even more special about it?

While the tingles in my red-orange skin slowly ascended into pain, the air biting as everything started to reform, a hard clanking noise outside the back door drew my attention. I slid into my thin underclothes, grabbed hold of my sword, then rushed toward the door. Knowing that sound was out of the ordinary, I was prepared to scour the garth and small area of trees behind the house, even search the neighbors' land to find the cause. I hadn't expected to open the door and find Xavyn standing a mere foot away, hood drawn and arms crossed as if I'd kept him waiting too long at the narrow back doorstep.

I pointed my sword toward his chest and glanced around him, scanning the darkness. "What are you doing here?"

"Following up." The words were slow. As his hand reached up and removed the hood, his human eyes traversed my face, swallowing the details of my reforming skin in an intense, almost penetrating way.

I realized then that I had no cloak, no mask. And for some reason, I wondered if I should take the time of throwing them on … before ending his life. He'd seen me in this state on Prince's Night, but that was an instant, a moment amid darkness and chaos. Not this closely. I growled at him, digging the tip of my blade into the black leather at his chest, my regrowth pain dissolving as my anger took control.

"Are you going to let me in or would you rather call attention to your treason?" he asked, his voice still holding a softness that grated me.

"Quit staring at me that way and you can come in."

A smirk stretched his lips. But a rustling sound stole his attention and he turned his body quickly enough to stir a wind with his cloak. I peered to the side of him and caught sight of what he'd heard. The raven sat atop a post in the stake fence bordering the trees, its inky feathers as dark as the night at its back. If it had not moved its head, I wouldn't have seen it.

Xavyn moved fast to him, snatching him up and turning back toward the house. The bird squawked in protest of his wings being pinned, loud and angry, kicking his feet. "Finally got you," Xavyn said to the bird with a smile then took hold of its neck and flicked his wrist once, hard enough to emit a snap.

I sucked air in reflexively. The shock of it, I supposed. Not that I cared for the bird. But as I had associated it with him, I never thought he'd take its life.

He glanced at me then chucked the carcass over the fence into the small group of trees and spun back, stalking directly to me until I stepped aside for him to enter. I stared into the dark for a few moments, looking for prying eyes again and collecting myself for what was about to transpire. Talking to him briefly outside was wildly different than having him in my house for any length of time. There would be no believable excuse to cover his visit.

His whole being took control over the house, both his physical size and his presence filling the entirety of the cramped, dim space. Slowly, he turned a few times, observing what little lay within the main area under the glow of a few lanterns I'd been brave enough to light. "Charming."

"Is that supposed to be funny?" I replied sharply, offended by his irreverence.

"If you think it is." An irksome answer that I wanted nothing to do with. I was about to open my mouth to get to the point of his visit, but he added, "It's nice, actually. Nicer than many others have."

I snapped my mouth closed, shocked for the second time in mere minutes of his arrival.

He chose to take a seat at the table, settling into a chair easily. "The raven," he said as his eyes continued to roam about. "His name was Oculi. He belonged to Elige."

"Why?" I asked the only thing I could think.

"Well, he was due to return to her soon. I couldn't let that happen because he'd give her information I'm not sure I want her to have."

"How could he—"

"They're bonded. She sees and hears things from him, through his mind, but only with physical contact. He was sent here with me, to monitor my actions and anything else he can pick up. He shows her everything upon his return. Most of it wouldn't be bothersome. But there are things I don't believe she needs to see yet. You, for example." His eyes finally cut up to mine from his seated position and held on. "And since I was uncertain of his departure plans, I chose to end him before he got the chance to skip across the sea."

"How is any of that possible?" My mind attempted to process it all unsuccessfully.

"There is magic in this world, Vala. I think you've had a little time to process that, even if you were in denial before." He grinned quite evilly as he reached for an empty goblet on the table then tilted it to look inside. "It returned not too long ago, but it is weak. There are very few of us who can do anything worth more than spit at all, beyond trivial child tricks. She's one. Though, she's not nearly as strong as she wishes. The sight bond with ravens is her main ability."

"Won't she find out what you did?"

"Not unless you plan to tell her. Do you?" he asked, lifting a humorous eyebrow. "No, she won't know. She'll think one of your humans got him, especially if that's what I tell her. Do you have any wine?"

My feet took me to the storage table pushed against the side wall where the breads and vegetables Haidee had stocked were still plentiful since most of the food I consumed was from the chateau. I grabbed an already filled carafe without thought and sat it on the table in front of him. A few days ago, I was prepared to kill him and now I was serving him wine. I tried not to think about that too much. Instead, I focused on getting answers. "What is she?"

As he lifted the carafe, his gloved hand shook. He clenched his jaw, the muscle in his cheek flexing as a ripple of charred skin waved across his face. As soon as it passed, he poured a heavy amount of wine into the goblet. "She's a witch, of sorts. That's probably the best way to describe her. She's a lot of other things too, but that's the main thing you're inquiring, I suppose." He gulped down a long drink then released a sigh. "The wine here is good. Reminds me of a place I used to live."

"How do you know her?"

"She lives in the north, in the fae lands. Though blurred, the territory divisions still stand, mostly because our people have chosen to cling to a history that was ripped from us long ago rather than come to terms with what we have become." He took another drink. "Oculi found me a few years ago while I was wandering the south, in The Borderlands of

Craw. Elige realized that my connection to magic was more than a distant ancestry, so she hired me."

"Hired you?"

"In a sense." His eyes fixed on the wall, holding a deep stare as if he were seeing the past.

"What does that—"

"I think I've told you plenty for now," he said, jerking straighter in his chair. "Your turn. Heard anything beneficial lately? I noticed that you were reassigned."

"How did you even know that? Are you able to get into the chateau with that fake skin you're wearing? How do you even do that? Is there something you eat to make it work?" If only it were that easy. Whatever it was, I'd be willing to consume it for the rest of my life.

He barked out a laugh, its resonance thunderous in such an enclosed space. "I didn't take you for the blabbering type. But I guess if you're quiet all day, watching and listening to others …"

I scowled at his honesty. My mouth had indeed sped up an unusual amount, I couldn't deny. It seemed to be happening quite easily around him. "Guarding others," I corrected, my tone defensive.

His fingers lifted from the table and he tilted his head a little, as if in surrender. "I can get around some. My ability to look like a human makes it easier. If I were to walk around looking like my true self, humans wouldn't exactly pour me wine and offer their beds."

I gaped at that, unsure what to think. Why would he even disclose that to me? Before I could even consider how deceitful that act could be, he smiled broadly.

"And I thought I'd already seen your worst repulsed

face." He laughed. "I'm not that evil. I meant it in the most basic sense. The vineyard's lord thought I was a newcomer looking for work." I relaxed a bit, unsure why I'd even cared. "Now, tell me what you've talked about with the princess. And spare me the female talk about how lovely the prince looks in his dress tights and tunic."

EIGHTEEN

I TOOK THE SEAT ACROSS FROM HIM AT THE TABLE AND poured my own goblet of wine. While there was never an acceptable excuse for being a traitor, even ignorance, I'd surely welcome wine as an aid to disregard my duties and morals. There was no other way to dull my mind's continuous thoughts of the possible consequences. I took a long drink, eyeing him as he did the same. I was risking everything. My home. My life. But part of me knew if what he said was true, if the future of Garlin and other lands were at stake, I had to take the chance and trust him.

After I explained the circumstances of my detail change and most of what the princess and I had discussed, I said, "There were books and papers in her sitting room, but I wasn't close enough to read anything."

"And that was it? She only wanted to know a little about you?"

"I left out the bits about Caulden and his tights like you asked."

He licked his lips and grinned, and it was a wicked sight only not so wicked at all. "Fair enough. I can see why she's so curious about you. I'm certain you've been baffling these humans for your entire life."

"Baffling," I echoed with a laugh. "Terrifying, more like."

"Yes, well …" He lifted his goblet and took another drink. "After what happened to their people so many years ago, I'm sure that fear is ingrained, twisted so deeply inside their blood the likelihood of them seeing anything beyond that terror is very slim."

"A few have seen beyond it at least." Saireen. Queen Havilah. Prince Caulden.

"Ah. Your queen," he said, squeezing those brown eyes into a squint to appraise me. "I've seen the differences in her skin, the contrasted colors so unlike most other humans. Could have been a part of why she allowed you on her Guard. The fact that you were young helped, too. However, I think the most feasible reason for her acceptance was fear. She knew you would be a benefit to her son, protecting him simply by standing at his side. Fear is one of the strongest allies to use against enemies. It can help to break them faster or make them think twice from the start. Your mere presence has made every human on this island not only question the rebirth of magic but also think twice about challenging you, challenging the prince, the throne. So for that reason, your queen has been able to look beyond her own terror. However, moving far enough past it to acceptance is a different matter entirely. I'm sure you considered those differences when you were being whipped the other day."

I held my calm expression even though the truth he spoke was like a dagger to my soul. I had doubts about truly belonging, truly being accepted. I'd always had those doubts. But with all the changes within the past days, with all that were to come, it seemed that everything had collectively flooded to the surface.

He sat straighter and stretched his arms out to the sides of the table, wrapping his fingers around the sides and gripping hard enough to knock his empty goblet over. Ripples surged over his skin again, this time the dark, rough texture spreading out and staying, wiping all the smoothness away. "Ah," he grunted with his eyes closed tightly.

I sat transfixed as the change took him in a few short moments. He inhaled fully then released his breath and opened his eyes to me, swirled with darkness. Even his eyes had changed into what I'd seen on Trader's Row—a replica of those I'd see within any basin of water or any pane of glass. "How is it possible?"

After releasing his deathly grip on the table and taking in another calming breath, he replied, "Close to twenty years ago, I felt a change. Not everyone in Vaenen or Craw felt it. Those who did knew that it had to be then that magic had re-emerged. Though, we have no idea what happened to cause it. There was also a lot of death at that time with no real explanation. Later, we realized those things could have been connected, that the ones who died ... whatever magic had lain within their blood may have been too potent and whatever had caused the change had been too strong for them to take. Some refer to it as The Wakening."

"So that was when you realized you could change?"

"No. I didn't see or feel any other immediate changes with an ability. I was young, and I thought it was a dream … or a nightmare rather, the pain of it … I was lost for a while …" His eyes flickered slowly around the room. "Some of my family died when it happened. But as I grew, I started to travel, eventually finding myself on the border of Craw. That was where I felt someone else's abilities for the first time. Knowing fae history and that my family's lineage included specialties, I did more research and discovered that I am a mimic."

"A mimic?"

He flipped his goblet upright and filled it then mine too. "I can adopt others' abilities and characteristics, fae or otherwise, from their energy. My body stays close in appearance, but some physical features can change depending on the individual's ability."

"Can you do it whenever you want?"

"I have to be in the vicinity initially, but keeping it varies. Human form I can keep longer without one being around because they have no real power. But you … around you I have struggled keeping human form. My body wants to pull your energy in. I was able to hold it off longer tonight than the other times. And when I leave, I won't be able to keep you for long."

I cleared my throat, shaking off the nervousness that had splintered through me following his words. The way he'd said them, as if we were connected, as if he knew what it was like to be me … It was worrisome, but there was also an inviting thrill too strong to ignore. "Is your ability the reason you were able to cross into Islain and come here?"

"Elige seems to think so." He lifted his goblet to his lips.

"Do you?" I eyed him, watching as he adjusted to his changed skin, his movements cautious and careful as he drank.

His eyes lifted to mine after setting the goblet down. "It's logical to associate the two. But it doesn't exactly have to do with changing. When I cross, I don't need to be in human skin. I do it as a precaution now, cross close enough to human areas to pull their energy, in case I'm seen. But when I didn't know much about the border, when Oculi had spotted me, I'd walked into the dense fog several times without realizing."

"So she saw that and still thinks it's the reason?"

"Yes, she believes it even if I don't need to change. Because no one has been able to cross, not even humans. Anyone who attempts to cross the border dies. Supposedly, there's a warning feeling, like a sickness. That's where most turn away."

I took another drink, savoring the sweet taste while considering all his information. "Was that why she was watching the border with the raven?"

He smiled to the table. "You are a smart one, aren't you? She has never told me specifics, but yes, she was waiting to see when someone was able to cross. As you already know, animals like Oculi can cross as long as they don't possess magic themselves."

"So what is it that you do for her?"

He rolled his shoulders back, stretched his arms, and stood. "I think maybe I should go. I wouldn't want your … sister or anyone else discovering that I'm here."

"Wait," I said as I stood with him, my voice sounding more desperate than I liked. But I wanted more information. I needed it. "Haidee doesn't stay here. I'm sure with everything else you've found out, you know that. No one else will come here this late, unless they want to lose an arm."

He pinched his lips together, containing a smile. "I don't think—"

"Just, please," I begged, shoving my shame aside, "a little while longer? There might be something else that we've missed. I just don't know enough …"

His eyes—my eyes—softened at that, his eyebrows pulling together the smallest amount as he studied me. He didn't reply, only settled back into his seat slowly.

"I …" I started, hearing the vulnerability in my tone and trying to quell all the unexpected emotions before continuing. "Like you mentioned on Trader's Row, I don't know much beyond this island, and I don't know much about magic or what happened all those years ago. These people don't talk about it here. I suppose that makes this island naive and me even more so since I know even less. But I want to know more. I may never know exactly where I came from or how I came to live here, but I'd like to know everything else. I'd like to find out what I am."

He looked at the table and peeled the gloves from his hands. "I'm not certain what you are." One set of fingers ran across the back of his other hand, feeling the texture I was so accustomed to. "With the way the flames call to you, with your ability to burn things with your touch … my only guess is that you have ties to fire elementals. I've read of some who had the ability. But there was no specifics about their skin." His eyes lifted to mine then flitted to the side of my face. "Or about their ears being rounded." I reached up at that instinctively, feeling the curve of my ear. "Back before The Final War, the fae families who possessed extra abilities were usually in charge of their own territories, managed their own courts within Vaenen. You might have ancestors from one, possibly have relatives still there."

"Thank you," I whispered honestly. Then I dared to ask, "So your ears aren't rounded?"

He laughed and shook his head. "No, they aren't." After a pause, he said, "That's why I'm intrigued by you, Vala, why I ended Oculi, also why I won't leave this island yet. I'm not sure how I can even cross the border. I haven't encountered any others in all my trips to Islain. But here you are. It has to mean something. I have many questions too. If you were born here, or only raised here. If you felt the change at the same time as I did. If maybe you suffered through it and that's why you are different. How old are you?"

"Nineteen. How old were you when you felt it?"

"I was five. It was close to twenty years ago. Maybe it was around the time of your birth."

"Maybe," I mused, thoughts spinning on end.

"And the princess asked you some of the same questions about how you came to be here," he said, recalling what I'd already told him.

"Yes, the same. She's been curious of me since her arrival. That first night when we were at The Siren Den on Trader's Row, she even asked Caulden if I'd been injured grotesquely." I laughed lightly, ignoring the sting that came with the memory of that night. As the laugh died, I found Xavyn's eyes pinned on me with a severe gaze. My smile disappeared.

"After a question like that, I'm surprised you defended them that night." He was more than serious.

"Of course I defended them. It's my duty. And really, she was curious because I'm covered. Those things don't bother me much anymore. They only fuel my need to be a better Guard." The intensity in his eyes didn't falter, so I continued, "And Prince Caulden informed her of me, my value on the Guard."

"I'm sure he did," he replied, still staring, his upper lip curling lightly, flaring his nostrils.

"What? You think I should have let you kill her?" I finally said, anger building under his scrutiny.

"I wasn't going to kill her. But had it been an option, yes, I think she would have found herself on the ground at some point, begging for my mercy or yours."

"I guess the differences between us still remain because I wouldn't betray the prince in that way."

"No? I find that more foolish than honorable." I scowled at his words. "It infuriates me to see you here, protecting the very people who have repressed you, contained you, molded you into something for their own benefit, only pretending to care for you."

I wanted to argue that they cared for me, that the princess could even see that Caulden quite possibly even loved me, but I didn't dare feed him that information. It was obvious that we were still so very different and he held no care for any duty but his own.

"I also think that if your positions were switched, the prince you so eagerly protect wouldn't reward you with the same amount of valor."

I shook my head, denying what I also couldn't debate. Would he? I'd like to think he would if he cared ... "That's not true."

"Is that how you came to be punished the other day, because of his protection?"

"Why do you keep bringing that up?"

"Why don't you?" he countered, his tone nearly as harsh as my own.

"Because I'd rather not. Mistakes happen."

"So you think he made a simple mistake? What was it? Not having the decency to stand up to his mother to save your skin from the whip?"

I ground my teeth. "Why do you care so much about that? What do you want to hear from me? That I deserved it? Fine. I am his Guard. I wasn't just saving the prince that night. I was the one who made a mistake. I entered the Sacred Lake, somewhere off-limits."

"Yet weren't you the only one who was taken to the prison chamber? I understand that the queen would spare her son from any punishment, especially after almost having been killed by assassins on the eve before meeting his potential bride, but why is it that the other Guards skipped out on such a generous fate?"

"I was the lead Guard on the prince's detail. The fault of decision-making was on me."

"Only you? No one else would be punished for entering this forbidden lake?"

"It's a spiritual place. Traveling there is not advised, but also not forbidden at the time … to them. But I'm different. I've been tainted. Cursed. Something that could potentially ruin its sanctity."

He eased back farther into the chair and crossed his arms over his chest. "Do you believe it's a spiritual place?"

I leaned back into my own chair, nearly drained from all the emotional flares I'd felt since his arrival. "I think it actually might be, yes. Prince's Night, when you almost killed Caulden and me." He lifted an eyebrow, but I pressed on. "The water is different there. It didn't hurt when I went under."

"Does it usually?" The intensity in his eyes had melted into something else. Curiosity. Or was it more? Perhaps empathy. He was wearing my skin after all, feeling what I was.

"Yes," I replied, taken aback by my own thoughts. "It didn't that night. It only hurt when the skin was reforming like usual."

"That's what that was," he said, more to himself than to me.

"And do you remember the glow of your skin?"

"Yes, I do remember. I wasn't as focused on it after getting out of the water and feeling the pain."

"Well, it's not normal either."

"So there is something special about that lake."

The lake was definitely special. And its water ... *The queen's questions.* I sat straighter. "They've been asking about our crops. The grapes, the wine." I lifted my goblet, sloshing what little wine was left inside. "When we were out at the vineyard, Caulden told the princess about Vitae River. How it twists through the island, sometimes above ground, sometimes below. It's our main river. It feeds the vineyards and farms. And it comes from Sacred Lake." The realization hit me hard.

He sat straighter too, mirroring me. "That could be it."

"But what is it? What are they looking for?"

His gaze shifted, looking at the small flame inside the lantern closest to us. I felt its hum, and I was certain it was calling to him also. I stared at him, watching the flame's reflection in his eyes.

"We didn't know what they'd be looking for. We only knew that there was more to this trip than a royal engagement."

"Maybe it is for the better crops. Maybe they knew there was something more. A reason behind the growth. They are trying to find it to take it, or cultivate it, to reproduce the process in Islain."

"That could be all it is. Still, I won't discount that there's something else behind their motives." His eyes snapped to mine. "Vala, Elige has been watching the queen for a while, using Oculi and other ravens. The queen has been gathering people, sending word to others, almost as if she's preparing for something."

I nodded. "Queen Havilah already knew Queen Meirin would be preparing for a hostile takeover here in the event our queen or prince refused the marriage. Queen Meirin knows we wouldn't last in a war against them."

He propped his elbows on the table and ran a few fingers over his lips with a squint. "Yes, but there are other things. Believe me when I tell you, there's more to this. Knowing that it might have to do with the lake is a good start to finding the answers, though. I'll need to go back, preferably during the day when I can actually see. And I'm sorry to say, but in the event I need to take a swim, I'd rather not be in pain. So you can't come." His lips tipped into a smile, and I couldn't help but to do the same.

"Not that I'd be able to anyway. Unless you'd like me to bring the princess along, of course," I joked. "She really wouldn't mind as long as I grabbed her some mourning flowers."

"Mourning flowers?"

"The ground cover plants, with wide, red-orange petals. Did you see them?"

"I have to admit, I wasn't paying much attention to the vegetation. I was focused on not being seen by the assassins I'd followed on the way in and on my changing skin potentially killing me during the climb out."

"Ah. Right," I said, both the pain on the assassins' faces and on his that night flashing in my mind. My smile was gone.

Xavyn stood, filling the room again. "I should go. I'll check in again soon." In a few strides, he was at the back door, drawing his hood.

I stood and moved his way, questioning why I was being so casual, so friendly, with each step. "I'll keep listening, but I agree that there's something with the lake. You shouldn't have to worry about anyone showing up. After the quakes, the queen deemed it unsafe and forbade travel there. This time, to everyone."

"Good. It'll be nice not having to look over my shoulder as much," he said, opening the door and looking out into the darkness. I wasn't expecting a goodbye, but after making sure all was clear, he turned back around. "Can I ask you something?"

"Sure." I gripped the door handle, leaning into the edge of the door as I inhaled the night's salty breeze.

He grabbed the top of the door and leaned in closer. "If it hurts … the water … is there a reason why you do it?"

My eyes widened a tad, reacting to the question that very well could have been on his mind all night—seeing me at the door, looking at me with that penetrating gaze that made me angry for feeling so weak, and then hearing that the water was painful. The question held more concern than curiosity, and that shocked me the most. I blinked a few times, then answered, "The pressure. It builds over time and eventually takes on its own life. Unbearable. Water wipes it away, resets everything. So it's necessary."

He didn't move for several moments, only looked at me. Then with a nod, he straightened. "Thank you, Vala. Sleep well." And then he was off, disappearing into the night between the dark and fog. No longer a shadow.

NINETEEN

"YOU WANTED TO SEE ME?" I ASKED, STEPPING over the threshold of Captain Baun's office. When I moved past the alcove of the door, I scanned the room and found more than his eyes had turned my way.

Captain Baun stood beside his desk, which was as narrow as he was wide, in a room smaller than the prison chamber residing beneath it. He wore no leathers, only a simple tunic covering his too tight pants and worn boots. He had the morning off from the queen's detail it seemed. Haidee stood with one boot propped behind her on the ledge of a tiny bookcase at her back, her long plaits loose, parting around her face when she looked up at me. Leint lounged in the only other chair in the room that wasn't behind the desk. His rust-colored hair stuck up in spots and the lids over his icy eyes drooped as if he had slept there all night.

"Good. I'm glad you got the message before reporting to the princess," Captain Baun said. "I got word that this Shadow may be staying at Lord Wyntor's vineyard. With the watch still on, everyone was notified to keep track of changes with their workers. It can be especially difficult for the farmers during this season when so many help out with harvest. But Lord Wyntor sent word yesterday and again this morning that he recently took someone in claiming to be a newcomer from one of the Islain ships, wanting to stay here permanently. He gave the name Xavyn."

They knew. I squeezed my nervous hands into fists. He'd given his real name, and now they knew his human form.

"There are newcomers on every trade ship, heading in either direction. Why should we think this one is who we're looking for?" Haidee asked without a single glance my way.

"He takes in many newcomers, and usually finds it beneficial to hire them. But this Xavyn has been acting differently than most. He's worked hard … when he's there. The messenger said that he's been spotted leaving late at night, sometimes not returning until early morning, as if he's barely sleeping."

I bit my tongue. *Traitor.* Was that what I had become?

"What about the taverns? Maybe he's just seeking friendly company in town?" Haidee asked.

"I was in town all night," Leint murmured from his slouched position. "One of Lord Wyntor's workers went with me and several other Guards to see if we could find him. He either got bored of each tavern very quickly or found a companion very early in the night."

A companion. I wasn't that to him, no. He was only using

me for information, and I was using him for the same. But that would all change if he was caught. Everything would change and nothing would be answered.

"Actually," Leint said, his eyes opening wider as his face tilted toward me. "The worker that was with me last night did mention that this guy was the one who tended to some of the horses when we had visited the vineyard. Do you remember the one, Vala? You were on the same side of the manor with him."

I fixed my eyes on him, steadying them so as not to blink or flinch my guilt while everyone's attention was directed toward me. "Yes, I remember him. Light-sandy skin. Dark hair in a thick tangle at the top of his head."

"That fits the description we got. I know you couldn't see The Shadow well during your encounters, but did this Xavyn appear similar in any way? His height or his posture?" The captain had perked up at having more inside information.

"I didn't consider him a threat in any way or even think he remotely looked like the one I'd fought. He carried himself differently, wore farming clothes. No leathers. No cloak." It was the truth to a degree. I hadn't known at first. I wouldn't have known if he hadn't made sure of it.

"Did you speak to him?"

"He complimented the horses. Mentioned the possibility of the prince leaving. I was shocked he spoke to me at all, but I didn't think much else of it."

"Perhaps it wasn't of importance before, but did his voice or the tone of it sound familiar in any way?"

I shook my head as an answer, not wanting to vocalize it fearing the memory of the vineyard might leap from my mouth and call me a liar. After a deep breath, I said, "What's puzzling to me, though, is if he were there that day, why not attack the prince or princess then?"

"Because we were all there," Leint said. "Don't tell me you still think that he's here for another reason."

I shrugged. "Why isn't anyone else considering that? He's had opportunities."

"Sure he has," Captain Baun interjected. "But those opportunities could have ended in his own death. He's biding his time, waiting for the best moment. That's why we will not give him one." His voice was as firm as his hand as he slapped it down upon his small desk, its legs wobbling like it was close to taking its last beating.

"So what are you thinking?" I asked, giving up on my attempt to open the captain's or Leint's eyes to an alternative reason for Xavyn's visit. There was no telling when I'd see Xavyn again, and there was no way for me to go looking for him. I'd have to wait and hope he'd have enough sense not to go back to Wyntor's Vineyard.

Haidee stole a glance at me, quick enough to miss yet long enough to see all the questions stirring inside. I wanted to tell her everything, to tell her all about the princess and every detail from the night before, including the answer she was possibly most puzzled about—that my skin wasn't permanent for Xavyn. We wouldn't have the time or the privacy, though.

"We have Guards searching the farms now with some of the other vineyard workers who can identify him. When they are done there, they'll move back into the town and all the areas between. For now, you all remain on your details. Leint, go get some sleep and report back to Haidee afterward. I wanted you three aware before the day really began. I was told that the queens, prince, and princess plan to visit the course where the Trials are being set up." I swallowed hard at his words. If the princess' information was correct, the Trials were being set up somewhere between the chateau and the lake, where Xavyn could be traveling. Hopefully, he still chose to look over his shoulder along the way. "I'll advise the queen to wait until after midday when I've heard back from the first searches and when Leint and some other Guards have had enough rest. After that, we'll have to be prepared to be out in the open with them."

Be prepared to be out in the open. Be prepared to make a choice. What would I do if he were caught?

I nodded my acknowledgment and looked down at my bare hands, thinking of everything Xavyn had said to me especially about a possible family in Vaenen. One who would accept me for who I was, not punish me. One who would care for me, not pretend to for their own benefit.

But here you are. It has to mean something.

TWENTY

TWENTY PEOPLE RODE ATOP HORSES TO THE PLATEAU situated about midway between the chateau and the eastern cliffs. The queens, prince and princess, Captain Baun, Haidee, Leint, and I were joined by Transton and Prins, Queen Meirin's two guards, and eight others of our own. The captain wasn't taking any chances of being caught unprepared. I just hoped Xavyn had enough sense to stay away from this excursion. With only a thin layer of fog and the midday sun peeking through, projecting slices of light onto the field spread before us, he'd be hard-pressed to find a shadow to hide in this time.

With some high points cutting its path, the Vitae River ran perpendicularly to the downward slope of the north, part of it showing above the ground during this section of its snaking journey through the island. Florisa's Cove and the town could be seen just past the river in some areas. Large boulders bordered the east, signifying the path to the crevasse fields on the way to Sacred Lake. Breezes of salted air blew into the plateau from the north, hitting the trees and backside of the southernmost peak and whirling around to find an escape. In a way I wished I could find one, too.

"Wow," Leint whispered with a low whistle as he dismounted his horse, taking in the nearly finished course in front of us. "People have been busy up here."

He wasn't lying. There were flats of land that looked like sparring areas, their borders created with stones and natural ditches. Wooden planks and logs had also been brought, creating raised walkways and climbing walls. Some had netting or ropes hanging in sections. Then there were other areas with painted archer targets at different distances, large woven bags stuffed and scattered throughout, and wooden spikes either upright from the ground to divide or diagonally to contain and corral.

"It's incredible," Prince Caulden said, his excited voice carrying in the breeze back to all the Guards.

Haidee gave me a sharp look as we slid from our saddles. We waited for the others to do the same, letting them walk forward toward the royals while we stayed back near the horses. She stepped to my side. "What is going on?"

A simple question for everything that had happened during the time we'd been apart. But I knew the main concern pertained to Xavyn.

I looked toward the eastern horizon, wondering if he was there somewhere watching, now with an even bigger target on his back. "He's not exactly what I thought he was," I whispered, looking everywhere but directly at her to conceal our conversation. "He can change."

"So they were right about what he looked like?"

"In a way. He can look human, but he can also look like me if he's close enough."

With a single glance her way, I could see the pull in her brow, the trouble in her eyes. She remained quiet.

"I can't go into detail. Just trust me when I say that he's not here to kill anyone. He's looking for answers to what the queen is searching for. We think it has to do with the lake."

"The lake?"

"They keep asking questions about it all. There's something else going on. We know it."

"We?" she hissed and boldly turned to stare directly at me. "What does that mean, Vala?"

I shook my head, denying what she hadn't outright asked. "It's not like—"

"Ahem." Captain Baun cleared his throat not far in front of us, his head turned, eyes flashing, the lines in his forehead creasing to show his irritation.

We both stepped farther forward, no longer able to speak. All the information I wanted to tell her would have to wait until she had her next break from Caulden, time alone to visit me at Saireen's house.

"I'm still not sure why you feel you must send your limited amount of people to accompany him," Queen Meirin said, then took a sip of water—or wine—from a flask handed to her by her guard. He was one of the taller ones, with golden hair much like her own. Though, with her hair knotted securely on the top of her head for today's trip, her height beat his.

"While I trust your guards, Meirin, I'm not about to send my son off this island without his own people when assassination attempts have been made," Queen Havilah replied, though I doubted she had any trust in them at all. She kept her eyes on the course, not bothering to look at anyone.

"After the Trials, we should keep this intact, Mother. I'm sure all the Guards would enjoy having this additional place to train. I wouldn't mind it myself," Caulden said, eyeing the activities he clearly wanted to test before the Trials even took place.

"I'm sure you'll like what we have at the palace back home too," the princess said, threading her arm through his. "It is very much like this one, but even more obstacles involved. It is a test to achieve the highest positions on our own guard."

"Tell us, Captain, what is the plan for this setup?" Queen Meirin said, beckoning him to her with a wave of her hand and a suggestive lick along her stained lips.

"Well," he replied, walking to her hesitantly. She grabbed hold of his arm when he was within reach, startling him and just about everyone else. "I—the Guards will test in different stations, some are individual assessments, others are against opponents." He tried his best to not look affected when Queen Meirin dragged her eyes up and down his body.

I watched the exchange curiously, knowing that she wasn't attracted to him based on what she had said the other day. But when I happened to glance at Queen Havilah, I knew exactly what the reason was. If Queen Havilah's eyes had been blades, they would have sliced everyone between them in half and then tortured her in ways I couldn't even fathom. Queen Meirin was purposely stirring trouble.

"Only the best will escort the prince … to your lovely kingdom," he added with a small cough. His eyes remained focused on the course as a pink tinge covered his cheeks.

"I bet it will test the best pretty thoroughly," Princess Anja said sweetly, her hands still gripping Caulden's arm, one rubbing gently over his sleeve. Her face turned a bit toward us and she winked at me before I could avert my eyes. "With how skilled Vala is, though, I doubt she will encounter any problems."

Even the horses seemed to stop breathing after her comment. The air was so still, so quiet. No one spoke.

"What?" the princess prompted with a tug on Caulden's arm. "You dare think your best Guard will have trouble with this course?"

"No, that's not … She won't be partaking."

"What? You've spoken of her as if she could take on all of this island with only a sword and yet you wouldn't want her to accompany us. She would be a great asset—"

"She's not permitted," Queen Havilah interrupted before Anja could go further.

"Oh. I'm sorry, I simply thought you'd want her with us after telling me of her skills and insisting on her protecting me." Anja's voice was a saccharine whisper to Caulden.

I supposed these were the charms she had mentioned to me, her strategy to grant my wish to run the Trials. My mouth went dry as I stared at Queen Havilah's face. I'd never seen her so angry. And why? Did she feel threatened by the others' questions and judgments or was she just expressing her frustration with me once again?

"You bring up a good point, princess," Caulden spoke and my knees threatened to buckle. "I do want the best to accompany me, and I think that Vala should be given the opportunity to run this course."

"No," Queen Havilah said, her tone flat, but her entire body projecting enough aggravation that most our Guards took a cautious step back. "Vala's capabilities are not the issue here, her infractions are. She is not participating in this course. She will not be leaving this island whenever you depart."

My body shook at her words, fury and heartache mixing into uncontrollable frustration. It was the first time I'd heard her comment on the subject of my fate. After Captain Baun delivered the bad news in the library, I'd wanted to believe that it could have been a mistake, maybe a quick decision based upon a minor error on Prince's Night. But with the harshness of her voice, the anger inside so potent it caused the last words to waver, I knew she intended to keep me here forever. There would be nothing I or anyone else could do or say to change that.

Caulden's eyes flitted to me. I felt them, the weight of their pity, but I kept my face down, eyes honed on the ground. I would not break. Not here. Not here. "Mother, if this is about what happened at the lake, I—"

"Enough!" she yelled at him, the thunderous echo traveling far down the slope. One hand instantly shot to her chest, the other smoothing her dress at her waist. She was collecting herself, her emotions, finding order again. "This is not the place for this discussion." She turned to the captain. "We're done here. Everything looks fine. Sign off on whatever else you need to." And with that, she mounted her horse and took off. A few Guards followed quickly.

"Well, that was rather entertaining," Queen Meirin said, mounting her own horse.

"I apologize for that. Entirely my fault," Caulden commented to no one in particular. "She was right that it was a topic better addressed elsewhere."

"Yes, well, sometimes we need to air it all out," Queen Meirin replied with a small smile. "Anja, shall we?"

"Hold on a moment," Anja replied.

"Vala," Caulden said, both he and the princess walking toward me. Haidee stepped aside, giving them enough space to invade mine.

I lifted my eyes to them … to him. Because whether or not the queen kept me here, my life was still for him.

The princess glanced between us, biting her lips nervously. "I'm sorry, Vala. It was the wrong time to push the issue." I wasn't sure if it was an act or a simple admission of fault. Either way didn't matter much.

"No, Anja, this is no fault of yours. It's mine," Caulden said. "Vala, I want you to know that I still want you with me. I will talk to her again. I will change her mind."

I was a Guard, I reminded myself, shoving everything away. The pain. The hurt. I served one purpose. One person. "Yes, Highness." I bowed my head back down.

"Don't," he said and reached for my hand to draw my attention. But his hand didn't grab my glove as intended. His fingers wrapped around the sliver of space that had gapped between my gloves and my arm guards. "Ahh," he said with a hiss and recoiled as if I'd struck him purposely.

I wanted to react, to reach for him, to look at his hand, to apologize for what I'd done. Only, I hadn't done anything. He had grabbed me. He knew what I was. And I wasn't sure I should apologize for that anymore.

"Caulden," Anja said, her tone worried.

I knew he was looking at me, and still I wouldn't lift my eyes.

"No, I'm all right. I'm all right. Let's head back to the chateau. I think we all need some time to unwind before dinner."

"Caulden, please, come to my room when we get back so I can help," Anja insisted.

"Yes, I suppose that would be best," he said, and they both walked to their horses.

"I suppose I'll go back to my rooms and enjoy the quiet also," Queen Meirin said. "Captain?"

Captain Baun had stood still the entire altercation, close to Meirin's side, as if he'd been stunned. "Yes, Your Majesty," he replied. He walked to his horse not far from me and Haidee and settled himself into the saddle. "Stay with your details. Vala …" His voice was calm, too calm. I listened without looking up, but nothing else was said as hooves clopped against the ground.

"Vala," Haidee called from atop her horse. "Let's go."

I stared one more time at the eastern cliffs, feeling something shift again, knowing that change had already come, then followed Haidee's lead.

TWENTY-ONE

N O ONE HAD SPOKEN TO ME FOR THE REST OF THE DAY.
Not even for simple orders. While Caulden had visited
Anja's room, Haidee attempted a conversation. But
when Transton and Prins were told to stand in the hallway
with us, she knew it wouldn't happen. We were both left to
our thoughts—her considering all the Xavyn information she
wanted, while I steered away from the queen's angry outburst
and toward more misery like Caulden and Anja's alone time
behind closed doors. Dinner had been the quietest and
quickest yet. Everyone retreated to their own rooms, skipping
the evening pastries, feigning tired and placing blame on any
lie they could come up with.

By the time I opened the door to Saireen's house, my
boots felt as heavy as stone and my head as watery as the

sea. All I wanted to do was sleep every hour before I had to report back, bury everything in the darkness of my mind. Forget. If even for a moment. Believe that my duty to protect the prince was again my only care in the world. Ignore everything else. But I realized that wouldn't happen sooner than I'd wanted.

I closed the door, dropped my cloak and mask, and spotted a flame in the single lantern above the stone oven, flickering, making shadows dance along the walls. Someone had been inside. I pulled my dagger from my belt—the quarters too close to wield a sword—and stepped lightly from the sitting room into the kitchen, inspecting everything in the subtle light. A goblet half full of wine stood on the table, the carafe beside it empty.

Xavyn. No one else aside from Haidee would dare enter my house uninvited.

I placed the bag of neglected pastry tarts I'd nicked from the chateau beside the goblet then moved to the bedroom door and pushed it open with my boot. The room was completely dark, the light of the kitchen lantern not even reaching the doorway. I kept my dagger in hand but kept it lowered as I crept into the room. His boots were the first thing I had the pleasure of noticing, tripping over them and taking a dive toward the floor. I threw out my arms and caught myself on the bed, cringing as the bed trembled under my hands. It trembled again as a figure sprang upward and swung a blade to my throat.

My breath sped up as fingers gripped the plaits gathered behind my head and the cool metal scratched the rough skin along the hollow of my neck. I lifted my hands in surrender, hoping he might feel the movement in the utter darkness.

"Vala," Xavyn said, his voice cracking with sleep. He released a long breath of air and the fingers tangled in my hair loosened.

"Can you drop your blade now?" As soon as he did, I got to my feet and added, "And get out of my bed."

"Yes. I'm sorry ..." He cleared his throat. "I had nowhere else to go. That vineyard lord gave my description and people have started looking."

"I heard," I replied. "Your late night behavior was suspicious to them." Even though I was standing and he was no longer touching me, I found being in the darkness with him too ... intimate. So I backtracked into the kitchen and poured myself some water to ease the embarrassment settling in after having felt the intimacy at all.

"That's what made him turn me in?" Jostling noises spilled from the room with his voice. "I thought it would have been all his missing wine."

"No, but I'm sure he is missing it like I'm missing mine." I tapped the carafe, wondering how much was left in the barrel stowed under the storage table. He laughed, and I closed my eyes to the sound, letting it resonate, trying to capture it, feel it. I wished I could.

"Don't worry," he said in a soft tone. "I brought you some of his. A full jug, next to the small barrel."

"You did not," I murmured, removing a pastry tart from the bag and taking a seat.

"Yes, I did."

"Do you even care if a jug of Wyntor wine—which is usually reserved for the chateau, lords and ladies, or export because it's from our best vineyard—links me to that manor, which now could link me to you as well?" I asked with a huff.

189

These were things I didn't plan to deal with and was almost too tired to care about.

"I'm sure you can take it to the chateau without anyone thinking twice about it. Besides, you should be out of here soon enough for it not to matter," he said, stepping into the kitchen and stretching tall, having to spread his arms for more space. His undershirt lifted over his waist and the shadows and dim light danced over the human skin of his lower stomach.

A rush of heat spread over me, and I quickly forced my devious eyes away from the sliver of his visible skin down to the table. To cover, I let out a little, bitter laugh at his statement.

He took a seat at the table across from me and swirled the wine left inside the goblet. "Bad day?"

"We were viewing the course for the Trials, and after the princess decided to subtly push the idea of my participation in them and potentially leaving the island, the day turned wretched. And I also happened to burn the prince when he tried to grab me."

"Why did he grab you?" His voice was flat, and his hand stopped swirling the goblet.

"I think he was trying to apologize for the queen's anger. I'd never seen her show such a vehement reaction. She's usually so ... calculated. That reaction stemming from something involving me was ..."

"Difficult to hear. To see?" he offered.

I nodded then took a bite of the tart, needing to occupy my mouth with the goodness of dough and blackberry instead of allowing it to lash out. I pushed the bag toward him.

"Anything else happen with Queen Meirin or the princess?" he asked, taking a tart and eating it in a single bite.

"No. They witnessed what happened. Anja apologized to me for bringing it up while we were out there. But I think they were uncomfortable with the situation and possibly horrified by what had happened to Caulden's hand, so no one bothered with me for the rest of the day. They went about the routine with even less interaction. No eye contact. No commands directly to me. I was even more of a ghost than usual."

"Sounds peaceful," he said soberly then took a long drink of wine. "My day was more interesting. Would you like to hear about it?"

"Do I really have a choice at this point? You're wanted by the Guard. You're in my house now, and I'm guessing you'll remain here until you leave."

"Until we leave," he corrected.

"I just told you—"

"I heard what you said," he replied, pinching another tart between his fingers and picking it up. "But you don't have to stay here if you don't want to."

"Really? I don't sail. If I get caught disobeying and trying to stow away, Queen Havilah … she will probably have me killed." I had no doubts about her feelings of me anymore.

"You can come with me when I go."

"You're serious?"

"Dead serious. You've been so kind to me since I've been here, trying to kill me most of the time, I figure it's the least I can do."

I rolled my eyes as he laughed again and popped the whole tart into his mouth.

When he finished chewing, he said, "Seriously. I'd be honored if you joined me, Vala. I'll take you wherever you'd like. I do have a boat. I didn't want to tell you before in case you decided to sink it."

I ignored his taunt and shook my head as I considered the consequences. "If I get caught in Islain … I'm not sure I could face him."

"We'll worry about that later. For now, know that you have freedom if you want it. They can't keep you here if you want to leave." His hand reached out to mine—his bare, mine gloved—scooping it up. I let him, not shying away from the contact I so desperately craved after such a horridly lonesome day.

I sighed and looked up to meet his eyes, the brown color barely seen in the dim light, but the empathy plain in his furrowed brows. What did I really have to lose now? Caulden? He was never mine. He never would be. And Queen Havilah would probably welcome my traitorous actions just to have an excuse to end me. As much as I respected the captain, he'd always stand at her side, honor her decisions. That only left Haidee. Haidee …

"Vala," Xavyn said with a smile, lifting my hand a bit before setting it down again. "Let's talk about my day, shall we?" I returned his smile with a nod. "That lake of yours …"

"Beautiful, isn't it?" I whispered, recalling Prince's Night—the water streaming in from the cracks of the inky cavern walls, the way the fire's light shone over the tiny island where Caulden was, pushing away thoughts of blood on my blade, the assassins' bodies sprawled over the rocks.

"Very," he replied and took a drink from his goblet. "There was something that was familiar that night, but I was too focused on the prince and escaping you that I didn't think much of it. Today, in the light, it hit me. Those flowers you spoke of before ..."

"Mourning flowers."

"You said the princess mentioned not having them in Islain?"

"After seeing the one in Queen Havilah's conservatory, yes. That's when she told us she hadn't seen them before. She instantly wanted to go where they grew, probably wanted one of her own due to their rarity and also because they're Queen Havilah's favorite."

"Oh?" he asked with a curious tilt of his head. After a moment, he continued, "What I realized as soon as I went back was that I've seen them before. Where I grew up, there's a lake named after Alesrah. They grow there too. Many of them."

"In Vaenen?"

"Yes, in the northern division of Windlan. The flowers ... they're the same as your mourning flowers, but their name is ember."

"Do you think they're connected?" I asked, pulling another tart from the bag and biting it in half.

He did the same but ate his whole, chewing it down quickly before speaking again. "I think they could be, yes. You are aware of the Disir?"

"The three goddesses? Who once watched over our world?"

"Yes. Many older books debate how the three came to be, but we know they were the goddesses we looked to, prayed to, and relied on. Herja, the mighty Valkyrie, was guardian of Vaenen and the fae. Verdandi, the Norn, was guardian of Craw and the witches and other dwellers. And then there was Alesrah, the Phoenix, guardian of the human lands. They kept an order between us, intervened whenever needed."

"We all know of the end, when magic was said to be erased from the world. But with no travel between the lands, humans don't know what happened in the north. And Garlin knows even less since our ancestors—their ancestors," I corrected myself, forgetting for a moment that I wasn't human. "Their ancestors were fleeing here just as the end happened."

Xavyn nodded with pursed, contemplative lips and ran a hand through his thick tangle of hair. A ripple streaked across his face and suddenly his human skin was covered in mine. He stretched his arms and legs, rolled his neck, and adjusted his position in his seat. "Sorry. Holding onto the human thing seemed rather senseless right now." A small smile formed on his now rough face. I smiled back but remained silent. "Growing up in the north, I learned a good deal about The Final War. Some from books, some from the land, some from other fae. There are fae who still pray to Herja, knowing that she, along with Izaris and the other two Disir, had died but never fully giving up hope that there would be a day when magic returned, and when the goddesses might return too. One legend claims that Izaris found his power by capturing a piece of each Disir. He'd tempted Herja with his good looks and the wars he created with his family. The battle call was something that enticed Herja, and he was able to strike his deal. It was said that Verdandi had been able to resist his charm, keeping herself well away from what was happening in Vaenen. Alesrah was a different story. She had kept her distance, watching and protecting from the skies as she usually had done. But he tricked her, luring her lonely heart with promises of love and companionship. She realized her mistake and was prepared to leave or fight. Only, it was too late. He trapped her. The war started soon after, and Izaris continued to gain strength from both Herja and Alesrah, stripping power from those he'd slain and cultivating that energy.

"According to the legend, Alesrah, seeing what Izaris had become and his plans to slaughter everyone and take all the lands for himself, raged against him. She found a way to free herself of his hold, and as soon as she was free, she flew to the tallest peak and sacrificed herself, ending her life cycle by first crying her lament song then burning. That song was said to be what had stripped magic from the world, what killed Izaris, the Disir, and what also killed many innocent fae and creatures unable to withstand the force of magic leaving their being. That cry ended the war and possibly created the impassable border between our lands. But it also ended our way of life in Vaenen. And with no further signs from the Disir, it killed spirituality in all the lands as well. While there are some who believe Alesrah did the right thing, that the world would have been much worse had Izaris lived on, others aren't able to believe that as easily. They feel that Alesrah holds the larger fault."

"They think the world would have been better with a ruler who slaughtered on a whim, took everything for himself?" I commented, shocked at the thought of what would have been left had Izaris not been killed.

"You have to understand that, until recently, Vaenen hadn't seen magic in many years, and we had to live knowing and feeling that we were lesser than we once were, that a different life had been ripped from us in a single moment, along with the lives of many ancestors. That isn't something easily lived with."

I nodded at that, unsure how to feel or what to say. This was so much history that I knew nothing about. Xavyn's history. And maybe my own.

"As with anything, there are many more stories, many other beliefs. But that legend is the basis of all the others, and the reason so many fae loathe the idea of her. Also why not many live near Izaris's old castle in Windlan. Alesrah's Lake and the ember that grow there aren't considered sacred or rare as they are here on Garlin. Most fae don't want to be anywhere near them."

"Are you saying that Sacred Lake is like Alesrah's? That it's another place where she …"

"Died. Yes, I think that's exactly it. I can't see another explanation. The phoenix was immortal, but it is said that she had many life cycles of birth and death. Sacred Lake could be another place she chose. But after scouring that place today, I'm still not sure what Islain's queen might be after. I did think of something curious, though. Because of the barrier between our lands, we've been separated, unaware of what was happening on the other side for all these years. With all that has happened recently, it is apparent that Islain's queen knows more than most humans. How can she? That's one question. But the more pressing question is why. She's hunting something as we thought."

"I've told you everything they've said while I'm near, and it's all been about the water. Do you think it's only about that?"

He shrugged and lounged back into the seat. "Or I could

be missing something. Elige doesn't give me many details." He paused with a long breath, scanning the room. "I need to tell you something. The reason I was sent here … I wasn't fully honest before." I waited, the blood in my veins pumping faster with each silent moment. "I did come for information, but I was also tasked to kill your prince. Knowing that this trip was also about a possible marriage arrangement, my killing the prince would have caused a good amount of chaos on the island. That would have disrupted the visiting queen and princess' plans, possibly speeding up their decisions, making them take risks that could accidentally show their true intentions … But I hesitated that night … after I saw you fight, saw you defending him …"

My breath caught as his words sliced through my thoughts, my mind instantly scouring all previous conversations with him, double-checking his intentions, his motives. It felt as though the walls were closing in. "Why are you telling me this now?"

He stared at me, unmoving, not blinking. "I needed to be honest with you. Your trust matters to me. Without it, my chances of leaving this island alive aren't so great. So, you're holding my life, Vala."

I inhaled a full breath to steady myself. While unsettling, I welcomed his honesty. Part of me wondered if it was simply because I had to accept it all now. I was in too deep. Even if I chose to betray him, forget everything I'd learned over the past days and decide to stay here forever, they would inevitably learn of my treachery. And that wouldn't go unpunished. "You're holding mine too," I admitted. And though the thought of someone else controlling my fate should have been paralyzing, I stared across the table at him, watching the lantern's soft flicker of light move over his calm face, and most of the worry drained from me. I could trust him.

"Thank you. And I promise to be gentle," he replied, his lips tugging into a full grin, lifting his cheeks, squinting his eyes.

I dropped my gaze to the table and smiled, his words, his stare, causing a stir inside I wasn't prepared for. "What now?"

"I suppose we have to wait. Queen Meirin and the princess might accidentally leak their intentions."

"You can't leave this house. It's too risky."

"Is that an invitation to stay?" The light made his smirk look sinister.

"I'm so glad you are able to joke about our fates so easily."

"I'm not taking this lightly." He stood and stepped to the edge of the table, reaching a hand out for me to grab. I looked up at him and laid my palm into his, trusting. He led me to my feet, then, one at a time, slid my gloves from my hands. "I know how serious this is." After he dropped the gloves to the table, he picked up my hands again. I stared at the contact, unsure of what would happen. But our skin was the same, rough to touch and warm, and neither of us burned. "Every day I stay in this house is another day I risk your life. I'm well aware of that. So we won't stay much longer." I dared to look up, knowing as soon as I did I would be caught with his stare. Closer, I saw how his eyes had become mine again, only they appeared to have a boldness within them that I lacked in that moment. It was attractive, more so than I would have imagined. My heart quickened. "You decide. If they stay closed off after what happened today, if you feel they won't let another word slip, then we leave."

I nodded, words failing me.

"Now, you need sleep. I probably should also. I'd offer to stay out here, but I think it's probably safer for me to be behind an extra door."

I quirked an eyebrow, my focus still very much on our hands, the way his cradled mine.

"I'm good with the floor. It's a step up from the ground and six feet better than a grave." He smiled as he released my hands then added, "Call out when I can come in."

So I readied myself for sleep even though my thoughts threatened to keep me awake for days. I'd found extra bedding Haidee had stashed beneath the bed and laid it all out onto the floor. Then, after I'd stripped down to my underclothes and situated myself beneath my own blankets, I called him.

Moments later, the door opened and closed, then what sounded like his boots clunked onto the floor. Other noises followed as he situated himself. And after a few deep breaths, he whispered into the darkness, "Thank you, Vala."

It didn't feel right to say that he was welcome. I was only doing what I felt in my heart was right. But I, too, was grateful to him, so I simply replied, "Thank you, Xavyn."

TWENTY-TWO

LIKE MOST OTHER MORNINGS, THE DAWN HAD NO trouble pushing its way through the threadbare drapery covering the tiny bedroom window. I opened my eyes to the gentle light and thought of Saireen standing beside it, her speckled russet skin glowing as she pulled the gray fabric back, looking outside to check on the many seedlings she had planted through the years that never reached maturity. She had cursed the goddessforsaken soil more times than I could count. If only she had known to use the water from the Vitae, from the lake …

I rolled over with a stretch, thinking about the day to come. I had to report to the princess soon, where I would find out if the day would repeat the silence of the last or if I had a chance to garner information that

Xavyn—we—needed before we decided to leave. I blinked at the window and drapery, suddenly knowing that it might be one of the last times I'd be in Saireen's house, wanting to memorize it all—the loose threading of the drapery, the basket of wooden toys beside the bed, the feel of the pillow under my head. Because if I fled, there would be no coming back.

Xavyn had been so kind the previous night, his energy calming after the day I'd had, his reassurance soothing. He was holding my life, as I held his, and for some strange reason, I felt safe, safer than I'd ever expected. Despite being different, I'd always felt a certain level of safety in Garlin. I was a Guard. I could protect myself and others. But this went beyond all that normalcy. Maybe it was simply because I was more like him than human, or maybe it was having the ability to leave the island, to find where my true home was. No matter what the cause, it was nice to feel some form of safety while standing on the precipice of change. To not feel alone on the cliff.

I leaned over the bed to where he was sleeping and gasped, covering my mouth with my hand to silence my shock.

Sprawled on his back was not the same man I'd seen the previous night. The green woolen blanket I'd left out for him was draped over his bare torso, which was no longer charred and rough but smooth and fog white with nearly translucent lines peeking out from beneath the blanket. His arms were the same, lacking all color, veined with identical lined markings on both sides all the way to his hands. His head rested to the side on the pillow, eyes closed, lips slack. From the side I could see that his face held the same features as with the different sets of skin—broad nose, narrowed cheeks to a firm chin. His eyebrow was startlingly black against such bright skin. The tangle of hair that bunched above his head on the pillow also held stark contrasts, most strands of white with streaks of black. And his ear … It did crest into a soft point, angled toward the back.

I let my hand fall from my mouth and breathed in deeply, awed by his real appearance. There had been so much happening—my normal duties, spying on the queen and princess, thoughts of life and death, leaving or staying— that I hadn't really taken the time to imagine what he truly looked like. I didn't even know what to expect, except for the ears, since he'd admitted they weren't round. But this … this was … powerful and enchanting. And simply looking at him was reassuring, knowing I wasn't so different after all.

A snore escaped his mouth, disrupting my appraisal of him, and I held in a startled laugh. I really didn't want to wake him, but, selfishly, I wanted to talk before I had to leave for the day. I also wanted to ask him more about his skin, the scars and markings.

A knock on the front door jolted me, my nerves springing me off the bed and onto my feet. The noise woke Xavyn too. He sat straight up, eyes wide—light gray eyes—staring at me. Another knock had me grabbing my gear, darting out of the bedroom, slamming the door, then throwing on my cloak before screaming at the oak door with as much anger as I could muster to hide my concern. "What?"

"It's me," Haidee replied.

Oh. Oh! I glanced back at the bedroom, hoping that Xavyn could stay quiet and also that Haidee didn't need something from inside. "Good morning," I said as I opened the door to her then turned, stripping off my cloak and beginning to pull on my leathers on the way to the kitchen.

"Is it?" she answered, instantly shooting my thoughts back to the events of the previous day.

"Already better than yesterday." I poured some water into a goblet and took a long drink, watching Haidee's eyes scan the room. They stopped on the table where the two goblets from the night before still stood. "Drink?" I offered, continuing with the rest of my leather gear.

"No, thanks. I was asked to come check on you after what happened yesterday, also escort you to the chateau this morning."

I finished with my armor then leaned against the chair, blocking her view of the goblets. "I'm all right. What about him? His hand was wrapped at dinner."

"He says it's fine." Her observant eyes danced around the room. "But I have a difficult time believing that either of you are. At dinner, you looked—"

"Like a dutiful Guard?" I said.

"He's concerned for you."

I laughed lightly, unable to hold it in, and Haidee tilted her head in question. "I don't see why anyone needs to be concerned. I'm only a Guard. Like you. The captain. Leint. We don't need to have feelings."

Haidee gaped, her full lips falling open for a moment until her mouth twisted into a scowl. "You know that's not true. You grew up with him. You're practically part of their family."

"No, Haidee. I'm their Guard, not family. I'll never be their family."

"You are mother's family. My family. I hope you haven't forgotten that." Her tone was sharp. "You seem to have forgotten everything else lately. Tell me, since we have some time to talk now, what is happening?"

"I'm still listening for information. Have you heard anything new? Anything about the lake?"

She tugged at the front of her leathers, composing herself. "Nothing of that sort, no. But on my way out this morning, I overheard other Guards saying that the Trials have been moved up."

"To when?"

"They start tomorrow. With so many entering, it will take a couple of days. Someone wanted to start the process sooner than later. I guess we'll hear more from the captain when we return."

"Then he's definitely leaving," I murmured. The prince's decision had been inevitable, and was likely more about protecting Garlin than the actual marriage agreement, but hearing that the plans had been set into motion cut through that last thread of hope tethered to Garlin's fate. Deep down, though, I knew Garlin's independence had vanished the moment the queen and princess' ship had sailed into port.

"Yes. The dates are still undecided. Last night, he mentioned that he planned to speak with his mother again about your participating. I suppose he'll have to do that right away, considering it's now due to start tomorrow."

I tapped my fingers around the goblet. "I need to tell him to stop. Queen Havilah won't change her mind. Begging her will only make a worse impression on his new family, especially after what happened yesterday." I stared down at my hands, remembering his shocked hiss as his flesh seared.

"You're giving up? You're not fighting for what you want? What you deserve? Because you deserve a chance, even more so than the rest of us," Haidee said, the hardened stare of her wide, grassy-colored eyes boring into me. "There's something you're not telling me. Is this about Xavyn?"

"He won't be here on Garlin for much longer," I said honestly, answering before she could ask.

"That's all you're going to tell me now?" she asked with a scowl. "All right," she added, then rushed to the bedroom and kicked it open before I could utter a warning. Xavyn stood a step behind the door's swing area, the breeze of air close enough to cause the now brown hair on the top of his head to stir. His skin was no longer his own but human and fully clothed.

"Hello," he said with an actual smile to greet her.

Haidee threw her arms into the air. "What are you thinking, Vala? Having him stay here? I can't … You can't …"

"Haidee, this is Xavyn," I introduced, biting my lip and turning to pour two more goblets of water. "Xavyn, Haidee."

"Pleasure." His reply was almost a whisper compared to what Haidee's had been.

Haidee's boots pounded the floor as she rushed back to me. "What is happening here?" She grabbed my arm and spun me around, spilling water everywhere—her shirt, the floor, my bare hands. Her eyes widened as she blanched. My body seized at the sensation, dropping the carafe and goblet, sending splinters of glass and splashes of water shooting across the floor.

Water wrapped around my hands, digging into my skin and separating it, the burning, familiar pain ripping into me as it always had.

"Oh, Vala, I'm so sorry," Haidee said, her shaking hands covering her mouth.

Xavyn was at my side in a single moment, now with skin like my own, gently taking my hands in his. I looked at him, shocked at first by his reaction, his choice to come to my side, then eased by his soothing touch and sympathetic eyes. The air took over, rebuilding the roughness that had been stripped from my tender red flesh. Still staring into his eyes, I blinked several times and offered him a small smile. "Thank you." He offered his own smile in response. I slipped my hands from his and reluctantly shifted my eyes to Haidee, who was gaping again, this time at Xavyn's appearance.

"It's okay, Haidee. You never need to be sorry," I said, looking down at her scarred hands. She glanced down too, remembering that time years before when she had grabbed me in anger, attempting to punish me for the burns Saireen had suffered. "I'm the one who should be sorry. Only ever to you and only because of Saireen, who was kind enough to take me in and love me when no one else would. But I will never again apologize for being who I am." I crouched to the floor and began picking up the pieces.

Xavyn squatted beside me, and Haidee grabbed a broom.

"I'm worried," she said as she dumped the last of the glass in the waste bin, breaking the silence we'd been working in. "I'm not asking you to explain everything, but I don't under-stand why you've changed your mind about the Trials, about wanting to go with Caulden when he leaves."

"There's a reason for everything, Haidee," I replied, choosing to hold my plans from her for a little while longer. In time—however long it was that I'd remain on the island—I'd tell her the truth. I'd tell her goodbye. "Queen Havilah is hurt-ing too. She's losing her kingdom. She's losing her son. I real-ize that she's angry and hurt by all of it. I have no idea what her plans may be. But it would be better for everyone if he just accepted I'm not going with him."

Xavyn's gray eyes slid to me, but I kept mine on Haidee, watching her lips tip down for a moment before she nodded and gathered a few stray plaits that had fallen over her face, tucking them behind an ear.

"All right, Vala," she said, straightening up. "We should leave so we aren't late. I'll be outside." I nodded and watched her pull the door open, but she stopped short. "Leint. What are you doing here?"

I froze for a moment then instinctively shoved Xavyn toward the bedroom. If he was seen by anyone else, everything would fall apart. Leint replied something I couldn't hear as Xavyn and I moved quietly, our eyes pinned on Haidee. We closed ourselves into the bedroom, leaving a crack to peek through where we saw Haidee take a last step outside and close the door behind her. Her voice remained loud enough to hear but not make out the words.

I turned around to Xavyn and found myself staring at the shirt covering his chest. I hadn't realized how closely his body had been leaning behind me. His hand propped high against the wall right below the ceiling and his face leaned close to the crack in the door. I tipped my head back and watched his face tilt down to see me. The light from the window was stronger now, highlighting the slope of his nose, the peaks of his lips, which tipped up slightly. My body wasn't prepared for the closeness and the feeling that came with it, like strength and weakness mixing as one thrilling rush of energy.

"I should … go," I whispered so softly I wondered if I'd said it at all. My heartbeat was louder, pounding hard against my chest, pulsing inside my ears.

"Will you be all right?"

I stared at his lips as he spoke, trying to focus on his words and not the feel of him surrounding me. "Yes."

His eyes closed for a lengthy blink. "Remember, you decide. Anytime." He glanced through the crack again, double-checking the empty room. "Even now."

"If I hear nothing today, then we'll go tomorrow," I decided, knowing it would be the best time. "The Trials will have everyone busy. You won't be seen leaving, and I can sneak away at some point."

He leaned in closer for a moment before pushing his whole body back, letting air rush between us. "Be careful today."

I smiled at his concern. "I will." Opening the door a little wider, I looked back at him. "After seeing you this morning, I couldn't imagine anyone, even humans, not offering you wine or a bed."

His eyebrows quirked then the corner of his mouth twitched just before I closed the door.

TWENTY-THREE

THE MORNING PASSED IN A BLUR OF SILENCE AND
hushed whispers much like the previous day, only with
more Guard and servant chatter about the impending
Trials. Haidee and Leint went about their usual routine with
Caulden, and I spent the morning posted outside the princess'
southern rooms. The only interaction I had was a trespassing
beetle traveling the hallway. I thought of crushing it, even
went as far as to lift my boot, but in the end, even though it
was positioned to squeeze its way beneath the princess' door,
I let it go.

The princess emerged hours after midday, clothed in a
simple dress made from very few layers of white and orange
silk with her hair plaited and wrapped in a large coil atop her
head. We met with Queen Meirin in the dining hall where

they ate by themselves. Queen Havilah and Prince Caulden were nowhere to be found. Since the Trials had been moved up, I would have assumed the prince and princess to use any extra time getting better acquainted. It made me wonder if there was a reason they were apart, but I stopped wondering when I remembered that it was no longer a concern of mine. Caulden would leave with Anja soon enough, but I was leaving sooner. And I could only hope from then on, I wouldn't have to worry about our paths crossing again. I didn't want to think what would happen if they did.

The queen and princess chatted lazily about communications with Islain, their council, and small issues that were being taken care of there. I screened all of their words, but none were about Sacred Lake, its water, Vaenen, any of the goddesses, or even the mourning flowers. When they finished eating, they chose to take a walk for some air.

"So, Vala," Queen Meirin called back to me after we exited the chateau and moved out into the gardens. I tensed, keeping my focus on her lengthy blue cloak as it dragged behind her like a gown's train, clearing some dirt from the slate pathway. Transton and Prins slowed, allowing me to pass them and move closer to the queen and princess.

I'd expected her to keep talking, so when she stopped, I gave a head bow. "Yes, Your Majesty?"

She squinted her eyes then turned to continue walking. "My daughter tells me you've always been this way."

"Mother! Honestly." Anja huffed. "The poor thing has been through enough without us bothering her."

Thing. Thing. Poor thing. I gritted my teeth beneath my mask and clenched my hands at my sides. That was all I was. *Thing.*

"I'm just trying to talk to her. I think she's exceptional. And if Queen Havilah can't see that then she is the one who has the problem. You have a gift, young one, no matter what anyone else says or thinks. Do you believe it was a curse that made you what you are?"

"Mother," Anja murmured in warning. "Don't."

"Anja, don't make me send you back to your room," she said with a squeaky laugh that made her whole body shake and shimmy.

What you are. "I do not know, Your Majesty," I answered, making my voice as stolid as possible.

They walked through the largest arbor, keeping a steady course through the garden without paying mind to any of the plants. They'd been here long enough to not care much anymore, I supposed.

"Pity you don't know. Because I think the idea of anything magic is simply amazing. We haven't seen it in a thousand years. You being so different is obviously a sign, don't you think?"

"I do not know, Your Majesty," I repeated.

"Well, I happen to think so. I also think it's fateful that you should be found here on this island, so far away from the magic lands that have been sealed for so long. Curious actually."

I looked at the chateau, watching the queen's two guards keeping speed with us while walking the pathway closer to the building.

"What else is curious about this place is its lack of birds. This island isn't so far away from Islain's coasts to prevent birds from traveling here. Any could make the journey, especially with the ability to rest on the archipelagos close to either coast and even the trade ships. You have some gulls down at the port that harass the fishermen. So where are the rest? You see, I'm a huge collector of feathers. That's why I'm interested. I love all kinds, but the rarer the better. Have you seen any here, Vala?"

"No, Your Majesty," I said, curious as to her point. It was something that we all here had wondered, but why would she have noticed or cared? Because of a collection?

Quicker than I even realized, we came to the end of the walkway, the last steps before the queen's conservatory. "Shame," Queen Meirin replied. "I would pay handsomely if anyone were to find one, of course. Big or little, dull or vibrant. I have no preference. I just like rare things. And a feather on an island without birds is rare indeed."

Feathers. "Do you like pheasant feathers?" I asked before I could stop myself. Asking her anything was a huge risk, but with how talkative she was being, I felt comfortable taking a chance to get some answers. Captain Baun had said the fletching used by the archer assassin had been pheasant feather, which Leint had said was a bird native to eastern Islain.

"Pheasant?"

"Striped," Anja said, as if the queen needed reminding.

"Oh, yes. They are pretty." Queen Meirin stopped in front of Queen Havilah's sentinels, Bransley and Lato, standing at the oak and metal doors, who bowed and opened them for our entry. "They dwell not far from our palace. We hunt and eat them quite often. The feathers are also used in arrows for our army archers, too. Nothing to waste. Maybe you'll get to see them or even hunt them … when you come with us."

Anja hissed quietly, and I stared at the back of both of their heads, stunned by what she'd said. "Mother, that's for her to decide. She has a lot to deal with as it is, and you haven't even extended a proper invite."

With only a thin fog during the day and a strong sun not long from setting, the conservatory had warmed considerably. But it could have also been my heat, fueled by an uncomfortable situation and by thoughts of feathers and assassins. When I thought the situation wouldn't get worse, I spotted Queen Havilah at the end of the building, sitting near her precious mourning flower. Her eyes were already locked upon us intruders. She was on her feet within a second, not waiting for us to approach. Her green dress billowed out alongside her, bouncing lightly with each hurried step.

She bowed her head and offered a twitch of her lips, barely passable as a smile. Her long black hair was loose, some locks tumbling over each shoulder. It was obvious she hadn't anticipated visitors. "Queen Meirin. Princess Anja. I do hope you are enjoying this lovely day."

"We are, thank you," Queen Meirin replied sweetly, bowing her head also. "We thought it would be good to visit here again, study all your lovely plants and flowers."

"Please enjoy yourselves," she replied with a low swing of her arm. "I have matters to attend to, but I also require Vala for the remainder of the day. I sent Captain Baun to fetch her only moments ago. When he reports back to me, I'll have him send a replacement should you require one."

"That's very kind. Thank you, Majesty," the princess replied.

Everyone stepped aside, allowing Queen Havilah

to pass. She moved swiftly, not waiting for me to follow. Transton and Prins eyed me as I stepped around them and hurried behind the queen. I caught up as the sentinels opened the doors for her. When we cleared the threshold, she slowed her pace, and as soon as the doors closed, she stopped entirely and turned.

"Vala," she said. "I have some things to tell you, none of which can be discussed here. It has to be somewhere private."

"Your Majesty?" I asked, thoroughly puzzled.

"You have to know it's very important that we speak." She smoothed her fingers down the front stitching of her dress. "I know you are not happy with me after the way I acted yesterday. But there are reasons … I want you to go home and get some sleep tonight. Meet me at the lake before dawn. That'll give us plenty of time to discuss things before tomorrow's Trials begin, before people assemble by the course."

"I—I'm not sure I understand."

"Do as I ask, and tell no one." She looked around again then started walking, this time waiting for me to follow off to her side. "I have much to explain to you, and it can't be done in the chateau."

Captain Baun exited one of the closest doors and met us along the pathway. He had walked along the border that Queen Meirin's guards had. I looked around, suddenly aware that they had not been inside the conservatory and were nowhere to be seen outside either.

"News?" Queen Havilah asked.

"None worthy of note." The captain looked at me for only a moment, face as stoic as ever. "The course is finished. A good portion of the Guard will participate tomorrow. They know to show at midday."

"And the man called Xavyn or the raven?"

"The raven hasn't been spotted since the vineyard. No signs of the man either."

"Do we think he is gone then?"

"There's no telling, Majesty. We're prepared for tomorrow. All the Guards have his description. And the port still has plenty of protection too."

"Good," she said, pulling some of her hair forward and running her fingers through it while staring at me. "I instructed Vala to go home for the evening. I need to meet with her tomorrow. Please send a replacement to watch the princess in her stead. Also, make sure they leave my conservatory soon. I don't cherish the thought of them poking around in there."

"Anything else, Majesty?" he asked.

"Find Caulden and give him the same updates. I want him aware despite the distractions."

I looked at the captain, watching his movements and remembering all the times I'd been instructed by him. His face seemed the same. Firm, placid expression. But maybe there was something less there now. I thought about the pheasant information, considered telling him on the spot. For some reason, though, the urge to report to him wasn't pressing in its usual way. Maybe I was viewing him as differently as he was me.

After a nod from the captain, the queen marched away and gave a brief glance back to me before entering the chateau.

Captain Baun stood in front of me, his body entirely blocking out the setting sun beyond the chateau wall. Rays of light and fog projected behind him, creating an almost cheerful glow that looked wrong surrounding his dark leather armor. "Did she give you more details for tomorrow?"

"Yes, Captain, but I was instructed not to tell anyone."

"Good." He pushed his shoulders back and adjusted his sword and belt on his wide waist. "Be alert, Vala. We've heard that Xavyn was spotted close to the chateau. It's best to be on guard at all times."

"Yes," I agreed while wondering where he'd gotten the information. Had someone seen Xavyn before he'd gone to Saireen's house?

"On your way then."

I nodded, almost expecting something else. Perhaps I was thinking about my own farewell, wanting to express one to him in some way in case I didn't see him again. Instead, I thought about the pheasant, curious about something else. "Captain," I called before he turned to leave. When he replied with a silent questioning look, I added, "Where is the palace located in Islain?" I'd learned it long ago on a map of Caulden's, and it could have been said a millions times before the queen and princess' arrival, but I didn't pay much mind, probably because somewhere inside I knew I would never travel there.

"Tamir Palace is in Sunsea, near the coast of the southwestern slope." He tilted his head in question. "Why is it that you're asking? Did Queen Meirin or Princess Anja mention something to you?"

"No," I replied, shuffling all the information in my mind. The queen said they dwelled near the palace, and also that her armies used the feathers. Did that mean they could have sent the assassins? And what about Leint? Had he been mistaken when saying they were native to another region? He hadn't lived in Islain for years. He could have forgotten in-formation he had learned in his youth. But doubt was also creeping into my thoughts. Could he be involved too? There was no way to accuse the queen or Leint without more evi-dence. But I was also readying to leave, so there would be no time.

"Vala? Is there something you want to say?"

"No, Captain. I think I should go get some sleep like the queen instructed." And tell Xavyn everything I'd heard.

TWENTY-FOUR

I'D INTENDED TO TELL XAVYN EVERYTHING—EVERYTHING Queen Meirin said, all about the cryptic meeting Queen Havilah invited me to, the information from Captain Baun—hoping he could help sort out what it all meant. Or if any of it should matter with our departure. There was only one problem. He wasn't in Saireen's house when I'd arrived, and he didn't return anytime during the night. I worried, pacing the floor for a good portion of the evening. He knew it wasn't safe to leave. By now, every Guard on the island could identify him in human skin. There was no way I could search the island. Not only was it impossible to do in one night, but it could possibly raise suspicion should anyone see. The most inconspicuous place to search was Florisa's Cove, but I didn't frequent the taverns, and there was no real guarantee he would even bother going there over any other place or even going back to Sacred Lake. Unless that was where he kept his boat.

That spawned a new concern. Had he left willingly? I really didn't know. Could he have been dishonest from the start, waiting to get information he needed before leaving? Or did he run out of time and have to? And then there was another option, the idea of it seizing my mind like a thick cloud of smoke. Maybe he hadn't planned to take me after all.

When the time came for me to leave for Sacred Lake, my eyes were heavy and I had worried a hole inside my cheek. But there was nothing more I could do, so, with a dispirited and hardening heart, I resigned to attend the meeting with Queen Havilah and figure everything else out later, whenever I could. I'd have all the time in the world if I was no longer leaving.

I kept an eye on the horizon while I traveled, watching as the darkness began to dissolve. I also listened for any unseen movement, especially when I neared the Trials course. A single Guard had been posted there to make sure none of the structures had been compromised during the night. I wouldn't put it past some of the Guards to manipulate the course to ensure a win or even ensure a loss for someone else. Our Guards were good and loyal, but not always righteous when a prized position was on the line.

The crevasse fields had indeed gotten worse, some of the gaps stretching farther than an average person could jump. It took more time to cross, searching the darkness for alternate routes, sometimes forcing me to move back several times in order to pass forward. When I reached the solid ground on the other side, I released a breath and then a soft laugh as I pictured the queen performing the same task. I shook my head, knowing she would have taken the less treacherous route. Looking along the horizon, the land now sloping subtly downward, I could see the light cresting over the sea, still so delicate. I started into a run, darting over the small beginning stream of the Vitae River, continuously listening and watching for any movement within the shadows and fog. In very little time, I stood before the entrance of the cavern, the red-orange mourning flowers spread beneath my feet like a path of fire, highlighted by the soft rays of dawn, welcoming me. Though, I wasn't sure how welcomed I'd actually be.

I could smell the fire before I could hear it humming from somewhere inside the cavern. The glow of it brightened with each new step on the uneven black rocks inside. I kept slow and quiet, not knowing if she would be alone, and after the other day, not fully trusting that this wasn't more than a simple meeting she wanted to handle away from chateau ears. The potency of the fire's stench increased. I sniffed the air hesitantly. It was … wrong. There was no comfort in the smoky scent. I sniffed again and realized why it had been off-putting. It smelled of every time someone had touched me and anytime I'd purposely struck someone else with my bare hands.

Burning flesh.

My heartbeat raged as my feet began to run, not caring about being quiet, entering the cavern in a whirl of noise and chaos as I had on Prince's Night. But this time I knew something bad had already happened. As soon as the walls opened wider, I scanned the area, my eyes shifting frantically. It had looked similar to that night—an enormous fire to the side, cracked walls slick with the cascading water of the Vitae River. And then, on the island in the middle of the lake, I spotted a heap. Soft smoke lifted from whatever it might be. Whoever.

No.

I pushed my legs hard, stepping closer and closer, until I tripped and dove down onto the loose rocks. Realizing I'd hit something hard, I rolled over and noticed the motionless bodies of the queen's usual Guards, Bransley and Lato. I scrambled back to my feet, ignoring the slack expressions on their faces, the blood coating my gloves, my cloak, my leathers. If they were dead then …

I sprinted the long stretch of land leading to the island then leaped over the water, falling to my knees immediately and looking over the scorched body and face of Queen Havilah. Her crown lay in the dirt above her mass of burnt hair. What remained of her dress was tattered and singed into clusters of melted fabric.

"No, no. Queen Havilah," I said, slipping my hand, my arm beneath her head, the smell of her skin searing my nose, making me gag. Her flesh was a mix of her dark and white skin, charred crust, and blisters. Her beautiful skin. "Who did this?"

Her eyes opened to me, their whites and light brown color the only clear things left on her body. "Vala," she whispered.

"Yes, yes. It's me. I'm here." I cradled her. Everything else faded away. My anger. My hurt. All the doubt and mistrust I'd felt during the last several days and all through the years, all slipped away as I held her. "Tell me who."

Her head moved back and forth the tiniest bit. "Listen to me. Tell Caulden I love him and trust … him to do what's right."

"No, you can't—" I said, my voice cracking, emotions stinging my eyes and nose as tears began to well.

"You," she continued. "You need to know. You are not like us. Or anything else. I found you here years ago. I heard your cry. Strong and fierce, and sad. And I saw you burn. After so many years, your life above ended. Your new life began, in a beautiful fire unlike any I'd ever seen."

"What are you saying? You saw who bore me?"

"No. No one bore you." Her eyes closed as she breathed deeply. "You were reborn, Vala bird. You are her. The lonely one. The one they called Alesrah."

I felt the first tear roll onto my cheek, burning and steaming into nothing. "Don't move. Just lie still. Someone will come help …" I glanced around the cavern, so empty. The fire continued to hum in the corner, its flames licking high up the wall. Someone had been here. Started the fire. Did this to her. "Tell me who."

"I want you to know." Her voice cracked like mine had, and I watched tears gather in the corners of her eyes. "I did care. Wystin would have adored you. Would have known how to take care of you. Like Saireen had. Better than I. I've failed you, Vala. I never found the answers, the reason you had come. Never knew what happened. Only that you gave us life. You fed the Vitae, and it fed us a better life. That was why I did what I did. It doesn't excuse my actions … I know … But I thought keeping you here … not telling you the truth … was the only way to protect you. To keep you safe."

"Your Majesty. No. I just need to find help. Please, just don't," I said frantically, scanning the cavern again, seeing nothing. No one. Tremors rocked through my body, my heart, churning my stomach.

"I only meant to save you. To protect Caulden. Never meant … to hurt you. Please forgive me." Her body seized then convulsed in my arms.

"Queen Havilah, please." I didn't know what to think, to feel. How could I believe her words? She was dying, and it was my fault. She was here to talk to me and someone did this to her. Burned her.

"Vala. Listen. Be careful of them. Protect him. I know I don't deserve ... to ask. I owe you my life for Caulden's. Please take care of our people like you always have. Guardian goddess."

Convulsions took hold of me. I tried to hold her steady, but I had no control. The sorrow was debilitating. "I will," I said, knowing it was what she needed to hear. This was her end. "Caulden loves you. I do too. And I forgive you."

The corners of her blistered lips twitched into a smile. "Thank you. And I love you, beautiful Alesrah. You are my queen, my mourning flower."

As soon as her eyes closed and her lips went slack, tears streaked down my cheeks, singeing my sadness into my skin. I placed a shaky hand to her chest, feeling as her last breath escaped in a quiet sigh.

"Ahh!" I wailed to the darkness, the cavern echoing the grief, the pain, back to me. The queen was dead. Life had left her inside my arms ... and I couldn't help her. I cried for so long, calling out again and again as the dawning light shone gently into the cavern's entrance, the rays highlighting the fog and smoke as they mixed in the air, dancing to my lament. I couldn't move. There was a part of me that wanted to go alert the captain, but my body refused to leave her behind, if even for a small time. I wouldn't leave her alone.

When my sobs began to dwindle, I heard voices calling. They were muffled and far away until one broke through clear and harsh.

"Vala!"

I lifted my head, seeing the captain standing before me, hunched over, a look of utter shock and sadness in his steely eyes. "She …" my voice hurt. Dry and scratchy and raw.

"What did you do, Vala?" Captain Baun spat in a whisper.

I looked from his face to the queen's face still cradled in my arms. "I found her here. I tried …"

He reached down suddenly and jerked my arm back, pulling me away, sprawling me onto the ground. My body was a waste of spent energy. "What happened?" He dropped to his knees.

"That looks plain to see," someone said from behind the captain. Leint's voice.

I rolled to my side, lifting my eyes to the group of people standing on the strip of ground leading back to the cavern's entrance. My eyes met Haidee's before she jumped the gap of water and came to my side. "Vala. What happened? We heard something … a cry …"

Captain Baun grabbed the crown then slid his hands beneath the queen and lifted her into his arms as he stood. One of her arms hung out of his grasp, swinging limply.

Haidee's hands wrapped around my arms, pulling me to stand. My eyes tracked the queen's body, watching as he took her away.

"Bring her," Captain Baun shouted over his shoulder.

And soon it wasn't Haidee's soft touch at my side to guide me. Firm hands gripped my arms on both sides, yanking carelessly, pulling forcefully. I didn't care. My eyes stayed on the captain's back, watching her arm swing as we traveled the long route, on foot and then on horseback, passing the Trials course where all activity had ceased, until we finally arrived at the chateau. She was home.

TWENTY-FIVE

THE SMELL. I COULDN'T ESCAPE THE SMELL. IT WAS worse than anything I'd experienced. I wanted to reach up inside and scrape it from my brain, or purposely dunk my face into a basin of water with one quick inhale to flush it away. But I couldn't. My gloved hands were tied at my back, my ankles bound around my boots, as I lay on the dirt floor of the chateau's prison chamber. My sword and daggers were gone. My cloak. My mask. In all my life, I'd never felt cold. Not really. Garlin's temperate climate was one reason, my naturally warm skin the other. Things had changed. There was nothing that could have warded off the cold that had settled inside, feeding on what was left of my emotions.

The trip to the chateau had been a blur of quiet whispers, the ten or so Guards that had come to the lake all talking, following closely behind, no one daring to pass Captain Baun as he carried her in his arms and then on horseback. I was led along, locked in a hostile grip most of the time. But I couldn't take my eyes from the queen.

Between the times of tears and restless points of sleep, my thoughts wandered. I thought about everyone else's thoughts, knowing they were of my guilt. And I wondered even more what Queen Havilah had been talking about. If I should believe it to be true or dismiss it all as the last, disorientated words of a woman dying a painful death. I cringed, seeing her eyes flash in my mind. I would never lose the sight of her eyes, the determination in them to tell me all she needed to say before letting go.

And still, I had no idea who would have killed her. Xavyn wouldn't … I didn't think. But since he'd disappeared and hadn't returned, I was doubting everything about him. Even the promise he'd made to not harm anyone. The other logical possibilities were other assassins or Queen Meirin. Getting rid of the prince's mother would make her life easier. Why, though, would she risk it? She was about to acquire Garlin by her daughter's marriage or by force. The cost of being caught ending the queen's life would kill all chances at an easy transition.

I shimmied to a sitting position, leaning my shoulder against the stone wall of my cell, and looked at the empty cells surrounding me. Alone again. I could hear some voices from the courtyard. I wondered what the captain had told Caulden. I needed to talk to him about everything that had happened at the lake, tell him what his mother had said about him, about them, about me.

Alesrah.

Even if it were true, how could I explain that to anyone? They'd think I was insane, think I did in fact kill the queen, and possibly keep me in this cell forever if they didn't take my life on the spot for ending hers.

The door's hinges squelched and I looked through the barred opening of my cell.

Captain Baun stepped inside, his feet scuffing along the floor—something he'd never done. His face was drawn, eyes bloodshot and puffed. I couldn't remember a time when I'd ever seen him cry. "Tell me what happened."

I cleared my scratchy throat. "That was where we were to meet." My voice cracked, hoarse and sore. "Before dawn. As she had requested yesterday. When I arrived, I smelled fire, but I knew something was wrong. I realized that the smell … I realized what it was and ran inside. That's when I tripped over … her Guards."

"And?" he prompted.

"I saw her," I replied, no longer seeing him. I was far away, looking over her again, watching her eyes close, feeling her last breath beneath my hand. "Her body … had been burned."

"You're claiming no involvement? You were there, Vala. You were found holding the queen. There was no one else. Guards searched the area when we arrived, before we left."

"I can't—I don't know who. I asked her. I asked but she didn't tell me. She was hurting, and I couldn't help her."

"Enough. I don't know why you would—"

"I didn't!" I screamed, the tone as rough as a rusty blade, tearing through my throat.

He opened the bars, stepped inside with his dagger drawn, and sliced through the ropes at my ankles. "I don't get to decide. You'll explain everything to the prince. Get up."

His anger, his hurt, was like another wave of cold, making my body shake as he stood me up and gripped my arm to pull me along. I had no idea what awaited me, but speaking with Caulden was essential. He would know that I didn't do what was thought of me. I wouldn't kill his mother, the woman who afforded me position, gave me a place that many others wouldn't. The captain led me upstairs and then out into the courtyard, where several faces immediately turned toward me. The only thing I saw, though, was the tall wooden post that had been erected at the center of the yard in front of the stone entry steps, the setting sun's hazy light illuminating it like a beacon. Flanking the post were two deep troughs filled with water. Behind one, Orimph, the prison guard, stood holding an empty bucket.

Captain Baun marched me forward down the steps. I clenched my fists behind my back as I focused on the eyes that tracked our movements. Chairs had been brought out, situated at the bottom of the steps. Prince Caulden. Princess Anja. Queen Meirin. The three were seated. Only a few Guards stood off to the side. There were no council members. No mass amount of people. No one else knew yet. For now, it looked as though Caulden wanted information from me, in a more formal, torturous manner.

While everyone else's eyes were pinned on me, his remained forward, staring blankly at the post. Some strands of his lengthy black hair had fallen over his face and he hadn't bothered to push them away. Rays of the sunset strong enough to break through the early evening fog also highlighted the red blotches of his face. His pain was clear to see and it broke me, buckling my knees. I fell on the final step. Unable to catch myself, the side of my face and shoulder crashed into the dirt. The captain let me fall only to yank me back to my feet again. I looked at the chairs, seeing the widened eyes of Queen Meirin and Princess Anja as they gawked at my fully exposed face for the first time. The yellow and blue colors of their dresses were blinding, too bright, too collected for this broken day made with pieces of death and dirt and smoke.

I returned my focus to Caulden, staring at his downward gaze while Captain Baun removed my ties only to back me against the post and fasten them to an iron hook above my head. I wanted to scream, to cry, but I couldn't find the words.

"Why did you do it?" Finally, Caulden looked at me, his eyes as vacant as his voice.

I inhaled frantically and shook my head, his calmness sending me into a panic. "No. No. Caulden—"

"Don't—" the captain started, but the prince lifted his hand.

"Your Highness," I corrected myself, the words shaking on my lips. "I found her. I wouldn't."

"After what happened at the course the other day, I'm not sure I can believe that."

The only time I'd seen him since that had been at dinner. We never had a chance to speak about her, about his hand. "I wouldn't. You know I wouldn't. She asked me to meet her this morning. She had things she wanted to tell me."

"Things she wanted to tell you?"

"None of that matters," Queen Meirin interrupted. "She's trying to distract you. We already know Havilah wanted to meet you. The captain informed the prince of that earlier. It explains why she was there, not why you burned her alive."

Caulden blanched in his seat.

"I didn't do it. My skin—I don't do that."

"We saw what happened at the course," Queen Meirin spat.

I glanced at the bandage on Caulden's hands. "No, that's not the same. I can't burn clothing. His Highness knows. Haidee knows," I said, looking over at Haidee, her position closest to the chairs, her eyes shifting between me and the prince. "A fire was used."

Neither spoke.

"You could have just as easily done that," Queen Meirin said.

"What about the Guards?" I asked. "Did anyone look at my sword? Check the blade for blood?"

"Another could have been used and tossed over the cliff. None of this matters. You were alone, with blood all over you," she replied.

The questions. Their eyes. My mind began to rage. How could he think I had done it? I thrashed, tugging at my suspended arms, my frustration taking control.

Water splashed across my body, ripping the breath from my lungs. "Ahh!" I released a ragged scream as the water attacked my skin, stripping my face, my neck, spreading down beneath my clothes.

I opened my eyes to the chairs, watching the queen and princess' expressions change as my body released my outer skin, revealing to them what lay beneath.

"Stop this!" Haidee called out, lunging forward only to be grabbed by Leint. He pinned her arms behind her as she too thrashed and cried out. "Your Highness, you know as well as I that she didn't—"

"That's enough, Haidee," Captain Baun yelled. "You will remain silent or Leint will lock you in a cell."

The air began to bite at my flesh as it reformed. I gritted my teeth, working through the pain, and shook my head at Haidee. I didn't want her punished for me. She didn't deserve it.

"Well, she's more different than we thought, isn't she?" Queen Meirin murmured. "What is she really, I wonder. Where did she actually come from?"

Anja hadn't spoken a peep the entire time, just watched with a curious gaze as she attempted to hold Caulden's arm.

Caulden recoiled from her touch, keeping his eyes on my feet. He couldn't even look at me. All these years together had meant nothing. All he saw tethered in front of him was a monster, not the girl he grew with, who had vowed her own life for his and his mother's. He didn't believe me.

"Coward," I said, scowling at him. Just as he looked up, another wave of water hit me, coating me, shredding me. I screamed again, this time letting the anger pour from my soul. Queen Havilah wanted me to protect him? Protect them? These people in front of me were too blind to see the truth. "Coward!" I screamed. "Your mother loved you. She told me to tell you how much. She told me she trusted you to do what was right!"

"Don't listen to her," Queen Meirin said, leaning in front of Anja to command Caulden's attention.

"She said she owed me for protecting you. She knew. All this time she knew." The last words came softer as sorrow struck again.

"No more!" Caulden shouted, standing abruptly and wiping a hand across his face to dry the tears glistening on his cheeks. "Captain, take her back in. No one is to touch her. I can't deal with this right now." His eyes flitted to me only once and then he was ascending the stairs.

Guards followed behind him as well as Princess Anja. Leint released Haidee and hurried to catch up.

Haidee took a single step toward me, but the captain blocked her path and said, "Go to your detail. This is your last warning."

Her eyes shifted to me before she turned around and followed the rest.

"You are something, aren't you?" Queen Meirin said from my side, her guards closer than usual. I hadn't even noticed her approach. "I wonder …"

Captain Baun passed closely behind the queen, eyeing her on his way to one of the troughs, where Orimph still stood with an empty bucket in his hand. "You can go back …"

His words faded as the queen moved even closer to the post and spoke again. "What did she tell you that was so important, Vala? Did it have anything to do with a feather?" She squinted and a little smile formed on her stained lips—their color as red as blood. "Come now, this is something that could help you. Like we talked about in the gardens, I had every intention of taking you along with us, no matter what Havilah wanted. Such a shame that this happened." Her head, piled high with golden hair, shook a little. "But nothing, even this, is permanent. If you tell me what she said, if you know where something is, I can certainly make things easier for you."

I stared past her, unable to look at her face. Despite what was happening, she was rooting for information. My stomach twisted, nausea building as my body began to settle following another assault of emotional stress. Her guards stood patiently behind her, hands loose at their sides, waiting, waiting, like I had been so accustomed to. I didn't think much of them. I didn't even know their names because Queen Meirin had never addressed them in my company. But they were bigger than the princess' guards, broader, with larger muscles hidden beneath their leather armor. None of which had caught my attention. It was the subtle smell of singed flesh that alerted me, making my eyes scour them. And then I saw the closest one's hands. He had them tucked, curling them inward protectively. But he kept flexing his fingers as if something was wrong. When they opened the next time, I saw the burns, the blisters.

"Just think about it, Vala," Queen Meirin said as Captain Baun's footsteps came closer from behind.

I looked up at her then, not strong enough to hide the rage that was probably so plain on my face. "I will think about it. I'll think about her death all night, and every day until forever. I made promises to her, and I'm making one more. Whoever actually killed her will pay."

Her eyes flashed with understanding. I had my confirmation.

"Your Majesty," Captain Baun said. "I'm taking her now. I'm certain dinner will be served soon. The staff would be more than happy to bring your food to your rooms if you'd prefer."

"Yes," she replied, her eyes blinking once before she tore her gaze from me. "I suppose I should go in." The fabric of her dress twirled as she turned and walked toward the steps.

"She did it, Captain. Her guards have burnt hands. You probably didn't notice, or didn't care to look," I said to him in a snarl.

He lifted his hands to mine and unhooked me from the post but didn't reply.

I let my arms fall, feeling the blood rush, nausea hitting

my stomach again. "I thought you'd be different. I always worried about Caulden. He always backed down. But you … I thought you'd at least get the facts before labeling the monster everyone else sees, and using my weakness against me so easily."

"You think this was an easy decision?" he asked, grabbing my arm again and pulling me forward up the stone steps. "You think I wanted to see my queen dead today and have to watch you suffer for doing it?"

My feet struggled to keep his pace. "She asked me to protect him. To protect everyone. She said I wasn't like anyone. Said she remembered when I was born."

His head snapped sideways for a moment as he continued his lengthy strides.

We both kept silent while moving through the chateau. Too many ears. *Do as I ask, and tell no one. I have much to explain to you, and it can't be done in the chateau.* "Her guards," I said when we arrived at the prison chamber. "Queen Meirin's guards had to have overheard the queen's plan to meet with me. That's how they knew."

"Vala—"

"No," I interrupted. "You may not owe me a goddess-damned thing. But you loved her."

He flinched at my words then closed the door and left without a second glance.

My thoughts ran through the day, over and over. Each time, the guilt pointing at Queen Meirin was undeniable. Her words were also difficult to ignore, especially when I thought of Queen Havilah's. One kept asking about a feather. And the other called me a bird. The queen bird. Alesrah.

TWENTY-SIX

*Y*OU WERE REBORN, VALA BIRD. YOU ARE HER. THE *lonely one.*

Those words. I awoke repeating them, having dreamed of them all night, lying upon the dirt floor in my prison chamber cell. Was I what—who—she said I was?

By midday, I wondered if Caulden planned to keep me in a cell forever. It was as if everyone had forgotten, but I knew that was farthest from the truth. The whole chateau was in mourning now. Preparations for the queen's burial had undoubtedly begun. I was of little importance.

Orimph came in a while later with a bit of water and bread, which I ate so quickly my stomach threatened to return it all even faster. "Time to go," he said when I'd finished, his low voice so contrary to his large body.

He fastened my arms and led me out to the courtyard. I had hopes that the captain would have helped in some way, saved me from being strapped to the post for a second time. But nothing had changed except the time of day. The sun was angled in the sky, sitting somewhere between midday and sunset, most its rays diffusing into the fog as usual.

Orimph walked me to the post and secured me this time. Captain Baun was nowhere to be seen. A few Guards were stationed at doors or at the edge of the courtyard by the gate. That was all. No one else. As Orimph lifted my bound wrists, my arms protested the position, still achy from the night before.

More time passed. Captain Baun emerged from the chateau alone a little while later, when the sun neared the top of the bailey, casting lengthy shadows onto the ground.

"How is he?" I asked.

He stopped in front of me and looked at his boots. "He's been in her conservatory all night and all day. I've checked on him, but he's denied most communication."

I sighed, dropping my gaze to the ground too. "Thank you."

"I wanted you to know that I looked into your suspicions. They are wearing gloves today."

"Did you ask them to remove them?"

He shook his head and glanced around the courtyard. "If I do that without cause or consent from the prince, I could be severely punished. But they did appear to be newer sets."

"Where is she today?"

"They've stayed in their rooms, mostly."

"There's something else I need to say." I had no idea when I'd get another chance, whether he'd ever believe my truth or if I'd die for another woman's crime. I had to tell him. "In the gardens the other day, the queen talked about birds and how she collects feathers. I asked her about pheasants. She confirmed that they live near the palace and that the feathers are often used for their archers, not in the east as Leint had said. I didn't tell you that day because I had just talked to the queen about our meeting and … I needed time to consider the information. Could they have been behind Caulden's attack and wanted him dead before the greeting? What would be the point?"

His scarred brows furrowed. "The point would be to pin it on someone else while getting the prince out of the way."

"Or he could have been a distraction," I said, thinking about their search.

"A distraction?"

"They came here for something else. Queen Meirin even asked me last night to tell her what Queen Havilah said, if I knew where anything was." I caught movement in the corner of my eye, down the pathway by the entry gate, but I pressed on. "I had to tell you. They are here for something more. And now that she's gone …"

"Captain!" Leint's voice called across the yard.

Captain Baun turned to watch Leint's progress, who wasn't striding the yard alone. He tugged someone along beside him, a canvas bag draped over the person's head and their hands tied behind their back. When he reached the captain, who had taken a few steps to meet him, he lifted the bag, and I found myself staring at Xavyn. I almost gasped. He hadn't left.

In human form, he blinked rapidly at the sunlight, holding a squint while his eyes adjusted, his dark brown hair sticking up on end from the bag being pulled away. There was a brief moment of calm where he didn't see me, and I wondered how he would react when he did—would his eyes shy away with guilt, or would they show me something else. When his eyes focused, I knew immediately he was genuine, that he hadn't left or crawled off somewhere to hide. Those eyes shot open and his body tensed and lurched forward, his movements at the sight of me reflexive and instant, his mind not processing the situation before reacting. His muscles relaxed and he looked away just as quickly, realizing he was being scrutinized.

Leint shoved him to his knees and tossed Xavyn's sword to the ground. "Doesn't he look familiar?"

Captain Baun leaned back, taking him in with a mixture of elation and awe on his face. "Where did you find him?" he asked, then waved another Guard down. "Go notify the prince that Xavyn has been caught!"

"That part is curious," Leint said and turned his eyes on me. "When you sent me to search Vala's house yesterday, I spotted a jug of wine from Wyntor Vineyard, which made me question Vala's recent behavior. Even though I didn't see anything else, I decided to return during my off time today. I just caught him leaving her house, traveling in this direction." The thought of him or anyone picking through Saireen's house made me want to scream.

"Vala?" the captain said, eyeing me. "Do you know anything about this?"

His view of me was already unsteady. There was no way I could lie about my involvement with Xavyn without him seeing right through it. I pressed my lips together in frustration, unable to think of anything that could free us from this situation.

A splash of water struck me, and I roared as pain flashed through me again.

"Tell me the truth, Vala!"

I opened my eyes to Xavyn thrashing inside of Leint's grip and grunting with heavy breaths. His anger had taken over, abandoning any hope of deception. His eyes were murderous. "No," I replied, watching the smile widen on Leint's smug face while the searing water tore at my skin.

"What is this?" Prince Caulden moved swiftly down the stone steps shortly after, wearing exactly the same tunic and pants he'd worn the previous day. His face was drawn, the deep tawny skin below his eyes darker than I'd ever seen. Haidee followed closely behind, her frantic eyes darting from person to person in the courtyard.

"Highness," Captain Baun addressed with a bow. "Leint found him leaving Vala's house moments ago."

"Vala?" Caulden's attention had turned fully to me.

It was my turn to ignore him, shifting my focus first to Haidee then to Princess Anja, who was slowly descending the stone steps clad in a purple dress with ornate accents of lace and stitching around its bodice. Too cheerful. Too pretty.

"Vala!" Prince Caulden yelled, taking a step closer to me. "You will tell me the truth."

"Why? So I can be punished because it's a truth you refuse to accept?"

His mouth opened and he took a step back, shocked by my disobedience. What had he expected?

Orimph slung another bucket of water at me, the splash knocking my head forward into a bow. My loose plaits swung forward, whipping water everywhere and curtaining my face. I laughed then—pain, grief, and bitterness escaping in a crazy mix of despair and amusement—staring at the mud below my boots as if it could be my last sight.

"Take this Xavyn to a cell then meet me in the dining hall. We'll question him later after we discuss the burial procession arrangements. Leave her here for now," the prince said, wiping a bit of water from his forehead then turning and walking toward the chateau. Princess Anja grabbed his arm. He let her. Haidee followed them hesitantly, glancing back at me every other step.

Captain Baun and Leint dragged Xavyn by his bound arms, not allowing him to get to his feet. Xavyn stole a look over his shoulder to me then stopped struggling.

When everyone had gone, I watched my tears fall freely to the mud and silently whispered, "I'm sorry, Your Majesty."

Haidee appeared with the dusk, using the shadows of the early evening to avoid the eyes of a few Guards, who were hauling and laying kindling and wood not far from my post. It wasn't a pyre for the queen. It would be a fire for … something else.

"Vala," she whispered, standing close, using my body to camouflage her own.

"Haidee," I replied, my voice rough from a dry throat.

"You need to talk to him. He's … going to do something. I'm not sure I can stop it."

"I don't want you risking your life."

"I can't stand and watch what is happening to you. I'm sorry for not stopping what has already occurred," she said, her hand gently pulling a few of my plaits away from my face.

"You have nothing to be sorry for. I'm the one who is sorry. To you and to Queen Havilah. I promised her I'd still take care of him, this island. That's not going to happen now. I can't change his mind. I thought the captain believed what I told him—that Queen Meirin's guards have burnt hands, that she's looking for something, that she asked me what Queen Havilah told me."

Haidee inhaled sharply. "She had the queen killed?"

"Yes. And she will pay in one way or another."

She was quiet for a moment. "Even if you get free, you can't stay."

"I'm leaving with Xavyn. At least, that was the plan before this happened. I don't belong here, Haidee. And the queen … she told me she's known all along. She said I'm not like people, but I'm also not like the others. She called me Alesrah and Vala bird. Said she'd seen my death and rebirth."

"Do you think it's real?"

"She was … dying. I'm not sure what to believe. But Queen Meirin's inquiries of a possible rare feather, it makes me wonder what can be real."

"I want to help. I want to go with you."

"No," I said, shaking my head between my arms. "You can't get caught helping me. You have to stay with Caulden since I can't, make sure he is all right after everything. The queen would have wanted you with him."

"I have to try to help in some way. Maybe I can be a distraction in the prison, help Xavyn then he can help you."

"I won't flee until I end her," I said, expressing the only thing of which I was certain. I would not leave the island while Queen Meirin still breathed.

"I know where she is," Haidee murmured. "Since Caulden has been in talks in the dining hall, she's been in the conservatory."

I tugged on my suspended arms, trying to bring them back to life. "She's searching. She thinks something is hidden in there."

"Do you think there is?"

"No. Queen Havilah would have told me if it were something that important."

"She'll have to work in sections, and it'll take her a while. She'll be in there all night, or at least until Caulden returns."

"Maybe I'll get there before he does," I said, planning what needed to be done. If I had my way, she would not see the morning. "You need to go. Try your best to help Xavyn. But stay away after that, Haidee. In order to protect Caulden, whatever else happens tonight, do not be seen helping us. Afterward … don't trust Leint. And keep talking to the captain. He'll need to hear the truth after I'm gone, even if it comes in small doses."

"I will," she agreed, squeezing the shirt covering my arm.

"I hope we see each other one day again, Haidee. I always thought of you as a sister."

"And I you." Her voice wavered. "Good luck, Vala."

She was gone before the Guards finished laying the wood.

TWENTY-SEVEN

I HAD LOST CONSCIOUSNESS. MY HEAD WAS HEAVY AND sleep had come easily despite having my arms tied high. When I awoke, two Guards stood between me and the positioned fire wood. They were igniting the bottom, their silhouettes dark against the quivering light of the infant flames. I scanned the rest of the darkened courtyard, readying myself, hoping for something to happen and expecting nothing. I had to be prepared for either. I had trust, though, that Haidee would be able to help Xavyn in some way.

I whispered to myself for a while, talking over the humming of the fire as it grew so close beside me, reciting everything that had happened within the last couple of days while planning what could happen from here on. Queen Havilah.

Queen Meirin. Prince Caulden. Princess Anja. Haidee. The captain. Leint. Xavyn. All the players. All their roles.

But as I grew weary again, losing the hope that anything would happen, I heard a crash and lifted my eyes to see the chateau doors burst open. Xavyn had been the force behind the crash, tumbling through the doors in my direction, almost falling down the steps as his legs gained control. I shook my limbs in anticipation, seeing the urgency in having the ability to help, to fight. My eyes tracked him eagerly, adjusting to the fire's light, and the blood in my veins thrummed as my heart pounded within my chest. The two Guards from the fire stepped in front of me, staggered, one farther than the other, blocking me—his apparent destination.

He drew the sword he had been carrying by hand, discarded its sheath with no care, and plowed through the first Guard with a single slice. He waited for the second to strike first, dodged the blade with ease, then turned and drove his blade swiftly into his back. Both rolled onto the ground, releasing small grunts and screams. They were two of my own, Guards I'd been aligned with, who I would have fought beside even without knowing their names. But no more. I was no longer a Guard of Garlin. I would no longer stand with those so prejudice and blind to the truth.

As Xavyn moved closer, Captain Baun barreled out of the chateau with Leint and two others right at his feet.

Xavyn slid the blade between my arms as I spread them apart. "Hurry," I said, feeling both his rapid breaths and heartbeat as his chest pressed hard against me.

Captain Baun was quick for his size. I'd always known he was, but he was steps from us in no time.

The ropes fell apart, freeing my arms. But we hadn't been

fast enough. Captain Baun slammed into the back of Xavyn, knocking him past the post, where they both fell close to the fire. As I spun away, shaking my arms to finish waking them, Leint was upon me, charging, the ferocity plain to see on his twisted face. I lurched sideways to dodge his attack, but his shoulder clipped my side, spinning me back against the post. I'd sparred with him enough to know that he was a hard and quick fighter, risking his stamina for blows that could end everything in seconds. But this was not a sparring session, and I wasn't conforming to routine or counting hits for bragging rights, I was fighting for my life and for Xavyn's. Because even though they weren't wielding any blades to kill us immediately, they still planned to.

I ducked as he punched, his fist colliding with the post. While he screamed in pain, I crouched, lifted a handful of dirt, and tossed it at his face. As I stood, a solid, strong hit landed between my shoulder blades, the strike coming from behind. I'd forgotten about the other Guards. The hit had stolen my breath, but I was still able to turn, seeing that one of the Guards had stayed with me while the other had joined the captain against Xavyn. I swung around with a straight kick to his knee, feeling it buckle and snap. He crumbled into the dirt.

With Leint still stumbling about blindly, I was free to charge the other Guard. I grabbed a log of wood piled close to the fire and slammed it into the back of his head, dropping him faster than the first. I recognized him, though. One of the many who had never spoken to me. Perhaps he'd been too afraid. Or perhaps he held more hate than fear like so many others. There was never a reason for him to hate or fear me before. Now there was reason for both.

"Stop!" Prince Caulden's voice shouted from the chateau steps.

Captain Baun was able to get an arm around Xavyn's throat, choking him. I moved to help, but the captain pulled a dagger and pointed its tip at the base of Xavyn's neck. Leint had made his way to my side, a sword in hand, knowing better than to try and hold me for fear of my skin.

"That's enough, Vala," Prince Caulden said, taking the steps slowly.

I glanced at Xavyn, the firelight so close and bright upon his face, watching his lips tip into a smirk even though the captain's trunk of an arm was capable of snapping his neck in a second. Before I could raise my eyebrows in question, the skin on his face rippled and the captain roared and dropped his hold.

I spun away from Leint's blade, but he realized what had happened and swung quickly, his eyes blinking rapidly, still coated with dirt. I dodged the swing and stepped into him to grab hold of his face with both of my hands, singeing his perfectly smooth skin. He fell to his knees before I let go.

"You're like Vala." Prince Caulden's voice came from behind me, closer than expected.

Xavyn had picked up a sword again and aimed it at the captain.

"He is … similar," I answered, turning toward the prince, confident that Xavyn had the captain contained. "Since you refused to even listen to me before you had me tied and tortured for killing your mother when all I did was try and help her, that's all you need to know for now."

"Vala, let the captain go. I know you don't want to do this," Caulden said, my words apparently unheard or unwelcome.

"I don't want to do this. I didn't want any of this," I said, indicating the people spread out on the ground, some bleeding, some immobile. More Guards entered the courtyard, their bodies and faces mere outlines so far from the fire and dimmed chateau lantern posts.

"Then let the captain go. We'll work through everything."

"Would we have worked through everything had I remained on that post? What were you going to do? Burn us?"

"No, I—"

His voice was cut off as Leint slammed into my side, his body as hard as a battering ram. He'd managed to get close enough while I was distracted. I had no time to react, to move. I was falling. Only I wasn't falling to the ground like I had thought. Heat had cocooned me, holding me hostage, the hum and crackle of the flames singing to me even louder, lulling me into a calm I'd never experienced before. It was rapturous and soothing, like a melodic kiss in my ears, and all throughout my skin. There was no pain as I continued to fall through the fire. I almost didn't want to leave, but I heard a scream, so I continued to roll with the momentum of the fall, spilling out onto the ground on the other side, into the open air once again.

"Vala. No," the prince said in an airy whisper.

I got to my feet and was greeted by intakes of breath all around me. Xavyn was who I saw first, his skin so coarse like mine, his eyes a swirl of darkness pinned on me, with his sword still pointed toward the captain. I looked down at my hands. My charred skin had gone, leaving the red-orange skin I'd see each time water had finished its assault. Though, the fire hadn't hurt as water always had. And the air wasn't stinging. I twisted my arms, noticing that there were no signs of regrowth. But there was movement, like a flame coating the top of my skin, twisting and wrapping around in a tender caress. Smoke rose from the bits of my undershirt that had caught fire, but my leathers—vest and pants—were intact with no damage. I ran my hands down my body, checking for any injuries. There were none. My hair remained as well, the plaits not even singed. Finally, I turned around and watched as Caulden fell to his knees in front of me. His tired eyes took all of my appearance in as if he were seeing through them for the very first time.

If we had any chance of leaving …

"Xavyn, bring the captain," I called over my shoulder, grabbing another sword from the ground as I started to walk. By Caulden's reaction, I doubted he'd tell anyone to stop us. But I wasn't foolish either. The captain was our insurance for a successful escape … after I handled what needed to be done first.

"Vala, I—" Caulden said as I passed by. "I don't know—"

"Protect your people. Protect yourself. It's what your mother wanted." I stopped for a moment and glanced into the eyes I'd seen almost every day since we were young, picturing all the emotions held within them through the years, thinking of the emotions I'd felt while looking at them. What was there before was now gone, the last string severed when he doubted my loyalty and watched my torture. The feelings that had once lifted me, that I'd once ached for, were like embers in the night fog, drifting into nothing, extinguished. I would always remember him, and possibly love him in some nostalgic way. But I no longer needed a connection. I felt free. Of him. Of this island.

After so many years, your life above ended. Your new life began here, in a beautiful fire unlike any I'd ever seen.

I held my chin high and breathed in my new life. "Don't try to follow us. We're leaving soon. After I avenge the queen."

TWENTY-EIGHT

AIDEE HAD RESPECTED MY WISHES AND STAYED AWAY during everything. Caulden's lead Guard had been absent. I was certain that after we were gone, she'd be punished in some way. Whatever it was, though, it wouldn't last long. Caulden had lost too much to let her go. Haidee was too smart, too valuable. She had even been right about the conservatory.

Xavyn and the captain were quiet during the march through the chateau and outside to the conservatory entrance. Anyone we passed along the way scattered like bugs under the light of fire. My fire. I felt it dimming as we moved, felt the air begin to dig into my skin again, felt the regrowth taking hold. By the time we'd reached the conservatory, I was almost fully changed.

The doors were unguarded and only a tiny speckle of light could be seen reflecting off of the numerous glass windows, shining dimly out into the pitch-black gardens. The silence made me pause. As much as I'd hated the conservatory as a child, I knew it had been her place, her reprieve. In a way, it didn't seem right for my vengeance to take place here, as if it would desecrate something sacred to her. But I also felt it befitting, a way to honor the queen who trusted me to protect, to defend.

I blinked at the oak and iron casted doors and took a deep breath. "Captain, it's good that you're here with us. Maybe you'll hear this truth."

When I pulled the door open and we passed inside, everything appeared in the same order. Trees and small shrubs lined the rows, individual leaves and branches silhouetted by the single lantern visible at the far end of the building. Queen Meirin was clever enough not to trash the place in a hurried frenzy. Knowing that I had been tied to a post in the courtyard and that the prince would be distracted over the next few days to tend to his mother's burial, she had time to return here, to search whenever she needed. She wouldn't want her secrets being found due to careless rummaging, especially with a wedding sometime in the near future … if there was still to be one.

We walked the length of the row, seeing no movement, hearing no sounds. My mind raced, the worry that she had already left starting to turn my stomach. There was no time to look elsewhere. If she was gone, we'd have to leave. Her judgment would have to wait. And she would live. But as one of her guards stepped out from around the trees at the end of the row looking curiously in our direction, I let out a relieved breath.

"Ah! You are here," I said, my voice echoing around the

panes of glass high above. "I was beginning to think you'd given up your search."

The other guard filed behind the first and Queen Meirin's voice followed. "It seems you are a clever one. More clever than I thought."

"You obviously chose the wrong path to find what you were looking for."

"I don't think I did at all," Queen Meirin said, finally stepping out from around the trees, wiping the dirt from her hands onto a cloth. The silver and white accents along the bodice of her Islain blue dress glinted in the lantern's light, as did her stacked golden hair. Her crown was noticeably missing, as if she didn't want to tarnish it. "The path I chose simply needed obstacles cleared out of the way."

I clenched my hands as I took one final step toward her, keeping a safe distance between us. "Good thing you have guards who are willing to burn those obstacles."

"A hostage?" she asked, ignoring my comment and looking behind me to where Xavyn held a sword to the captain's throat. "Things haven't gone quite as you'd planned either then? I suppose we're dealing with somewhat similar situations. We both need the other out of the way to finish our goal."

"I suppose that's right. I need you out of the way so I can leave. And I'm guessing you need me out of the way to continue searching for Her Majesty's secret."

There was a twinkle in her eye and a hint of a smile on her lips at that. "She told you something after all. Are you planning to tell me?"

"I am," I confirmed with a smile. "But I don't think it's going to be in the way you want to hear it."

"You know, your queen would be disappointed to know you plan to tell me." Her lips relaxed, abandoning the civil pretense. "She held on for so long without saying anything."

I moved to charge only to watch a potted plant fly over my head, aimed at Meirin. One of her guards pulled her out of the way while the other swung his blade through the hardened clay, spraying pieces of clay and soil all over the floor. With the sound of grunts and breaths close behind me, I didn't need to turn around to know it wasn't Xavyn who had launched the plant. But I looked back anyway, staring right into Captain Baun's face, so twisted and red with fury that he was almost unrecognizable. I glanced at Xavyn, who only raised his eyebrows.

"You killed the queen!" the captain said and bowled past me, armed with another plant and nothing else.

I turned and charged after him, unwilling to let him fight alone. He threw the plant at the first guard, using it as a mere distraction as he launched his body into him. Before the second guard could join in, I swung my blade at him, slicing through branches and flowers, backing him away from the captain. Xavyn ran up from behind. Unable to engage in the captain's ground fight, he turned his blade on the guard I was fighting, backing him up farther as he tried to defend himself and protect Meirin, who was tucked into the corner of the well alcove, behind the mourning flower pedestal and the queen's bench.

As the guard blocked a swing from Xavyn, I sliced my blade into his side. He lurched and swung, but Xavyn blocked, clearing me for a straight shot to the guard's chest. He dropped and through heavy breaths I said, "I would have taken your hands if I had more time."

"Stop her!" the captain yelled out from his position on the ground, his eyes on Meirin as his arms and legs grappled with the guard.

Seeing her first guard drop, Meirin had left her corner, edging along the walls, heading toward the back row to escape.

Xavyn ran down the front row, blocking the doors, and I followed Meirin into the shadows.

She frantically looked around then stopped dead when she saw Xavyn at the end of her escape. "If you kill me, they will know. You will be hunted! But if you let me go now, I will do the same for you. You can leave here and I won't send my army after you as long as you stay away. Never show your face."

"Let's go," I said and stepped aside as Xavyn pushed her forward with the tip of his blade.

The captain and guard continued to wrestle until the captain found a hold around the guard's neck. With a snap, it was all over.

"I'm telling you now. All of you," Meirin shouted, as if someone outside would hear and respond. "You are free to go. Leave now."

"No," I replied, watching the captain stalk toward her. As he grabbed hold of her wrists and pinned them behind her back, I moved to the queen's mourning flower still perched atop the pedestal, the open iron lantern hanging from a wall hook at its side. "You were looking for a feather," I said, sliding a finger over the red-orange petal, thinking of the queen's words. "Only there's no feather here." I turned back around to look at her. Her whole body shook as the captain's massive frame stood behind her. I almost felt bad for her until I thought of Queen Havilah's burnt face and body. Her pain. The only mercy Meirin would receive was how quickly she'd die, simply because I could not control the time. If I could, she'd burn for days.

I reached up to the lantern and pushed my hand between its iron slats, my palm open to the flame below. I was no longer afraid. The years I'd spent staring into the flames, petrified, believing that I'd been cursed … it had all been so foolish. "What feather do you seek? Was it one from the goddess bird, Alesrah? Is that the kind of rarity you're looking for?" The flame engulfed my hand, shedding my charred skin again, the crackle and hum growing louder in my head.

Meirin's mouth went slack, her stained lips opening wide. I glanced at Xavyn and Captain Baun, noticing theirs had as well.

"You see, you were searching for the wrong secret." The flame traveled up my arm, spreading like wildfire across my body, soothing, sedating. "I was the queen's secret."

"How can it be?" she stammered the words.

"Why were you looking for a feather?" When she didn't respond, I asked again. "Why were you looking for a feather?"

Captain Baun wrenched her arms from behind, jostling her body. She made a pained face and then a slow smile formed on those hideous lips. "You don't know. And she didn't tell you or she didn't know herself. Well, that is surely interesting."

"What is so interesting about it?" I said with a growl.

A loud banging noise spread across the gardens outside. "Vala," Xavyn warned, his eyes toward the doors down the row.

With the smug look upon Meirin's face, I knew she was

prepared to take the information to the grave. "Captain? Do you want the pleasure?"

"This won't be over for you," she screeched. "They will hunt you—"

"Yes," the captain answered my question, ignoring Meirin. He turned her around, pinned her against the pillar with a single hand, and grabbed the sword I extended to him. "She'll be there to meet you on the other side," he whispered then leaned back before shoving the blade into her chest.

We watched her eyes lose focus, the last breath escape her lips, and her bowels empty.

But we were out of time.

Xavyn's hands were on my face, pulling my hazy focus to him. His gray eyes were wide. "We need to leave. Now." He grabbed my hands, unfazed by the flames moving across my skin.

"Not that way," Captain Baun said, letting Meirin's body fall. "There's another way, here. I'll take you." He moved around the stone pillars and pushed in on the wall at the back, sliding a door open.

Xavyn pulled my hand, leading me forward while I glanced back over my shoulder at the lone light shining upon the lone mourning flower, happy that our queen had been avenged.

TWENTY-NINE

WE FOLLOWED WITHOUT QUESTION. THE pathway dropped underground into a short and narrow tunnel with barely space for the captain to walk without hunching over or getting stuck. It had to have been an alternate exit for the queen in the event of an attack. I'd never known of it. I wondered if it had been the way she traveled when she was to meet me at Sacred Lake.

Not long after, the tunnel started to climb. Xavyn's hand still held mine, his grip tight and secure on my newly reformed skin. The captain shoved hard against a wooden door, pushing it open to a view of a few tree trunks and the sky and fog beyond, a tinge of light beginning to seep into the darkness.

"Where are we?" Xavyn asked, surveying our surroundings.

I pointed to the north. "There's the wall and the top of the conservatory. Farther down the hill is Florisa's Cove."

He nodded, looking east.

"I'm sorry this exit is so far from port," the captain said. His face tilted a bit down to look at me. "I'll tell the prince everything when I return. He deserves to know the truth. All of it."

"Be cautious of the princess. And of Leint," I said, still uncertain of his statements, his actions.

"I will," he said with a nod. "I wish I knew what she meant ... about the feather."

"I do too," I agreed. "But wherever I go, I will search for more answers. I'll also send word here to you whenever I can. You'll stay, right? Even if the prince weds Anja and travels to Islain?"

"That's my intent."

"Good." I smiled up at him, staring at his face to memorize it, as if I'd forget. "I'm sure the queen would have wanted you to stay, to protect Garlin and its people."

"I'm sorry, Vala. I hope one day you can forgive me for what I've done," he said suddenly. "I was weakened by the loss of her and I couldn't see around my grief. But even that will never be a good enough reason for betraying your trust." His hands lifted as if to touch my arms, but he gently hooked a few plaits hanging at the side of my face instead then released them. A tender gesture, one a father might bestow upon a daughter.

I nodded. "I think I understand how and why. I feel it too, but I'm sure your love for her far exceeds my own."

"Yes, well ..." he said, wiping his eyes. "She meant a lot to me. I'm not sure what Garlin will be without her."

After a moment, I looked toward the horizon. "We should go, and you should get back. Thank you, Captain, for everything you've taught me. I'll always remember."

"There's something else I want you to know, Vala. I don't know what Havilah told you … After seeing your skin, I suspect whatever it was that it's all true. But she did keep these secrets from me too, at least some of them." He paused and wiped beneath his eyes. "Those years ago, my detail was King Wystin. He was an honorable man as I'm sure you've heard many times through the years. Queen Havilah used to travel to the Sacred Lake often. It was one of her favorite places, and she often spent many hours there. One day, there was a terrible but beautiful cry that spread over the island followed immediately by a quake. We had no idea what it was, but, being heard and felt across the island, it scared everyone alive at the time. I went to alert the king in the library, afraid magic had returned and possibly the dragons that had once terrorized the main land. But when I entered, I found him dead, his body slumped over his desk. He had shown no prior signs of illness, so the chateau physician thought his heart had failed. When the queen returned, she had a baby with her, wrapped and crying. As soon as she learned of Wystin's death, she shut down for some time, never explaining where you had come from. We gave you to Saireen that night, knowing she would care for you as she cared for most other things in the chateau, including the infant prince."

My eyes stung while he spoke, tears welling for the women I knew so little about but owed so much. They may not have done things the best way, but they kept me safe, gave me a reason for being. "All I knew before was that Saireen found me on the road. I didn't know that the queen had found me until she told me. She said she saw me burn, watched me be reborn. She didn't have time to tell me much, only that she was sorry."

"I'm glad that she was able to tell you in the end. I'm sure it weighed heavily on her heart. She was good, and she loved Garlin more than anyone else could."

I blinked the tears out, tipping my face down to avoid their singe.

"That cry that the island had heard when she had found you, I was reminded of it the other day when she died. There was a cry … it was the reason we traveled there and found you. From what I remember, it wasn't as strong as the other those years ago, but it sounded the same. I thought you should know. Maybe it's something else to research."

"Thank you," I replied then wrapped my bare arms around his clothed body. I felt his chin rest on the top of my hair.

"Thank you."

After a few moments, Xavyn cleared his throat. "We should get moving."

I released my hold of the captain and backed away.

"Be careful at port. There will be many there."

"I'm glad my boat isn't at port then," Xavyn replied, staring out through the trees toward the chateau. "There's a nice little cove near your Sacred Lake that seemed like the best place to stow her."

"That is good news. Either path should be clear. No one will expect you to shove off from the cliffside. They'll have everyone searching the north."

"Good. Let's hope it stays that way for some time."

"Take care, Vala. Xavyn, I'm sorry for hunting you," the captain added with a sincere smile.

I laughed at that, and Xavyn joined me with a shake of his head before saying, "I can't really say it was nice meeting you, but I will say farewell and I hope your island sees better days."

"Thank you."

"You take care, too," I said to the captain. "And tell Caulden …" What did I want to say? I was sure I'd said everything that could have been said, but it still felt as though I hadn't said nearly enough. "Tell him I said goodbye and that maybe we'll meet each other on better terms again one day."

He nodded once with understanding.

I held the sword with a loose grip, smiling one more time his way before turning and walking east, toward the gentle light forming on the horizon.

Xavyn caught up to my side. "Are you ready to find your answers?"

"Yes." I turned my head, watching the fog swirl in the dawning sky over the chateau I'd once called home. "I am."

THIRTY

THE SUN HAD JUST CRESTED THE SEA'S HORIZON WHEN we arrived at the lake. It was a view I'd only ever seen once before from this spot, but that had been with blurry eyes that were not focused on the beauty of the sky, only the queen's arm swinging freely from the captain's hold.

Standing at the entrance of the cavern, amongst the sprawling mourning flowers, I focused entirely on the beauty this time, channeling the sorrowful feeling of never seeing the view from the same place again. There was no noise in the peace of the morning. No busy servants readying the chateau for the day, no Guards training in the courtyard, no ship sails within view. I liked to think that she was here, in her once favorite place, showing me the beauty in the silence and the hues of the morning.

"I heard you too," Xavyn said, stepping away from the cliffside.

"What?"

"The other day," he replied, approaching me. He had dropped the use of his energy sometime during our trek, his skin returning to his own. I stared at him openly, the sight still so new and mesmerizing. His brilliant skin was almost too much for my eyes to handle. I wondered if it became brighter when the sun was higher, with less mist in the air. I wondered if my eyes would ever adjust, not sure I'd want them to. I looked at the lines in the skin of his arms, below the rolls of his blood and dirt covered sleeves. I looked over his face. All the contours I was already familiar with, comfortable with, seemed even more pronounced, more defined. And his hair, the mix of black and white was something out of dreams. I had seen older people with a mix, but it was always softer, blended throughout, each new year bringing a touch more white. But his wasn't the same. It was harsh and stark and … beautiful.

He stopped in front of me, and I blinked several times. A slow, alluring grin pulled on his lips as he noticed my ardent perusal, but instead of addressing it, he said again, "I heard you the other day."

"The other day? To what day are you referring? When you should have been hiding in the safety of Saireen's house?" I asked, my senses coming to me, needing to address some unanswered questions. "Where were you anyway? I thought I'd never see you again."

This time, his smile was with pressed lips. "You thought I'd left you? You didn't trust me. Even after I told you I would be gentle with your life."

"I—well, I can't say I've known you long at all. I wasn't sure what to think about your disappearance. There was so much happening, so much I'd wanted to tell you that day. I was worried."

"Ah, I see. I should have maybe left you a note?"

"Are you teasing me right now?"

"No, I'm completely serious. I will leave a note next time I go stock the boat for our long journey and then move it for safety."

I could have shriveled inside of myself because of my foolishness, and judging by the smile turned into a wickedly handsome smirk upon his face, he knew. "I had no idea. I'm sorry."

He waved a hand. "I should have told you my plans."

I was lost for a moment, looking at him, the sun rising at his back. Then I realized he was staring at me too, his cool gray eyes appraising mine affectionately. The smile on his lips went slack with seriousness, and I remembered he hadn't finished what he'd started to say. "You mentioned hearing me."

"Right," he replied, shaking his head and looking at the ground. "I was in the boat, looking for somewhere to hide it, maybe halfway between here and the port." His body turned a bit to face the sea. "I heard the cry like your captain had. I heard you … crying for her."

"Had it been me?" I asked, mostly to myself. How could I not realize?

"He said he'd heard it before. And that coincides with what your queen had said about finding you, watching you burn those years ago. I'm willing to guess that's also when we felt a change in Vaenen and Craw. It would make sense that magic might return when Alesrah died again."

"So you think this is true? That I could be what the queen says I am?"

"Yes, I do." He held a hand to his mouth and looked up at the sky, thinking. When he let his hand fall, he added, "It's possible that Alesrah was reborn when she ended The Final War and stripped magic from the world. She could have lived another life cycle between, watching from above, then chose Garlin as the next place to die. And if it is true, things … might become more complicated from here."

"Reassuring," I murmured.

His hands grabbed hold of mine, his smooth fae skin not burning. "Either this is normal, or my skin holds a memory of yours," he said when I looked up at him in shock. "About everything else … I will help you piece it all together."

"We can't go to Islain after killing their queen. And if I am who Havilah said … aren't I hated everywhere else?" The thought of being the one who had ended magic, killed so many, and stripped their lives …

"That adds to the complicated part," he said with a tiny smile. "But we'll find answers. We'll search the history. We know that Islain's queen was looking for a feather. There are legends about Alesrah's feathers, stories that they'd been lost or taken. If Islain's queen knew something about them, she found the information from somewhere. Elige might know."

"Elige? You killed her raven so it wouldn't return and show her what happened here. Do you really trust her enough to tell her?"

"Not entirely. But there are other ways of finding out. We'll just have to go in that direction."

"Are you certain that I will be able to cross the border between lands? I thought it was deadly."

"We'll know when we get close, if you get sick. But I have a theory about why you'll be able to." After squeezing my fingers tenderly, one of his hands released mine and lifted to my face, his palm pressing just below my cheek. I leaned into his touch, welcoming his warmth, his gentleness. "I told you about Alesrah's Lake in Vaenen, that the area is not a … revered place. I lived there for many years, swam in its water. If the stories are true, and the lands were separated by her, I think it's the reason I can cross the border."

"What if I'm not her?"

"I believe your queen was telling you the truth, and I think you believe it too. There's something about you, Vala. I felt it from the beginning, a connection. I know part of it is because of my ability, feeling you, knowing more of you, inside and out. Your strengths, your weaknesses. I can feel you. I also know there's something more, though, something familiar." He tipped my face up, his fingers pushing back into the plaits of my hair. "You've been guarding people your entire life, maybe even long before this one. And from what I've seen in my time here, no one has done the same for you. I want to, if you'll let me. Help you. Protect you. And maybe more."

I slid my arms around his back and took a step closer, letting him know I wanted the same. There was a time when I'd wanted this feeling with Caulden, this building energy, this contentment. Apparently, that was little more than an attraction built upon a history. I'd known Caulden my entire life. Although he may have cared for me in some way, I was always an outsider, never an equal, never someone more than his Guard. Xavyn had known it all from the start, saw my differences and never treated them as such. He understood me, he felt me, and made me feel at ease. That wasn't something

I'd ever needed, but it was something I wanted. And I wanted it from him.

His eyes searched mine, waiting. I reached a hand up to his face, as he had mine, and slid my fingers through strands of his short hair and touched his ear, wanting to explore, to feel him too. He turned his face with a smile, grabbing my hand and pressing a kiss to my palm before leaning in and kissing my lips.

I could have stayed there forever in the dawn, in his arms with his mouth on mine, my body responding in ways I'd never dreamed as he held me tightly, our tongues meeting, our hearts beating, setting my soul ablaze. But I knew we had to go. So I left his arms feeling fuller than I'd ever had, seeing the same sense of emotion in his smile and his eyes as he watched me enter the cavern.

I needed to say goodbye one last time.

Standing on the edge of the waterline, I gazed at the small island where Havilah told me her final words and whispered my final farewell. The massive fire in the corner that had taken her life was burned down to a crumble, but there was a hum somewhere deep inside the fluffy mounds of ash. I dug into the airy pile, feeling the embers' heat push against me before I drew back my hand and watched a flame catch and spread across my skin again. Though it was goodbye, I knew I'd hold her with me forever.

Xavyn was perched on the edge of a boulder at the entrance, his legs dangling off, his hands cradling a mourning flower, waiting for me to emerge. He lifted his eyes from the flower and focused on me for my last few steps. "They're connected to you, too," he said, nodding to the flower. "Red and orange flames."

I stared at the petals spread out in his hands. *You need to know. You are not like us.* I was not human after all. *You are my queen, my mourning flower.*

He slipped off the boulder and held the flower out, waiting for me to extend my palms. As soon as he placed it in my open hands, the petals lit up, the fire on my skin catching. We both watched as the flower continued to burn, showing no signs of wilting. I started to walk, stepping over the crest of the cavern's entrance then turning back toward the island and bending to the mass of flowers at my feet. I lowered the one in my hands and tossed it onto another, watching my flame catch and spread over the ground, like a wave of fire, lighting it all.

Through the morning fog, from far out at sea, they continued to burn.

ACKNOWLEDGEMENTS

As always, I need to thank my incredible family for always encouraging me to chase my dreams. I couldn't do this without you.

Big squishy hugs to Tonya Carey, Cari Schroder, Amanda Clark, and Debbie Durham, for offering your input at different stages of the process.

Huge thanks to those who helped shape and package *Fallen Flame:* Aunt M, thanks for all your questions and notes. Kim Chance, your crit skills are the best. Jenni Moen, you are *the* badass. Amy Concepcion, I can never thank you enough. Megan Addison, you may be stuck with me. Regina Wamba, I am in constant awe of your cover brilliance. Emily Lawrence, please don't hate me for my repetitive errors. Tiphs, I'm so grateful for your phenomenal map artistry. Stacey Blake, thank you for always making the paperback interior so special.

To Ena and Amanda with Enticing Journey — You ladies are amazing! Thanks bunches for your hard work.

To all the bloggers reading and reviewing and those participating in the release blitz — Thank you for sharing *Fallen Flame* with the book community. It means the world to me.

Blowing mad kisses to That Translyvanian Chick, Iza, for being so awesome!

To the Dreamers — Thanks for being a part of my reader group! I appreciate all your kindness and support.

And to everyone reading this — I really hope you enjoyed *Fallen Flame*. The start of Vala's story was challenging and extremely fun to write. Stick around, there's definitely more to come!

ABOUT THE AUTHOR

J.M. Miller currently consumes her coffee in Florida.

When she isn't spending time with her family or being distracted by social media sites, she writes Young Adult and New Adult romance novels. She loves to travel and will jump at the chance to go anywhere, whenever life allows.

Find her:
jmmillerbooks.com
facebook.com/j.m.miller.author
instagram.com/authorjmmiller

Sign up for news and giveaways-
http://smarturl.it/6s137t

OTHER BOOKS BY
J.M. MILLER

CPSIA information can be obtained
at www.ICGtesting.com
Printed in the USA
LVHW090946210222
711610LV00002B/48